Lust in Her Eyes

Story of a Women That

Wants to Satisfy Her Deepest Needs

Rebecca Hadden

Table of Contents

Chapter 1

Scarlett couldn't understand whether she was under the extraordinary circumstances voluntarily, no compellingly, or willingly got herself into. How long had it been? Fifteen minutes? Thirty minutes? Sixty? How much longer would she need to impatiently and eagerly wait before she was allowed to cum? Would she ever appear to help her or was she just playing a teasing game with her? Who was she? What did she want from her? Why was Scarlett feeling that her body was insanely getting out of control?

Scarlett Vargas was twenty-six years of age then and married to Jacques Vargas for over three years. Jacques was also twenty-six and was a marketing executive in the same company in which Scarlett worked in advertising. They lived in a luxurious and posh neighborhood in suburban Denver. Tragically, they purchased their home at the end of the lodging bubble and just as the easy home loan money was crunching. They were not late on their loan, yet the inflated installments made it a daunting challenge to cope with other household bills. Since Jacques's income varied month to month, some months were affluent and some were exceptionally tight.

Jacques and Scarlett both endeavored to increase their income by undertaking freelancing jobs. The ultimate outcome was they never frequently saw each other these days. Their schedules were negatively affecting their marriage. It wasn't the companionship that she missed dearly, but the quality sex. Scarlett, in particular, had always been open and outspoken about her sexuality. In school, she cherished the opportunity of being out of the home with vigor. She had several boyfriends on a regular basis and preferred to keep and be around the ones who truly knew how to fuck with vigor and vitality; however, in the end, she got too bored with all the vanilla mentality of her boyfriends and advanced toward another conquest.

After Scarlett graduated, she became employed in her current job. She owned a small apartment and was resolved to focus on propelling her career and profession. Her escapade of boyfriends continued until she met Jacques. He was the most complete, absolute, and adorable fit that she had ever met. Jacques appeared to have an insatiable thirst for sex like her. Even though she had an unwritten, basic rule to never bed with the man on her first date, with Jacques, she simply fell into his arms and they had been together since then.

Unfortunately, as their money crunch escalated and their schedules veered, the absence of quality time and nervous vitality implied their sexual experiences endured a significant blow. They retrograded from twice every day – once in the morning prior to the day's work and once during the night before going to bed on every day, to simply the mornings, to every couple of mornings, and further to every couple of weekends. More awful yet, the amazing standard of their lovemaking was also degrading. Jacques, while generous, was regarding their sexual adventure and coexistence as a chore to be endured rather than the youthful passion and feverish excitement of their previous life. To say Scarlett was frustrated at the sheer unsatisfactory and undesirable sexual union would be utterly undermining. Her dildo could give her an exercise when she found the time and energy; however, she always longed for the physical lively human touch instead of the lifeless plastic or metal touch.

Of course with her elegant, charming, and sizzling character and unbridled passion, Scarlett knew she could easily discover a replacement for Jacques. But, she heavily disliked cheating on him and as a husband, he was an excellent man. She continued on reasoning that if they could simply hold tight, the economy would improve, and things would become as they had been before. Luckily, when Scarlett was at her absolute limit, Jacques had a huge, lucrative, and profitable sales month and his bonus enabled them the luxury of a getaway vacation. They successfully afforded to rent a small luxurious duplex just outside The Rocky Mountain National Park for five nights. After the first couple of long days of climbing, hiking, and revitalizing their batteries, Jacques and Scarlett returned to their old passionate and exciting selves. They didn't leave the room for the next three days, except for dining and drinking. Their buried passion again erupted like an active volcano.

Shockingly, the following month Jacques's businesses were down and they were back to striving hard to meet their needs. Surprisingly more terrible, their ardent sexual life was dwindling again. One night while Scarlett was home alone (Jacques was engaged with his freelancing job away from home), her immediate and close neighbor Helena welcomed her over; a sudden, gracious, and welcoming invitation she gleefully acknowledged. Helena and Ron, her husband, were about two to three years older than Jacques and Scarlett. They appeared to enjoy a perfect marriage. Scarlett didn't have any acquaintance with them that well, yet she and Jacques generally got along with them whenever they interacted.

Helena said that Ron was away on an official trip and she was feeling lonely. She had a bottle of the finest French wine already opened and poured Scarlett a glass.

"I would rather not drink alone," Helena said.

For the following couple of hours, they drank and discussed life like good old friends enjoying a much awaited reunion. As the alcohol lessened their inhibitions and helped them relax, discussions turned increasingly sexual in nature. Inevitably, Scarlett revealed about her absence of sex issue. Helena just chuckled.

"That is no issue. I can easily solve that," Helena remarked.

Scarlett was somewhat dizzy, yet she wondered whether she just heard what her eardrums resonated in her brain.

"Listen, Scarlett. Every woman desires a little kinky help in the bedroom. Ron is incredible, yet sometimes I need to boost him up."

"What type of boost?" Scarlett inquired, getting quite intrigued.

"Sex toys, silly girl. What else did you think I meant?" Helena teased.

Scarlett stammered for an answer, fumbled with her vocabulary that wouldn't make her sound like she thought Helena was cheating on Ron. Helena seemed as if she couldn't make believe her confidant. Scarlett hurried to change the topic of discussion feeling somewhat uncomfortable and Helena hurried with equal enthusiasm to open another bottle of exquisite French Burgundy. Before they had polished off the two bottles, Scarlett's head was spinning. She asked for her leave politely and wanted to head home. She knew Jacques would be home soon, perhaps, within an hour, and she needed to get to bed so he wouldn't catch her getting drunk. Scarlett tried to maintain her balance on wobbly legs and began strolling toward the doorway. As they were passing through the stairs to the second floor, Helena somewhat delicately pushed her toward the stairs.

"Before you leave, I'd love to give you something," Helena teased.

In her wine-fueled giddiness, Scarlett was hesitant, yet she was insistent and she ended up gripping the banister as Helena escorted her to her room. It was elegantly designed and had a spacious closet. There were three dressers, garment racks, and an enormous piece of cloth shrouding a recliner. Scarlett was getting anxious, and she was sure her appearance promptly exhibited that. Helena remarked on her undeniable distress and asked her to chill and relax.

"Here, take a look at this," she said. "This is our way by which we keep our bed crisp and I keep my pussy perfectly satisfied."

Indeed, even though drunk, Scarlett was stunned that Helena referenced her pussy. She watched curiously as Helena slid open the bottom cabinet of the dresser. She dragged forth a lovely piece of satin lingerie.

"This one is for sweet Helena," she chuckled.

Then, she shut that cabinet and opened the next one. It was stacked with lingerie as well, yet it looked like leather and perhaps vinyl. Helena pulled out a stiff bra with openings cut out of the center.

"This one is for naughty Helena." She giggled mischievously.

Closing that cabinet, she moved forward to the next. It was stuffed with dildos of a wide variety of length, girth, and design, vibrators and a short cylinder with stubs on the end somewhat larger than an AA battery.

"This is for when my beloved husband isn't home or can't get his pinky excited. I'll be in this cabinet later tonight," Helena teased.

Ultimately, moving on to the fourth cabinet, she demonstrated to Scarlett a wide collection of handcuffs, blindfolds, a paddle, a leather cane, and a thick black strap-on dildo.

"Also, this is for when I'm very naughty and kinky." Her smile had a touch of mischief.

Scarlett could just nod her head, unsure of what to say.

"All I'm saying is I'd prefer having Ron's dick, yet that isn't always possible. However, when he is home, I would cum much better with the help of these abundant resources," Helena asserted.

She grabbed the short cylinder and held it up for Scarlett to inspect. "Feel free to take it, silly girl." She teased. She turned on the bottom and it sprung to life. Scarlett grasped. Its vibrations were amazingly strong, even for its small size.

"You position it perpendicular to your clit when your man is busy pleasuring you with his tool. He'll feel the incredible vibrations and it will drive you wild. I assure you. There is one problem, though; it eats out batteries. I had to purchase the rechargeable ones for it." Helena giggled.

Scarlett switched off the malevolent little device and attempted to hand it back to her, but Helena wouldn't take it.

"Keep it. Just give it a shot when Jacques returns home. And tomorrow, let me know what you think. I have a lot of options for tonight," Helena confirmed.

On the off chance that Scarlett was polite, perhaps she would have refused. That would have been the safest choice. But she didn't think likewise. Scarlett brought her new mischievous friend home and went to the bedroom. Possibly, it was the wine, but watching Helena effectively describing her toy collection had intensely aroused and stimulated Scarlett. She was desperate to explore and inspect the impact of the small vibrator. She undressed and hopped into her bed. When she brought down her fingers, she had the remarkable proof of what she had already suspected; she was wet. She opened the cabinet in her bedside table and grabbed her dildo. She typically used it just after Jacques nodded off or in cases when he was unable to give her the ecstatic delight. At times, she utilized it when Jacques was working late, but she always felt guilty. Tonight her mind wasn't crowded with guilt, remorse, or some other unpleasant emotion as she slid her dildo into her soaking pussy.

"Oh, it feels incredible," Scarlett wondered. Jacques hadn't fed her his cock for almost a week and she was unsure about his emotions and passions when he would return home. "What if he is too tired to explore our fantasies?"She wondered desperately and started fucking herself vigorously. When her perverted mind assured her of her arousal and being a bitch in heat, she was stirred up and turned the little vibrator on that Helena had presented her. Her clit was engorged and cresting out of its hood. Its first touch with the small buzzer was practically stunning, intensely exhilarating. She buzzed herself a few times, each time removing the vibrator rapidly, even though holding it on her clit a little longer each time. Goosebumps coursed through her skin, electric stimulations rocked her senses, and Scarlett felt those inexpressible pleasures again that she had been missing for so long. She shuddered terribly, biting her lips involuntarily.

At long last, her body adjusted rhythmically to the sensation and Scarlett was successfully able to position the vibrator directly over her clit while she kept on slamming ceaselessly on her pussy with the dildo. Helena was right. It was superb, heavenly, and mind-blowing and soon her heart was pounding like bass drums as she neared the zenith of excitement. She had used a vibrator a couple of times while she was a teenager, but she overlooked what having an incredible toy could accomplish for her. Soon, Scarlett was squirming on the bed in sheer ecstasy and then exploded brilliantly. It was the best orgasm she had experienced since they had their vacation a couple of months prior. She lay in the bed, gleaming, gasping, and shuddering until she heard the carport entryway open.

"Damn, how the hell did I forget about Jacques?" Scarlett cursed herself. She bounced up and slid both the toys in her cabinet. Her mind was still dizzy, her legs still weak, and her heart and stomach were doing somersaults in her throat. She grabbed a robe out of their washroom and wrapped it over her sizzling, naked curves. She hurried downstairs and found Jacques in the kitchen. She deliberately left the band of the robe open so he could have easier access to her seductive curves and tempting edges. With the robe blowing open and her succulent bosoms flapping, she rushed into the kitchen still feeling the heat in between her legs and wrapped Jacques in her arms.

"If you ain't taking me to bed, you'll lose your wife forever!" Scarlett whispered enthusiastically as she licked his earlobes.

Scarlett pushed Jacques against the wall and planted a deep, slow, and fervent kiss on his lips before he could respond. Luckily the story didn't end with Jacques ignoring her. He took her to the bed and rammed her like a hunk, endeavoring to calm a bitch in heat. Scarlett used the little vibrator on her throbbing clit while Jacques pounded her and was buried deep within and he was stirred by its electric sensations. His invigorating touches showering love all over naked body enlightened her, her smile was radiant, and that charged the air in the room with amorous desire. As her defense unfolded, her heart sang melancholy with a sweet rhythm of blossoming intimacy. She exploded twice, even before he dumped his load within her. She hungered for his taste, his smell, the feel of his soul touching hers. "I just can't live any further without these dangerous and attractive toys," she thought as she nodded off. She was already starting to get infatuated by the toy, obsessed with the toy.

The following morning Jacques was up and out of the house early. Scarlett had a couple of intimate moments before she would need to drag herself to the shower so that she could manage her schedules on time. Accordingly, she delighted in another exquisite sizzling round of self-pleasure with her new intimate companion. Her life attitude was certainly improving.

That night Scarlett was absolutely engaged with her second job, so she was late to return home. She stopped by the local store and grabbed a packet of overrated batteries. She figured it was the least she could accomplish for Helena and return her enormous, heavenly favor. Scarlett didn't return home until 11 PM and all the lights in the house were turned off. She concluded Jacques must have already hit the bed. She curiously investigated at Helena's home and a few lights were still sparkling. She thought to return her toy, but decided it was too late to knock at her door. Besides, she wouldn't like to trouble Jacques and explain to him the cause of her delayed arrival in case she ended up exploring some more toys in Helena's Pandora box.

Thus, Scarlett returned home and headed upstairs to the bedroom. Jacques was snoring, sleeping soundly. She entered into the washroom and stripped off her filthy clothes. She took a quick shower and then slithered into bed, feeling comfortable, warm and still naked. She wondered breathlessly about her dildo and the vibrator; however, feeling dead tired, heavy eyes overwhelmed her contemplations even before she could decide to follow her wonderful temptation.

The following night Jacques and Scarlett were both engaged with their second jobs, but she finished up early. Seeing Helena's lights on, she decided to pay her a visit. Helena was delighted to see Scarlett, and she expressed her profound gratitude toward her for allowing her to use her magnificent soft toy. Scarlett was secretly hoping Helena would allow her borrow something else from her Pandora box, but instead, she invited her to a toy party at her home on Saturday.

"What's a toy party?" Scarlett inquired. Her perverse mind had already started fantasizing about dozens of women sitting around and around using different sex toys for sexual pleasure and gratification on themselves, but she truly had no idea of what it was all about.

"Actually, I bought all my toys from an online gift shop. The saleswoman sells sex toys door-to-door." Helena giggled.

"Really, you got to be kidding me. Door-to-door selling of sex toys," Scarlett breathed out in sheer shock and disbelief.

"Well in a way, yes, she does sell door-to-door. Actually, she owns a sex toy website and you know that online stuff and all. Besides, she also sells her exquisite products through parties like the one I'm hosting on Saturday. It's sort of a Tupperware party, but we just call it FUCKERWARE."

"I truly can't get you," Scarlett countered.

"Bella, one of my most trusted friends, brings samples of what she sells on the internet to someone's home. That individual welcomes a few of her friends she thinks will be available to experience them and will be benefiting from the party. You get considerable, extraordinary discounts because she doesn't own a retail store and you get the opportunity to seriously explore the toys in a discreet location," Helena countered.

"That seems really exciting and innocent enough," Scarlett remarked.

"Just a word of caution, it's not that innocent. Obviously, no one is going to compel you to do anything, but sometimes most of the women prefer to test the viability of the product. Bella brings a couple of 'demo' models and sometimes either lets you borrow one at the discretion of a bedroom or even demonstrates either on herself or on the models."

Things were beginning to get exciting and weird, yet Scarlett assured Helena regarding her participation. After all, Jacques would be engaged with his freelancing work all through the weekend and it was better to explore something kinkier rather than getting bored. The rest of the week, Scarlett wondered about the deviant gathering and how she would blend herself into it. She was absolutely sexually open, and she truly enjoyed her little vibrator. She knew she was desperate to purchase a new one for herself, but what else would Bella bring? Would the rest of the ladies in the party be "typical" or was Helena welcoming a lot of deviants and perverts? Was that her opinion about Scarlett as well, a perverted, promiscuous, and sexually insatiable married woman? Her mind was crowded with all sorts of awkward and obvious questions. No, Scarlett was a typical woman with typical needs and Helena seemed to be too normal hosting these lewd parties. But then again, a deeper depraved part of her brain countered she was going to attend a party of liberated women who had the courage to express and explore their sexuality and fantasies and who took keen interest to discover new methods of utmost pleasure. At least that was what she rationalized.

Chapter 2

Saturday finally arrived. Jacques had already scheduled his work from 10 AM to 8 PM. The party was at 2 PM, so Scarlett thought she would have ample time to evaluate her new toys. She wondered what to wear for the party. It appeared as though she should wear a skirt on the off chance that she was tempted to test a toy; however, she would not like to appear too obvious. Finally, she decided to slip into her jeans and a t-shirt. In the end, she was walking toward Helena's house at 2 pm. She was amazed to find eight to ten cars parked outside Helena's house. Her body was shivering with excitement as goosebumps coursed through her radiant skin, her fingers felt icy cold, and then she rang the doorbell.

"I'm so thrilled to have you, Scarlett." Helena greeted her and gave her a big friendly hug. "Don't be shy! Let's get you introduced."

Helena walked Scarlett around the room introducing her to her friends and the party attendees. Most of them were around her age and a few even had wedding rings on their fingers. Scarlett was never that good when it came to remembering names; however, she made it a point to remember Bella, the saleswoman who ran the online sex toy store. Likewise, she got acquainted with Kathleen. She lived a couple of blocks from their neighborhood. Scarlett recalled she had seen her in the neighborhood, but never got formally introduced. As Kathleen shook her hand, she was stunned by how firm her handshake was. She was strong, like an athlete. She wasn't curvaceous and she wasn't traditionally gorgeous in that sense, but looked incredibly vigorous and flexible. The strength of her handshake provoked Scarlett to wonder if she lifted weights.

Helena said there were two others expected, so they settled down on the couch and discussed life and other things until they showed up. Everybody was remarkably friendly and the atmosphere of the room was certainly easygoing. Helena had her exquisite collection of French Burgundy opened up already and everyone polished off a few glasses, except Bella. Then when the time arrived to get serious, they

20

formed a circle like a round table conference in the living room. Bella started with an introduction of her online business and her philosophy on women's satisfaction, pleasure, and ecstasy. Her hypothesis proclaimed that for a significant amount of time women had undermined their very own sexual pleasure and sensualities. This was something to be rejoiced and celebrated rather than criticized as lascivious or vulgar. Irrespective of being alone or with a partner, a woman should be enabled to discover her pleasure zone. Obviously, her recommendations were applauded with extraordinary fervor by the party attendees.

Bella lifted an enormous case onto the footstool and opened it up. Inside were around six dildos and vibrators, conveniently held in high-density foam. Scarlett also found the little vibrator Helena had lent her, the primary thing she realized she was desperate to purchase. The ladies gang inclined forward and started to give more consideration. Bella picked up the first vibrator and started to discuss its quality design for a considerable length of time. She proceeded to exhibit each toy in detail and passed them around the gathering. The women were looking at the toys as if they were inspecting an organic product or vegetable at the store before purchasing it. Some were weighing them in their grasp, analyzing the general benefits of the toys and estimating on which would suffice and fulfill their needs.

After describing everything in her Pandora box, Bella brought forth a catalog. "Obviously, I can't carry all that I just demonstrated with me, but I can get you anything you need."

Scarlett didn't have a toy in her grasp then, so she gestured to have the catalog. She had never observed such a wide variety of collectibles in her entire life. There was every size, shape, and color possible according to everyone's needs. She was absolutely clueless about how to pick her toy. She was too captivated looking at the catalog to focus on all when one of the ladies approached Bella for a demonstration. She looked up with sheer wonderment when Bella was opening another case, also filled up with vibrators.

"I keep these as models," she said. "They all get cleaned after each party so you don't need to stress over health and hygiene."

A lady, Scarlett didn't recollect her name, picked an enormous vibrator and approached Helena. She murmured something in her ear and Helena said "up the stairs" and pointed to the room just beside her bedroom. The lady calmly exited and the exhibition continued.

Bella opened the third case. This one was unique. Scarlett wasn't even certain what every one of the things were. As Bella clarified about the items, she was illuminated about nipple suckers, clit suckers, magic wands, Ben WA balls, chastity belts and many more. She was certain she wasn't the only one intensely excited and aroused to discover this magnificent collection. She surmised that because as soon as the first woman returned downstairs, another of her neighbors, Linda, a cheerful blonde, grabbed a different model and left the room.

Scarlett sensed her pussy was beginning to feel exceptionally warm, and she now regretted her decision to wear the jeans. They were tight, and the groin was scouring her pussy every time she squirmed in the seat. Like the dildos and the vibrators had been, this collection of toys was passed around for investigation and another catalog was passed alongside it. The room appeared to get hotter as Bella requested volunteers to demonstrate some lingerie.

Scarlett checked out the room and just one hand was up. It was Helena's. Bella excused herself and exited with Helena and a bag. They vanished upstairs and the rest of the group members sat quietly. The only sound breaking the awkward, yet exciting silence of the room was Linda's footsteps returning. She unquestionably had the expression of somebody who had been jerking off.

"This thing is fantastic. You girls should give it a try," she said.

About that time Bella returned. "Helena will be down in a moment. I wish another person to volunteer so you could see more. In case not, we'll do fine, don't worry."

Bella got busy to hand over her lingerie catalog and then Scarlett saw Helena descending the stairs. She was elegantly clad in a black merry widow, thigh-high stockings and almost 4" stiletto boots. She looked extraordinarily attractive. Scarlett didn't remember regularly thinking about another woman that way. Possibly, it was the strain in her jeans, or perhaps, it was the whole atmosphere of the room getting intensely stirred up around the toys, but she felt her pussy spout a little when Helena finally arrived into the room.

Helena cat walked in front of the gathering as best as she could while Bella explained why her lingerie was far better than any brands out in the retail market like The Victoria's Secret, Natori, or the Skims. What she was explaining seemed practical and justifiable irrespective of the high prices; although Scarlett seemed somewhat reluctant due to the prices. The group of women appeared to feel uncomfortable to have Helena, their hostess, modeling before them. Scarlett thought about whether it was because they were all having similar tempting feelings and illicit thoughts, and moistening in between their legs or whether it was because of some other underlying reasons. Helena demonstrated four different outfits that evening and before the end of the show, all Scarlett could consider was returning home and getting her hands in between her legs.

She endeavored to imagine how much money Bella made from that party. It was considerable. The vast majority of the toys she had "in stock" in her mini-van was at par with her lingerie collection in her bag. The rest that Bella needed to do was to deliver the orders with absolute discretion within a week. Scarlett thought she was expected to apologize as she could only manage the cost of her new little smooth vibrator to replace the one she had acquired from Helena. Bella consoled her not to stress concerning it. And if she was interested to host a similar party, she could easily get her help and could win more toys and if she would decide to volunteer as a model for the event. Scarlett confessed her feelings to consider Bella's proposal; however, she was really unsure of her budget. Besides, she was unsure if she could be able to exhibit her sizzling curves publicly, no matter how tempting they looked. Definitely, she wasn't bold enough like Helena.

Scarlett strolled back home. She was desperate to run, yet she was apprehensive someone from the party would see her. Once inside the house, though, she hurried to her bedroom and immediately slipped out of her clothes. Her climaxes rushed to demonstrate how aroused she was. She realized she wasn't really satisfied, but with Jacques returning home in due time, she concluded to experience an overwhelming release. After a light supper, she practically assaulted Jacques as she rode him like a wild bitch in heat. He performed well, yet her corrupted psyche was on Helena exhibiting the lingerie. She didn't have a clue why she fantasized about her while being with her husband, but she kept fantasizing about her removing her lingerie and enticing her to approach her. Jacques and Scarlett both peaked simultaneously; however, she needed to consider what he would do in case he discovered she was imagining her attractive neighbor while having sex.

Their work routines continued to be in a chaotic mess and the passionate nights were hard to come by. Fortunately for Scarlett, her ecstatic buzzer kept her sane, even though it was beginning to lose its impetuous attraction. She realized she required something new and energizing. She called Bella to organize a party, yet she truly didn't know enough people, kinky and eccentric like hers, who might take a keen interest in her alliance and would make it profitable for her. Bella kept on insisting Scarlett be a model. She couldn't disclose to her that the key reason for her reluctance was her furtive fantasies about Helena, and she didn't want other women wondering about her that way.

Being the great sales representative that she was, Bella convinced Scarlett to visit her office, her home really, and explore some more samples. She affirmed Scarlett could give them a try and "test" model them with absolute discretion to get over her unnecessary uneasiness. She further revealed to her that Helena had earned $300 worth of merchandise at her house party. Bella also revealed to her that she had a big party planned for a bridal shower in two weeks. If Scarlett agreed to be a model, she would give her 5% of the receipts in cash or a 10% rebate on any merchandise. Scarlett was desperate to try it. She surely required the money or if she chose to purchase some items instead, she would be set to experience her supreme pleasure for years to come. She consented to visit Bella and discover more.

After two days, Scarlett was sitting and savoring tea in Bella's living room. She lived in a spacious house which was elegantly decorated. After some usual introductory babble, Bella escorted Scarlett to the cellar where she managed the business. The cellar was designed like a recreation room except for the endless supply of racks stuffed with every sex toy possible. There were three standing closets filled with lingerie, a small stage with lights and a stripper post, a sex swing hanging from the ceiling and a king-sized, comfortable bed. It took a few moments for Scarlett to keep her jaws from dropping onto the floor. Finally, when she came out of her bewilderment, she spoke.

"It's quite overwhelming."

Scarlett was absolutely stunned at the wide range of collections at Bella's place. She never anticipated the quantity of her business. Bella clarified she did at least three shows every week and sometimes even four. It got exhausting since she needed to fill the orders from the shows and website throughout the day and then be out on a couple of days every week to attend the parties, but she was clearing almost half a million sales every year off the web and almost the same amount in party sales. As the sole representative of her company, she was earning about $300,000. Scarlett started her mathematical estimation in her mind. 5% of party receipt times two or three hundred thousand... Kink modeling could be the solution to her financial problem.

Evidently Bella could sense the wheels turning in Scarlett's mind. She offered her the opportunity again to be a successful model for her. Her portfolio would include enticing and tempting the visitors and getting them in a sexy, purchasing mindset, much as Helena had done. Bella further disclosed Scarlett would need to be open to model the lingerie and to demonstrate the toys, although she wouldn't always expect her to exhibit and demonstrate the toys. Obviously, at some parties, the women get somewhat wild and they will demand hands-on demonstrations. It would be completely up to Scarlett whether to acknowledge those solicitations.

"Let me also tell you, I had a model that was delighted to flaunt her masturbation aptitudes to a lot of repressed housewives. Apart from being an exhibitionist, she also preferred teasing them. When she got herself off, whatever vibrator she was utilizing would fly off the shelf. I typically got the chance to double my profits because a lot of money flowed those weeks. I always gave her a lucrative reward after those parties since I realized she was the sole reason for the immense profitable sales. Most of them don't get that insane; however, I can promise you will be propositioned at some of them. So, let me know your opinion."

Scarlett paused. The money seemed excellent, but she was still unsure if she could be able to perform masturbation publicly. When she clarified her apprehensions, Bella was exceptionally reassuring and encouraging.

"Look, Scarlett. You are a gorgeous woman and I figure you could do well indeed. Be that as it may, you need to overcome your shyness. That would fly off on the chance that you were facilitating the party. Heck, it could even help because your friends understand what you like and it would feel authentic. But, in case we're teaming up together, there's no need for you to be nervous and have a sales target," Bella supported.

Scarlett finally acknowledged that she understood the terms and was eager to try.

"Alright," Bella said. "We should begin with having you try a modest nighty. Take off your clothes."

Bella was stern in her command. Scarlett had her prying eyes investigating the room for a changing room, but couldn't find one. Bella wasn't focusing on Scarlett. She was rummaging through the closet. So Scarlett immediately got rid of her clothes and put them, neatly folded, on the table. She was standing in her bra and panties when Bella returned with a long, streaming house gown.

"No issues with the panties for this outfit, but get rid of the bra," Bella exclaimed.

Bella's eyes were locked on Scarlett's as she unclasped her bra, leaving her succulent bosoms to dangle free. Bella took her bra and kept it on the table with the rest of her clothes and helped her slip into the house outfit. She tugged and squeezed the outfit, trying to get it to hang appropriately.

"You'll have to figure out how to dress because you won't have the help at the parties; however, today I'll help since I have to understand how to fit you," Bella teased.

Scarlett stood devouring her self-reflection in the mirror behind the stage. The gown wasn't fitting properly and Bella looked upset. She continued her futile attempts to adjust it appropriately. And, in that process, she continued touching Scarlett's delicate feminine spots. "Shit! Is she doing that deliberately? Stop it, girl! She's just trying to help you, Scarlett." Questions crowded her restless mind. A few times she "accidentally" brushed against her abundant bosoms, trying to get the fabric to hang properly. Immediately, she shivered and her nipples started to harden, which was most likely the look she was going for.

Finally, she surrendered with a disheartened huff. "This one simply won't fit. I have to measure you."

Bella pulled off the gown, leaving Scarlett standing there naked, apart from her panties. She pulled a measuring tape out from a desk cabinet along with a paper pad. Weight, height, inseam, arm and leg length, waist size, bust size, hips, calves, and so on, Bella measured it effectively. Her fingers continuously touched her. Not in a sexual manner as such. She was so cool, mindful, and professional, but Scarlett's lush body wasn't familiar to the fine sensual feminine touches. Her body was responding in kind. Her pussy was lubricating and her nipples were rock hard. When Bella stooped down before Scarlett to measure her inseam, she spread her legs somewhat further to give her space to adjust the measuring tape. In doing as such, her leaking pussy interacted with the back of her hand. For a moment, Scarlett thought, "I'm certain she could sense my arousal from my wetness. Even though I couldn't smell myself, I'm sure at such intimate closeness of her head's position, she could." An electric shudder went through her spine as Scarlett surrendered to the sensational sensualities of the moment.

Standing there, almost naked before the fully clothed Bella, was her most terrible nightmare, yet a charming fantasy. Her body was reacting in ways she couldn't control. Bella stayed detached and proficient, which was making Scarlett insane. A conservative part of her mind wanted to escape the situation and the more perverted part of her mind wanted her to toss her down and fuck her, yet her body was restrained on the spot incapable to move to either extremity. Bella returned with a red leather corset she swore would fit her better. She had Scarlett remove her panties. Her soft hands kept on enticing her yearning body as Bella helped Scarlett to slip into it. Once again, she brushed her hardened, sensitive nipples as she adjusted the corset's cups around her ample bosoms. She was enjoying the fascination of teasing her new model as she laced the corset ever more tightly constraining her succulent bosoms to swell upward and out giving her a voluptuous cleavage and tugging the tight crease of the corset's groin strap further and deeper in between her pussy lips. Finally, when the garment was properly adjusted, it was so tight that Scarlett struggled to breathe as Bella left her gazing at her self-reflection in the mirror while she hustled for a few shoes.

Scarlett restlessly continued to stare at her own reflection in the mirror. It wasn't her. It was some sex-infatuated bimbo lurking in the shadows. Her pussy was drenched. Regardless of whether Bella had not noticed her wetness before, the corset would have been wet when she removed it from her. Visions of purchasing the corset and wearing it home to hide her extreme arousal overpowered her mind. She realized she couldn't bear the cost of it, as a matter of fact, and where might she wear such provocative clothing? "I'd scare Jacques away in the event that I wore this in the bedroom," she laughed at herself.

Bella came back with a couple of red leather stilettos to perfectly match her corset. "Fuck Me," Were the words she could wonder and the pumps were all she could think about as Bella steadied her flimsy legs enough to slip them on.

"Come on hottie, walk for me. How about we check whether you can demonstrate this one?" Bella teased.

Scarlett wavered over the stage, unable to take her hungry eyes off the reflection in the mirror. She could see Bella grinning as she observed her catwalk. Even though she had worn heels this high previously, the constricting nature of the bodice compelled her to make exceptionally small strides. At whatever point she made an ordinary stride, the binding of the groin put sensational pressure on her anticipating clit. Scarlett gasped at the first step and needed to strive hard to not lose control. Gradually, she turned out to be all the more sure-footed. As she strolled to and fro over the stage, Bella continued yelling out recommendations and commands on the most proficient method to demonstrate and "exhibit the product." Scarlett didn't know whether Bella was discussing her or the bodice. Her mind was spinning with desire as the corset kept on scouring her touchy shrewd bits in the most exciting ways. Bella kept on yelling requests and pulling on the ends of the corset, and her ample bosoms, sensitive nipples, abundant ass, and soaking pussy, with the alleged reason for ensuring it fits "perfectly." Scarlett was rapidly losing control and going to surrender to her wild desire and simply start pleasuring herself when Bella reported that was sufficient. She helped her off the stage and began un-strapping the corset.

Scarlett's body was hot with a blend of sweat and love juices as Bella stripped the culpable piece of clothing from her aroused body. The groin of the bodice suck to her pussy lips until Bella stripped it way, dim stains of moisture affirming what they both knew to be a reality. Scarlett dropped into a seat. She was gasping hard, her midsection at long last released from the tightening of the corset. Her yearning pussy was throbbing and her legs were spread wide. She had begun to return to her earthly senses and again her conscious personality instructed her to grab her clothes and leave while her unquenched desire inflamed her subconscious mind to simply surrender and finger fuck her.

Bella hung the corset back on the garment rack and brought forth a baby doll nighty. This couldn't have been more significantly different from the corset. It was silk, fine, and hung delicately from the new model girl's curves. Once again Bella brushed her delicate regions, driving Scarlett wild, as she adjusted the piece of clothing to her lush body. One more time Bella had her cat walking before the mirror while giving her guidelines on the most proficient method to move and even pout for sexual impact. Her excitement was much more in overdrive when she wrapped up the nighty modeling. Bella stopped the pretense of overlooking her overheated aroused state and informed her there was nothing wrong in getting tempted while modeling or doing her job. That was the manner by which her clothes should make a lady feel. Scarlett was desperate to reveal to her it wasn't the clothes, but the tempting circumstance. Yet, she just nodded reluctantly rather than admitting the naked truth out in the open. Bella stripped off the nighty and once more Scarlett was naked before her. Her desperation to jerk off was much more frenzied this time and as Bella turned her back to her to hang the nighty back up she discretely gave her clit a brisk rub. The electric sensation it sent through her aching body was fascinating and she shuddered in ecstatic delight. Obviously, Bella turned around too early and caught her with her finger close to her hungry lips. She didn't appear to be outraged or upset, yet Scarlett turned beet red with embarrassment.

"You're reddening is adorable; however, don't stress over it, honey. I have exactly what you need," Bella teased.

"What I need is one of her dildos, my fingers, or heck her fingers, anything for two minutes, so that I could cum." Scarlett wondered desperately. But what she got was surprisingly delightful.

"I don't carry this thing to too many parties. It's somewhat excessive for some people; however, I think you'll like it." Bella grinned.

Scarlett sensed her heart pounding like bass drums. Her stimulating excitement was trickling from her wanton pussy and her nipples were excessively hard. Bella opened a cabinet and Scarlett saw her pull out a couple of black panties. She could sense the material was not fabric. Bella also brought forth a case that had been on the rack beside them. She brought the clothing over to her.

"This is an exceptional toy. I promise you will have perhaps the best orgasm of your life with it. Wanna try?" Bella teased.

Scarlett gazed at the panties in absolute wonderment and took it from her hand. It was made of vinyl, she guessed. It was full size and seemed as though it would fit extremely tight. Around the waistband was a fine zipper and in the groin were three sets of metal contacts. Scarlett was bewildered and confused simultaneously. Bella opened the case and clarified how the panties worked.

"These panties cost $300 which is undoubtedly a tough sell. Covered up in the waistband is a series of 12 watch batteries. They are slim, quite cheap and give around 12 hours of power whenever utilized appropriately." Bella explained.

"Power? Power for what?" Scarlett inquired.

Bella turned the case around. Inside were ten attachments of varying shapes and sizes. Bella clarified that the accessories set onto the metal contacts which give power and control to vibrators covered in each one. There were three various sized and shaped butt plugs, two g-spot vibrators and three ordinary molded vibrators for the pussy and two more for direct clitoral stimulation. Scarlett looked at the arrangements wide-eyed and they appeared to be crafted to either fill a woman up or to be worn throughout the day. Bella then dragged a remote control out of the case.

"After putting on the underwear, you choose what level of stimulation you need. You can control every one of the three vibrator areas exclusively, program the panties to rotate which is on, turn on randomly with different measures of intensity or my undisputed top choice, is a long moderate tease," Bella explained.

Scarlett was not in the temperament for a tease, but she was charmed by what that implied.

"In tease mode, the panties pick indiscriminately, which vibrator to switch on and for how long. In any case, it just uses the most minimal setting. You can get half of a day out of the batteries in this mode. The panties are tight enough that you won't leak around the edges. That is something worth being thankful for because you will be more excited than you ever have been previously. I, for the most part, wear a couple when I'm hosting a get-together because it keeps me concentrated on sex and wearing this under your garments is an excellent temptation and provocative encouragement. Obviously, when I'm back in the car, I need to hit the full power button on the remote to release my arousal immediately," Bella described.

Scarlett wondered who might make such a gadget; however, in her exceptionally overheated state, she was dying to try them.

"Would you let me try them?"She inquired. She then embarrassingly acknowledged that she was desperate to cum.

"Sure, darling. That is the reason that my organization exists. Obviously, you can try them."

Bella selected three attachments. The smallest anal plug and the smaller clitoral vibrator were first. Scarlett shrugged off the plug.

"Um, Bella, I don't do anal," Scarlett advised her emphatically.

"Young lady, you don't have the foggiest idea what you're missing. However, that is cool. The panties realize when nothing is attached to the third contact. You really can extend the battery life by running with just a couple of attachments. I do need to discover your g-spot, in any case, so I can pick the right pussy vibrator." Bella spoke softly.

Scarlett was all the while processing what she just said when she saw her hand, two fingers outstretched reach toward her exposed sex. For the first time, another woman's fingers entered her pussy before she got an opportunity to respond. Electric shivers raced from her feet, through her pussy, up her spine, and into her head as Bella expertly investigated Scarlett's drenched pussy looking for her most sensitive spot. She was an outstanding specialist. Scarlett had a compelling impulse to pee as her finger tapped the soft tissue around her g-spot. She felt her legs go powerless as Bella moved her fingers around looking for her excitement epicenter. Scarlett needed to wrap her arms around Bella's neck to prevent from falling over and she felt a crisp spout of juice coat her fingers.

"That is the spot. You need a number 3. It will make you climb the walls before you blast off," Bella teased.

Perhaps Scarlett heard Bella's voice, yet she was excessively busy trying to bump her hand, silently trying to persuade her to continue her exquisite and expert fingering for only a couple of seconds longer. Oh dear, Bella pulled her flickering fingers out, holding them up for Scarlett to witness.

"You are unquestionably prepared for an advanced toy." Bella chuckled mischievously.

Scarlett looked as Bella dragged the number three vibrator out of the case. It was flimsy and not exceptionally long. Possibly, it was three and a half inches long and somewhat three-quarters of an inch in girth. It was curved, however, and Bella promised Scarlett it would fit her perfectly. Bella placed the vibrator before Scarlett's mouth and requested her to lick it to warm it up. Scarlett felt embarrassed, somewhat humiliated as she sucked it into her mouth as though it was her husband's erect organ, yet she couldn't have cared less.

After fifteen long seconds, it was well lubricated with salivation with definitely no obstruction for her to penetrate her pussy and was then slid into position. The first touch with her sensitive and boiling g-spot was sufficient to make Scarlett climb the walls. Scarlett bit her lips, closed her eyes, and her mouth was left gaped open in sensational stimulations that she was experiencing after so long. For a moment, she could only hear her heart pounding like bass drums and she shivered like a leaf in a hailstorm.

"Quiet down little one. We're nearly done." Bella snickered as she witnessed the remarkable results of her splendid work.

Bella then grabbed the clitoral vibrator. It was a thin round bar around two inches in length and somewhat half an inch in girth. It snapped into the front of her underwear. Clearly the metal contacts were electric. Bella pulled the g-spot vibrator back from Scarlett's burning pussy and sent her to the washroom to experience the peak of her excitement; by then she needed to fight the desperate temptation to masturbate. Bella then had her step into the panties and she guided them up to her legs. At the point when they were up to her knees, she reinserted the g-spot vibrator. The panties were excessively tighter than any other pair she had ever worn and Scarlett was fortunate she was there to help her.

Bella needed to stand behind Scarlett and draw the panties from both sides to get over her hips. Subsequently, Scarlett needed to bend forward marginally to facilitate the lift. She felt like a bitch hound in heat. She was already penetrated and now a lady she barely knew was pulling the most prohibitive panties she had at any point witnessed up her legs with an assurance to make her orgasm harder than she ever had previously.

At last, the panties were nearly set up. Bella took care to position the g-spot vibrator in the best possible area and again Scarlett nearly exploded from her tremendous electric sensations just from that. She heard that vibrator click onto the panties center adjustment and with the last pull they were on. The clit bar was positioned impeccably over her swollen stub. Her mind-blowing ejaculation was imminent and Scarlett was ready.

Chapter 3

Scarlett stared at Bella who was holding the remote. She looked as she pushed a button and right away, the two vibrators sprung to life. Just as fast her knees buckled, and she flopped to the floor writhing in a shuddering orgasm. As she lay groaning on the floor, Scarlett gazed back at Bella who squeezed another button and the vibrations appeared to double the extraordinary intensity. Her body was wracked with another flood of ecstatic delight as the g-spot vibrator did something superbly amazing. Scarlett sensed that she would lose bladder control and snatched the front of the panties with both her hands.

"No more! I can't take it anymore! Please! Turn it off!" Scarlett screamed.

Just as fast as it had turned on, the vibrations ceased. The trembling in her body didn't as Scarlett kept on moving on the floor as the orgasmic pulsations and shocking waves kept on rocking her body. Gradually, she returned to Earth and witnessed that Bella was all the while grinning at her.

"What a shame that you didn't allow me to proceed! That desperation to pee is the thing that happens directly before you have a g-spot climax. You were going to squirt." Bella smiled wickedly.

"I've never felt anything like that before. It was stunning," Scarlett answered.

"On the off chance that you'll allow me, I can take you back there and much further," Bella teased.

What was there to think about? "Holy shit! Yes," Scarlett moaned.

Scarlett assumed Bella would simply turn on the vibrators once more, yet instead, Bella helped her to stand on her feet and started pulling off the panties. Even though it had effectively held back her pleasure juices, the delicious smell that was released was overwhelming. Again Scarlett felt humiliated, yet again Bella assured her there was no reason to be.

Bella pulled the panties down just to Scarlett's thighs and afterward returned to the case and recovered the small butt plug. "You need to try this," she teased. "Trust me."

Regardless of whether Scarlett confided in her or not, that wasn't an issue. Her body resembled clay impatiently waiting to be molded by Bella and she submissively bent over on one of her tables as she applied sufficient amount of lube to her butt cavity and the plug. Bella asked her to relax, easy enough in her excited state, and in it went. Immediately, came the panties and Scarlett heard the obvious snap of the two vibrators connecting themselves. Scarlett cautiously stood back up. Despite the fact that she had a small butt plug in her anal cavity, it felt colossal. Bella gave a speedy push of a button, and it sprung to life for around 5 seconds. Just then, she turned it off. It was a terrific, yet a different feeling. She had never had those nerves animated in a sexual manner and it felt breathtaking. Whatever Bella had arranged, Scarlett was going to experience a tremendous orgasm willingly.

Bella checked the time. "I didn't realize we would continue playing for so long. What about some lunch?"

"Um, would I be able to put back my clothes on?" Scarlett inquired.

"Do you yearn for a significantly explosive orgasm? Do you confide in me?" Bella questioned.

Scarlett knew the response to the first question was an inadequate yes. With regards to the second, she wasn't so certain.

"But firstly, we should get you another bra," Bella stated.

Bella opened a cabinet loaded with frilly undergarments. She explored around for a minute and pulled out a full coverage push-up.

Typically, Scarlett preferred a demi-cup so she could exhibit a little of her tempting cleavage and she was shocked Bella had picked a progressively conservative model. Then, when Bella wrapped it over her chest, Scarlett realized she was horribly wrong. From at a distance, the bra looked ordinary; however, inspecting closely, Scarlett saw the patterns for her sensitive nipples. As Bella pulled the bra tight, Scarlett also sensed that Bella had picked the one which was at least two sizes excessively small. As her succulent bosoms were crushed into the cups, her sensitive nipples were out popped and the majority of her areolas were exhibited. Past the exposures, the surface of the bra on the nipple appeared to be somewhat itchy.

"That's perfect. It will keep your psyche off your pussy," Bella teased seductively.

Bella returned to the rack and pulled off a light yellow sundress. This confounded her more than the bra.

"I consider this outfit my beast tease collection. It's not about exhibiting you off; instead, it's about getting you off," Bella stated wickedly.

Scarlett didn't comprehend until Bella slipped the dress over her head. It was baggy and slid down her body effectively. She was impatiently anticipating that the dress should be more body fitting; however, it moved easily, practically streaming over her body. The key, Scarlett immediately sensed, was a band of unpleasant material planted over the chest of the dress. The first time the placement of the dress moved over her widened nipples, an electric shock coursed through her body. She was presently adjusted for four areas of discrete incitement. Scarlett stared at Bella with concern.

"Don't worry, sweetheart. You look incredible and I realize you're going to cherish this. Now, let's enjoy our lunch," Bella expressed.

Scarlett figured they would walk upstairs for sandwiches; however, Bella deftly guided her into the carport and afterward into the car. Strolling up the stairs, her sensitive nipples started screaming for passionate consideration as the dress scoured on them in all the possible sensual ways. The butt plug was also dancing its animating move in her rear end as Scarlett climbed the stairs and the vibrator continued poking her discovered pleasure chore. Furthermore, they were not even on yet. Scarlett was essentially shivering with savage want. She realized she should call a quit to this game; however, she was too consumed with wild desire to make the call.

Scarlett passively sat down in Bella's SUV and clasped the safety belt. Bella got in on the opposite side and before she accelerated out of the carport, she pulled the panties remote out of her satchel. Scarlett had nearly ignored it; she gulped hard.

"We're just going a couple of miles into town for lunch. I know an extraordinary small café on a lake. I'll put you on random, so you can appreciate the ride." Bella smiled wickedly.

Scarlett watched Bella press the button and the clit vibrator sprang to life. It was an exceptional buzz, about as hard as she had felt before. And afterward, it ceased. She gazed with questioning eyes at Bella. At that point, the butt plug fired. Not as hard, or perhaps Scarlett simply was less sensitive there. Again it was for only a couple of moments. A moment later the clit vibrator and g-spot vibrators both sprang to life concurrently and both were extremely intense. Scarlett couldn't suppress the groan they caused. Thus it went. After every fifteen minutes, at least one of the vibrators would bounce to life. The position and force continued changing, always keeping her senses on high alert. Scarlett was in a mess when they arrived at the parking area. Her hands were caught up with squeezing her bosoms and scouring her nipples through the dress. Her yearning pussy was spasming, and she was surely leaking her passionate juice into the underwear; however, the sizzling excitement wasn't sufficiently long to allow her to peak. She despised herself for giving such authority to Bella, yet she cherished her for seizing such an opportunity.

Bella stopped in a parking area about a block off the lake. As they pulled off in a relatively private and discreet area of the parking lot, Scarlett begged Bella to let her cum.

"I already said it would be far superior to the one you had at my home. You're not prepared at this point," Bella teased.

"I'll do anything you need," Scarlett begged earnestly. After a moment's delay, she again implored, "I'll even lick your pussy!"

"Thanks for the offer, but I'm not in the mood right now to be eaten," Bella answered. "I'm simply trying to demonstrate to you why my business is exceptional. I gained from my very own experiences what women need to accomplish their best orgasms and I've transformed that into a fruitful business. I could tell from the party that you simply required somebody to give you a little push and break down your hesitation about your own sexuality."

"So why wouldn't I be able to cum?" Scarlett inquired.

"Try not to stress, you will. However, you need somewhat more seasoning first." Bella chuckled.

To state Scarlett was disappointed would be putting it mildly. As she ventured out of the car, the butt plug changed into high gear and she nearly lost her balance. She glared back at Bella.

"I'm not sure if I would be able to do it. I'll never make it. I'll cum before everyone." Scarlett literally begged.

"Would that be an awful thing, Scarlett?" Bella teased wickedly.

"Um, no doubt. You know it'll make me an exhibitionist slut. Simply let me cum here to offer some relief." Scarlett begged again.

"Or then again, you could take off the panties. That would work as well," Bella pressed with a wicked smile.

The tone of her voice and the harsh look all over affirmed Scarlett that she was going to keep wearing the panties and in case she couldn't control herself, she'd be cumming in broad daylight.

"Okay, we should go. Where's this café?" Scarlett asked.

"One second and we'll leave," Bella said.

Scarlett looked as Bella squeezed two or three buttons on the remote and afterward set it on the front seat and locked the SUV. Gently and gradually, Scarlett felt the vibes all turned on. They were not buzzing quickly. They were practically delicate and calm. Scarlett figured this was the tease mode that Bella had discussed.

"Now we are all set. How about we go?" And Bella moved toward the café.

Bella led the route as they strolled down to the lake. It was an excellent day and the recreational zone was beaming with life. Scarlett didn't recall any cafés on the lakefront; however, food was the least of her interest. The vibrators, although barely on, were hitting quite a few spots as Scarlett strolled and the breeze was blowing her dress scouring her now exceptionally hard and sensitive nipples. The sensations were intense; however she realized they wouldn't be sufficient to let her cum.

Bella led Scarlett for a decent stroll along the lake. She was certain in the sun, the pale dress would be at least translucent and she was sure her nipples were by and large unmistakably exhibited, yet she didn't look down to affirm what her aroused body was proclaiming. Scarlett was certain the men jogging in the recreation park were getting a spectacular show, but everything she had the energy to focus on was the sexual vitality coursing through her body. Again she offered herself to Bella. She was using her as her play doll, subjugating her for her own pleasure in a twisted way and yet, Scarlett was getting stimulated with every one of the acts.

Bella ridiculed Scarlett saying she was a married lady and she would not like to exploit her. She advised her that her organization was involved with educating women to explore their sensualities and helping them to be progressively intimate with their partners. Scarlett disclosed to her that was actually what she needed; to get physically involved with her. Bella just laughed mischievously. Scarlett couldn't believe her hard-luck as her advances for intimacies got rejected for the second time. She realized she was more aroused and wildly excited than she at any point had been previously. She was desperate to do anything Bella would ask. Anything. And again, Bella rejected her.

After about a mile stroll through the recreation center, they turned around up a side road and Bella escorted Scarlett into a small bistro. It was dark, classical, and romantic. Scarlett saw numerous couples enjoying a romantic get together along with some delicious snacks and thought about how many of them were cheating on their partners. She had never cheated on Jacques, yet anyone in that café who asked could have had her. They settled down in a booth and the movement pushed the butt plug further up her anal cavity.

"I'm never going to make it Bella." Scarlett was desperate.

"Trust me Scarlett. I know what I'm doing. I've trained numerous unhappy housewives. On the off chance that I didn't leave the remote in the SUV, you would, in the long run, persuade me to turn up the panties. You'd be shouting your head off worse than Meg Ryan in When Harry Met Sally. You don't have any desire to make a scene, isn't that right?" Bella teased mischievously.

Scarlett immediately shut up. The waitress showed up. She was a youthful teenage girl. Perhaps, eighteen years of age and just out of secondary school. Scarlett heard Bella ordering a plate of fruit salad, yet everything she could focus on was the fit of her dress. Scarlett was in her very own reality devouring the young waitress's lush body until Bella snapped her fingers before her face. She apologized for her absent mindedness (regarding the menu and not to the waitress) and just ordered her to bring two. She didn't have a clue what she ordered.

Bella continued discussing her business and how she thought Scarlett was perfect to be a model. Scarlett was successful to pay enough attention to her discussions, yet she didn't know whether her opinions made any sense to Bella. Her thoughtful and restless mind was on the fire in her crotch and the lust-filled gazes she was giving to her ardent appreciators and the ones she was receiving. At the same time the panties kept cheerfully buzzing ceaselessly keeping her on the edge of a monstrous orgasm, yet so far from achieving that.

Lunch was boring; if she could call sitting out in the open while her aching pussy sautés itself boring. "Did the waitress continue coming over to have a decent view of my hardened nipples or was she simply being mindful about the customers? Did each one of the men want to fuck me or was my mind simply losing its hold on the real world?" Scarlett wondered and her heart kept on pounding like bass drums making her insane with wild desires. "As we strolled back to the SUV, was Bella's arm around my waist to balance me or was this scheming plot to hold onto control of my body?" Scarlett licked her lips and wondered inwardly letting her perversions consume her sole existence. At long last, they arrived at the SUV.

"You've done particularly well, Scarlett. You've been on a tease and denial session for over sixty minutes. I have got a choice for you. We can return home where I'll turn the panties on full. You can have the greatest, most intense climax of your life in the discretion of my cellar within half an hour." Bella spoke wickedly.

"Yes. Please! Bella! Please let's go home," Scarlett immediately concurred.

"One moment. The price of that choice is I'm turning back on the random mode for the panties while we drive home. Just this time I'll choose level two. I won't mention to you what else that includes, yet I'm almost certain you'll like it. Oh, and you need to take your dress off as well and ride home in only the bra and panties." Bella's eyes were filled with mischief and she chuckled deviously.

"And, what about my other choice?" Scarlett almost pleaded.

"That one is even kinkier. We stroll back to the recreation center. We are located a decent spot close to the jogging path and the panties take your breath away at the most unfavorable minute. Despite everything, you'll get the greatest climax of your life, yet this time it won't be so private. Unless, of course, you can refrain from being too vocal." And Bella chuckled as she made her proposal.

There was no chance Scarlett would be calm and once again, she hated herself for being in this circumstance. Bella owned her orgasm, actually, in the palm of her hand with the remote. She could make her cum with the slightest push of a button. So far she had not requested anything in return deciding not to utilize the power she held over her, but to tease her to insanity. Scarlett realized her body couldn't take considerably more of these panties, yet might it be able to wait for another thirty agonizing minutes and save her from the debasement of cumming before a gathering of strangers? "Would Bella even let me cum in thirty minutes or was this some devious scheme of some master strategy to make me considerably more vulnerable against some malevolent mysterious plan she had?" Scarlett wondered as she strove to make her decision.

"Back to your home," Scarlett responded with a shaky voice and gulped hard.

She plunked down in the SUV and buckled her safety belt.

"Aren't you overlooking something?" Bella teased again.

Scarlett gazed back at her with questioning eyes for a minute and the unfastened the safety belt. She got back out of the SUV. And after cautiously checking the surroundings in the parking garage, she pulled the dress over her head.

"Just toss it in the back," Bella instructed.

As Scarlett did, Bella disclosed to her that she altered her perspective and to have the bra go along with it. This wasn't a part of their deal; however, she wasn't in any position to argue semantics. Before long she was locked back in the seat, naked except her high heels and the teasing panties as she chose to wonder about them.

"Alright, now for part two and we can go." Bella chuckled.

Scarlett gazed at Bella, but observed just delight in her appearance. She was certain she was giggling inside about how simple it had been to transform her into a sex-crazed pervert.

"Open the glove box. You'll find a small dark container. Pull it out," Bella instructed.

Scarlett obeyed. Inside were eight glue patches. They looked like what a doctor utilizes when doing an ECG.

"Two of the cushions go on your tits just over your nipples and two just beneath. The other four go on your thighs on either side of your pussy and simply over your pussy on your abdomen. Then, attach the four cushions on your tits with the short wires and do likewise on the pussy cushions," Bella instructed.

It took Scarlett a few minutes to make sense of how the wires clipped into the cushions. Bella then grabbed a longer out wire and ran it from her left bosom into a plug in the waistband of her panties. She did likewise for her thigh and midriff cushions with a shorter wire. As she was bent over with the wires, Scarlett was desperate to simply get her head and compel her to lick her burning pussy, yet she realized the panties would not permit any touch aside from by its wicked gadgets.

"Finally, connections are done." Bella reclined up. Venturing into the glove box for another little dark case, she pulled out two little clear cylinders and a syringe. She gave the first cylinder a lick around the open end and squeezed her right nipple into it. Utilizing the syringe, Bella then started to draw the air out of it, tugging on her nipple deeply into the cylinder. Scarlett's breath was erratic and snappy as she endeavored to change in accordance with this new electric sensation. It was a blend of pain and pleasure that escalated as Bella finished a similar treatment to her left nipple. At last, she accelerated the SUV. Scarlett desperately hoped to reach her home and experience the orgasm she had been begging for hopelessly.

Just before they pulled out, Bella talked. "You could have already cum; however, I respect your determination. Just sit back, relax and enjoy the ride."

With that and a couple of more pushes of the buttons on the remote, the vibrators sprang back to life. Quicker than Bella had set them while they were in the café, yet Scarlett realized not quick enough to let her cum. As she had been throughout the previous two hours, her restless mind was flooded with musings on how to rush her orgasm. As if Bella had been guessing what Scarlett might be wondering, Bella stopped at the entrance of the parking area and unfastened her safety belt.

"I know how ladies like you think. Get the third box out of the glove compartment," Bella instructed.

Scarlett was excessively too far gone to argue. She did what Bella commanded. This case was huge. Opening it, Scarlett discovered a blindfold and a lot of handcuffs. At long last, her game was evident.

"I overlooked section three of your decision to cum in my home. I don't need you to pull off the nipple suckers too early. So, bind your hands behind your back with the cuff. The blindfold will allow you to focus on what you are feeling." Bella chuckled.

Scarlett took a full breath. As unusual as the day had been, on the off chance that she had the strength, or weakness, to do what Bella asked, their relationship could never be the same. Instantaneously, an electric impulse rocked her succulent bosoms and thighs and the clit vibrator was turned on to the fullest for just the briefest of minutes. Scarlett's torso contracted while tossing her forward. She bounced back against the seat as a wave of raw desire gushed through her body. Goosebumps coursed through her radiant skin and her mind was flying the peaks of excitement.

"I must cum. You win. Take me to the park. I'll cum any place you want!" Scarlett pleaded.

Be that as it may, Bella just mischievously gazed at her as though to say her submissive had settled on her decision and now needed to experience the consequences. Scarlett pulled the blindfold over her eyes with trembling hands and icy fingers and snapped one of the cuffs on her wrist.

"Put your hands behind your back, please... Here, I'll help." And Bella helped her submissive.

Scarlett felt the second cuff fit properly. Her unconditional submission was complete. Her mind was numb. Her aroused and excited body's actions were now controlled by her savage desire. She, at that moment, felt the safety belt was buckled back up in place and the SUV started to move. The voyage to home appeared to be much longer than usual as Scarlett was denied the luxury of her vision. There appeared to be more turns in spite of the fact that it could have quite recently been her failure to focus on something besides the electric shocks and stimulating vibrations coursing through her aching body. At last, the SUV stopped and she sensed the safety belt being removed.

"We're here, Scarlett. You've made it," Bella said.

"Great, please get these toys off of me." Scarlett pleaded, her heart pounding faster than normal as she was flying on the edges of her excitement.

"Obviously. Let me help you to get out of my car."

Scarlett heard Bella giggling. She shivered and gulped hard. Bella licked her lips; this was a delight of a sight to witness a submissive housewife being toyed with in her lair according to her desires and wishes.

But that wasn't what Scarlett implied. She heard the driver's car door open and close and afterward hers. She felt Bella's hand grasp her arm as she dragged her out of the SUV. She could feel grass through the open toe of her high heels.

"Why the hell aren't we in her garage?" Scarlett was shocked at the new sensations and vibes.

"What the hell!?! Where are we?" Scarlett sounded furious.

"We're at my home just as our deal." Bella chuckled.

Scarlett felt herself being driven forward in the grass.

"Horse shit! Where did you take me?" Scarlett was growing restless.

Click. Scarlett heard the sound even before she felt every one of the seven stimulation points vibrating with life. She battled it as hard as possible. She didn't need Bella to make her cum in broad daylight, she thought desperately for a moment, and especially, when she didn't have a clue where she was heading. Scarlett battled and struggled against the extreme pleasurable sensation. It was possibly ten seconds before her body tumbled for the second time that day into a quivery mass of climaxing tissue. Anyone within a three-block region presumably heard her screams of passionate excitement and relief as Scarlett rolled around in the grass. She didn't have a clue how long she laid on the ground. Her body was clenching and quivering as though she was going through a seizure. Scarlett realized that as the vibrations and stimulating shocks ceased, she felt Bella lifting her back on her feet and walking her up a sidewalk and afterward through a doorway. She guided her into the room where she was pushed once more into a comfortable couch. Scarlett had no clue where she was or how many individuals were looking as the g-spot vibrator was turned on again. It was this time when she profoundly learned and experienced the full power of the vibrator with a fierceness she had never felt before. Instantaneously, she had an instinctive and an overwhelming feeling that she was going to pee, her pussy was excited and soft from the long hours of teasing and two tremendous orgasms she had encountered. The torment was exquisite and her breathing grew erratic.

"The need to pee will pass rapidly. Now, brace yourself for the huge one," she heard Bella say and giggle.

And yes, Bella was right. Scarlett could feel the greatest satisfying and powerful orgasm of her life building up rapidly. And afterward, the vibrations ceased.

"Uh oh, sorry about that," Bella prodded.

Scarlett viewed with a gaping mouth in the direction of the originating mischievous voice. On the off chance that she didn't have the blindfold on, Bella would have been burned into ashes from the ferocity of her glaring eyes.

"I couldn't help it. Sorry, here you go. Have a great time," Bella teased again. Yes, Bella was experiencing her share of joy and voyeuristic pleasures while seeing her submissive tormented and teased passionately.

Another snap and each of the three vibrators sprung to life at maximum throttle. Scarlett was off like a rocket and felt her pussy clench down on the vibrator as she experienced an overwhelming release unlike anything she had ever experienced previously. Scarlett was certain her pussy was squirting its juice just as Bella had guaranteed as she felt the insides of her panties getting flooded by her juices. Over and over again, her aroused body quivered and shook like a shattering earthquake and she counted the stars as she was devoured by her apocalyptic orgasms. She had a feeling that she couldn't inhale as wave after wave of joy fell over her. And then nothing.

"This is no love, baby girl. This is your absolute surrender to me…my touch…my voice," Bella whispered in her ears and Scarlett fainted from the overwhelming orgasmic delight.

Chapter 4

Scarlett woke up after two hours or so she thought, leaning back in Bella's living room couch. The room powerfully and wonderfully smelled of female excitement, a carnal response of the pent up savage desires in the torturous underwear. She likewise smelled a trace of a distinct aroma. Yes, Bella had serviced herself while watching Scarlett's naked and resting body. She lay there opposite to her in a state of frantic confusion, clinging onto the control of her hands and the vibrator; control that was slowly slipping from her conscious mind into the clutches of her animalistic subconscious. Finally Scarlett, after recovering her consciousness, felt her arms were free and the torturous panties, the electric cushions, and the nipple suckers had all been removed and she was wrapped under a microfiber sheet.

Her legs were still somewhat shaky as Scarlett wandered naked through Bella's home searching for her. She discovered her back on the first floor. Bella was busy dispatching orders. Scarlett sensed her garments had been flawlessly folded and any proof of her erotic sensational experiences had been cleaned and taken care of.

"Howdy, Scarlett! I hope you weren't pushed too far today?" Bella asked.

"On the off chance that you had mentioned to me what you had planned when I showed up, I never would have believed and confided in you. I'm sore from cumming so much, so I surmise I can't be angry or mad at you," Scarlett answered.

"Great. I have a marriage party going to the house on Friday night for a show. These occasions are normally great cash makers because the young ladies all figure the guys are fucking around at their bachelor party and they need to settle the score. You can easily earn a hundred and fifty dollars," Bella proposed.

"Alright, Bella. What time?" Scarlett was optimistic.

"Come over around 7 PM. They are supposed to reach by 8." Bella replied.

"Fine, I'll be here." Scarlett sealed the deal.

Scarlett returned home, arriving just before Jacques. He, at long last, felt savagely passionate that night, but Scarlett was still excessively shagged out from the evening to return the romantic favor. She faked a brisk orgasm and let Jacques experience some good times before nodding off.

The rest of the week, Scarlett was worried about the upcoming bridal show. She was anxious about exhibiting the panties and demonstrating the toys; however, every time she experienced some kind of hysteria, she thought of the torturous underwear and realized she needed to have them. So, at 7 PM as per plan, she rang Bella's doorbell. She ran her through the schedule. Marriage parties were about embarrassing the lady of the hour with stories of small-dicked husbands, drinking wine, and getting insane. Generally, there was more action toy experimentation because young ladies would be somewhat drunk. Scarlett was to demonstrate a series of provocative lingerie and afterward some fantasy outfits. Her pussy began to cream at the splendid idea.

Scarlett was anticipating an insane affair; however, she thought it would turn out as subdued as Helena's house party had been. There were fifteen ladies in participation, or so she counted. As she demonstrated each outfit, everybody was exceptionally well mannered, and no one touched her inappropriately. Before the night was over, Scarlett was so turned on that she desperately wished someone had touched her improperly; however, it wasn't supposed to happen. She completed the night wearing a small French maid's outfit as Bella took the last orders. At her provocation, the ladies gave Scarlett a round of generous applause and she wavered out of the room on the unthinkably high heels Bella had given her to wear and returned to the cellar to change. She was looking for one of the sample vibrators to deal with her aroused state when Bella came down the stairs with her share of the money. It counted to $175 in products or $100 in real cash. Scarlett inquired as to whether she could bank the $175 toward the torturous underwear she explored the other day and Bella concurred. Scarlett then probed if she could have one of the "sample" toys for a couple of moments and Bella just grinned acknowledging her excitement.

"There's nothing wrong when you're making the most of your work. I'll be waiting upstairs for you." And Bella left.

She gave Scarlett a hare vibrator before heading back upstairs. Scarlett put the toy to great use. It didn't take long before she could bring some relief from her savage and passionate desperation. After that, she got dressed, went upstairs, said her farewells, and returned home.

Scarlett ended up working for Bella all the time. The parties all resembled the same to Scarlett. She ended up purchasing the torturous underwear and two or three different toys and afterward began to bank some money. Each one of the gatherings turned into a blur. Sooner or later, Bella ended up handing over documentation and testimonials about the toys and how she got a lot of joy from them. Scarlett was an outstanding salesperson when it came to marketing the toy products. Sales appeared to blast off after that which satisfied both of them. She got an email from Bella that the following weekend would be a fetish party and inquired about her possibilities to participate and demonstrate. Not sure about what that implied, Scarlett inquired regarding the intricate details and discovered it was leather, rubber, vinyl, and plastic garments. She would likewise be required to wear cuffs and collars and role-play the job of a slave while strolling around the room. Bella assured her that it was strictly looking and no touching. "These fetish parties," she clarified, "Don't occur frequently; however, when they do, they are lucratively rewarding." Scarlett would be working with a second model but there would be a lot of commission and rewards to earn. Scarlett apprehensively concurred.

That weekend Scarlett ended up in the home, well a luxurious and spacious mansion as a matter of fact, of a rich lady whose husband was the CEO of a global investment company. Her partner was an eighteen-year-old attractive redhead with a fantastic body named Clara. She didn't appear that smart to her and her face looked so innocent. Be that as it may, the way in which she moved her body oozed provocative seduction and temptation and wisdom beyond her years. They were both crawling on the floor like dogs as their party dominatrix drove them from lady to lady by their leash. Scarlett was dressed or naked in fact, in a leather G-string which filled no other need than to tease her clit while she crept and a leather push-up bra whose purpose for existence was to pound her succulent bosoms together into a profound seductive cleavage. Her partner, Clara, was much more uncovered, wearing a similar g-string and a swimsuit top which marginally secured her nipples and enabled her youthful, perky nipples and juicy bosoms to hang out all around the small circular patch of material. As usual, Scarlett sensed her pussy was drooling.

She could sense the sales were flying extraordinarily. In any case, splitting the exhibition fees with her partner would grant her a lucrative share. The hostess recommended both the models to enjoy a brief recess so everybody could invigorate their wine glasses and go to the washroom if necessary. Bella dragged Scarlett aside to ask her something kinky.

"Scarlett, this is going to sound strange, yet I've had a request to explain and exhibit the bondage bed. The person is even willing to pay you $100 if you act as the model. So, would you like to model that? Are you interested?" Bella was optimistic for an overwhelming yes.

"I don't have any clue whatsoever," Scarlett answered. "What's a bondage bed?"

"Well, fundamentally it is a portable mat, sort of like the gym mattress just somewhat wider. You fix it to a tabletop or a bed. Then, someone is restrained utilizing Velcro cuffs to the corners. You can undoubtedly get away from the bondage whenever you wish because the Velcro never tightens that incredibly, yet it allows you to have the fantasy of being bound and without any risk," Bella explained.

Scarlett recalled how she felt in Bella's SUV while wearing her cuffs. She was willing and the $100 reward unquestionably made a difference.

"Don't worry. I'll be just beside you to ensure no trouble occurs," Bella assured.

Scarlett concurred and Bella went out to her SUV to bring the bondage bed. When the party attendees returned from their break, Bella had secured the bondage bed to the broad dining table and was fitting leather straps to Scarlett's wrists and ankles.

"I thought you said this was Velcro?" Scarlett seemed apprehensive. "These are real cuffs."

"Indeed, the cuffs are real, yet they are bound to the bed with Velcro. As a matter of fact, you can likewise hook them to eyelets on the bed for increasingly conventional bondage so your partner can't get away, but I generally use the Velcro at parties," Bella countered.

Bella started her discussion and explanations about the bed and its numerous uses. She focused on the flexibility since it was convenient and because it could be utilized on the floor, on a table, on a bed or even vertically mounted to a wall. She additionally clarified how the submissive could be secured if the dominant was willing to have the escape route or if the dominant was determined to bind the submissive thoroughly. She then held out her hand and helped Scarlett up on the table.

The bed was softer than she anticipated. Bella held Scarlett's arms back and wrapped Velcro through the cuff's carabineer hook. The Velcro at that point adhered tightly to another Velcro positioned onto the bed by the metal ringlets used to absolutely restrain the partner. Scarlett's red-headed partner, Clara, restrained her legs. Scarlett was now spread-eagled on the dining table. She pulled softly on the cuffs in an effort to display struggle. She didn't pull too hard because she needed to ensure to give the illusion and fantasy of being truly restrained. She couldn't see herself; however, she was certain she looked charming and surely every visitor at the party was giving her their complete consideration.

Following a couple of moments, Bella proceeded on to more bondage and restraints related devices not requiring a model. She left Scarlett on the table. Scarlett realized she could get up whenever she wanted to, yet she was resolved to play the role of an enslaved young lady. While the party attendees were back in the room, Clara snuck into the dining area. She hung over her head and murmured in her ear that she was hot and that watching her on the bed made her aroused and animated as well. Scarlett didn't know how to respond. Being on the table made her more sizzling than she had been and she was anticipating the end of the party and some help. She felt thirsty and swallowed hard. She felt Clara take her head in her grasp and she planted an exceptionally profound passionate kiss on her lips. Scarlett felt herself reacting to her passionate feminine touch and intuitively pushing back, their lips locked in an ardent dance.

Clara lifted her head. Scarlett attempted to tilt hers to pursue her, yet she lost her as she dodged behind her. Scarlett heard two snaps over her head, but hardly cared about it. Clara must have slithered under the table since she now heard two snaps close to her feet. Scarlett had the choice to raise her head and look down the table enough to see Clara reappear with a mischievous grin all over.

"Now you can't escape from me," she laughed.

Scarlett tried the bonds, but they held quickly. Clara had deftly bonded the cuff clasps to the metal ringlets. She battled once more, this time for real, yet couldn't get away from it. Again Clara moved over her to kiss her, but this time her right hand wandered all over her lush body. Breaking the kiss and spellbinding Scarlett, Clara crept over her body.

"I know you're aroused from exhibiting this stuff. So am I. How about we get off before Bella completes the process of approving her orders?" Clara teased.

She didn't allow Scarlett to react. Clara jumped over her and started to dry hump her yearning pussy against hers.

"I wish I could have a strap-on and fuck you appropriately, but for now, this should do." Clara moaned seductively.

Over and over again, Clara drove her pelvis into Scarlett's. The exquisite friction from the little leather g-strings they were wearing was carrying out its responsibility to tease their clits and soon, Scarlett experienced a wonderful, if not explosive orgasm. Clara was grinding herself against Scarlett desperately to peak her lust-filled excitements. Both of them attempted to stay quiet and Scarlett could sense Clara exploded more earnestly than her, yet it was still very pleasurable. As they were descending from their passionate peaks, they heard commotions in the living room proving another wine break was going on. This would have the party attendees heading to the living room once more. Clara hopped off Scarlett only minutes before getting captured. They attempted to act easygoing and if anyone had witnessed Scarlett were now really restrained to the bed and that her body was flushing with a post-orgasmic shine, they didn't utter a word. Bella popped her head in to say she could get up since they were done. Scarlett sort of shrugged. She promptly realized what her non-verbal message implied. Giving Clara a mischievous, mean look, Bella strolled around the bed and released her bonds. She murmured in her ear and apologized, saying she experienced issues with Clara once before and that she ought to have cautioned her. But Scarlett affirmed not to worry concerning it. Clara and Scarlett split $500 money from the party. It was the most formidable deal Scarlett had ever made— she had a climax and Clara got familiar with her and what they both cherished the most. Besides, it was an incredible night.

Throughout the following couple of months, Scarlett kept on exhibiting and modeling for Bella. Clara filled in as her partner a few times at the more insane and wilder parties; however, their scene on the table from their very first party wasn't repeated. After each party, Scarlett generally carried herself to an intense delightful climax with whatever new toy she successfully earned. Increasingly more, as often as possible, Clara emerged unmistakably in her savage and perverted fantasies. Now and then, she was with Jacques and Clara. Some of the time it was only both of them.

Last Saturday, Scarlett was running late to another wedding party. Then, when she landed at the maid of honor's home, Bella had just started and Clara had already started flaunting her seductive body to the assembled gathering of young ladies. Without breaking stride, Bella tossed her a white ribbon teddy and guided her to the bedroom. The rest of the party went easily and was uneventful. Bella made her lucrative deals and Clara and Scarlett shared the profits. It wasn't as much as some of the past bridal parties; however, it was still incredible cash for two hours worth of work.

Strolling back to her car, Scarlett saw an envelope under her windshield wiper. Her first idea was "Did I park beside a fire hydrant? Am I being booked for wrong parking?" She didn't see any fire hydrant or a no parking sign when she pulled up, yet she was in a hurry so it was possible. Picking up the envelope, Scarlett was relieved to discover it wasn't a ticket. She plunked down in the driver's seat and opened it. Enclosed was a handwritten message on an expensive piece of paper. The penmanship was streaming and indicated an exquisite touch of calligraphy. Her initial impression was someone of knowledge, elegance, and supreme class composed the note. As Scarlett read the note, she was amazed. It surely was not what she was anticipating.

"Hi, Scarlett,

You don't know me because we haven't met. My sister went to one of Bella's bridal parties. She educated me concerning how you endorsed Bella's remote vibrating panties and how exceptionally stimulated you generally got when wearing them. It sounded intriguing, so I had her request me a couple. Thank you for prescribing them! I've never cum so hard in my life. My husband loves to have me wear the panties in broad daylight and tease me until he makes me cum while attempting to hide my passionate feelings from the individuals around us."

Scarlett's pussy had just been wet from exhibiting herself at the party and now she was getting absolutely overflowing reading a note from a lady who appreciated the panties as much as she did.

"In the event that you are willing, I might want to talk with you about the panties. Enclosed is my email address. I would like to get more enthusiastic reviews from you... p.s. As I'm sitting in my car composing this note, I'm wearing the panties. My beloved husband sets them on simmer and keeps the remote with him at home. I know when I return home, I realize I'll be prepared to do anything he desires. Thank you so much. I love these panties."

As Scarlett read the note and afterward read it again, she envisioned an exceptionally sophisticated and refined lady jerking off in her car while composing the note. She hoped the elegant writer made it home safely. She carried the note to her nose and inhaled deeply. She realized the distinctive, powerful smell of her excitement, but then again she wondered if her perverted mind was pulling pranks on her. She crafted an image of her in her deviant mind as she landed back home to be stripped and taken by her husband when she strolled into the doorway. When Scarlett returned home and stripped out of her very own garments, her secret lesbian fantasy was stimulating her mind and body and she carried herself to an incredible orgasm fantasizing the female writer and her beloved husband.

She didn't know whether she needed to contact the lady. During that entire week, Scarlett had a few extra powerful and pleasurable climaxes fantasizing about her husband teasing her the way Bella had teased her. Scarlett had a feeling that any contact between them would unavoidably prompt dissatisfaction since she would never accept and believe the fantasy that Scarlett had cum thinking about her. In the long run, Scarlett's curiosity conquered her concerns and she shot an email to the mysterious note writer. Her email address was a generic Yahoo mail account. It provided no insight as to her identity, age, or physical address.

Scarlett was on a tingling sensation waiting impatiently for a response. The following day she received an email from the mysterious email writer. They made a deal to avoid sharing personal information. She knew Scarlett's name and Scarlett realized she was married, yet other than that, Scarlett knew nothing about the mysterious note writer. Indeed, that didn't continue for long. They really turned out to be dear companions since they shared intricate details about their love and sex life, their fondness for the remote-controlled panties, ways and places to pleasure and satisfy them, different toys and their twisted fantasies, perverted kinks and fetishes. Somehow or another Scarlett had her most intimate connection with a lady she had never met and didn't have any acquaintance with her name.

Chapter 5

At the desperation of her mysterious companion, Scarlett wore the remote-controlled panties to work last Friday. The mysterious note writer said her beloved husband had her do it frequently, and it was always a thrill. Jacques was away on a boot-camp training course for his freelancing work, so Scarlett was feeling hornier than expected. At her office Fridays were casual days, so she figured this would be a perfect time to try something kinky and have some fun. Usually, her office was less populated during Fridays compared to other weekdays, so it appeared to be an ideal opportunity. Scarlett was eager to wear a hidden toy at work and she needed to feel attractive. She picked one of her hottest trim bras, a pair of pull up stockings under her pants, and high heeled leather boots. Up top, she wore an ordinary white pullover. Outwardly, Scarlett looked absolutely normal. Underneath, however, she was mischievously excited.

During her drive to the workplace, Scarlett had set the panties in random mode. Multiple times it caught her off guard and she nearly got in accidents; however, the panties carried out their responsibility. When she made it to the workplace, Scarlett was insanely aroused.

She got into the workplace much ahead of time. Two or three of the administrators arrived by that time in the workplace, yet none of the general staff. Scarlett immediately snuck into the restroom and sought refuge in the handicapped stall. She pulled out the remote and turned each of the three attachments on full. At that speed, everyone could hear the humming, yet the odds of getting captured were insignificant and Scarlett was desperate to cum. She needed to put her clenched hand in her mouth to prevent from shouting as she enjoyed her first powerful orgasm of the day. Scarlett was gasping and overheated as she descended from her peak. She switched off the panties and endeavored hard to calm down her restless mind and nerves. Looking at her watch, it was the starting of her shift time, so Scarlett immediately washed her hands and headed back to her desk.

After returning to her work area, Scarlett stashed her satchel (and the remote) in her desk cabinet and tried to concentrate on her regular office work. Although the vibrators were not running, their negligible nearness in and around her sore pussy and ass had made her anxious. She was battling to focus on her work. As silly as it would appear, Scarlett discretely slid her hand into her satchel and immediately customized the remote into the tease mode. She kept the vibrations low, in fact too low to even think about having any audible sound. She also kept the clit vibrator off. The straightforward buzzing in her yearning cavities really quieted her down. They felt extraordinary, practically like meeting an old companion and she were, at long last, ready to concentrate on her routine work and chase them down. She knew at this level, she couldn't cum. Instead, she simply let the underwear keep her excited and jovial.

About an hour later, Scarlett decided she had worked hard enough to have a break. She declared to her cubicle colleagues that she needed a long washroom break, grabbed her satchel, and leaped toward the washroom. She desperately prayed that none of her colleagues would suddenly decide to accompany her. Lady luck seemed to favor her and Scarlett immediately replayed her eternal ecstatic bliss from before that morning. Back at her cube, she futilely tried once again to concentrate on her work without her euphoria buzzers on, yet she disastrously failed once more. She grabbed the remote and set the buzzers on tease mode. Indeed, getting off in the washroom every now and then truly was a fascinating method to lead the day.

Just before lunch, Scarlett was preparing for her third washroom trip. She decided she had enough of the teasing underwear and was going to take them off and then toss them in the car in her other purse. Sadly, she had not thought to bring another pair of panties so she was compelled to carry on with the teasing panties until she could purchase another pair during the lunch break. The teasing underwear had already done their job. Scarlett was highly excited about another astonishing washroom visit. In any case, just before she could recover her handbag, her floor manager hurried into the cubicle and declared there was an emergency company-wide video conference and they should be present in the conference room.

Scarlett and her cubicle colleagues stood up and pursued the rest of the office into the conference room. She didn't have the foggiest idea why they were all summoned in the conference room rather than a team discussion in private. There were just twelve seats at the table which the managers immediately grabbed. The rest of the average workers were left to gather around the table standing side by side. Scarlett ended up sandwiched between two of the sales representatives. Tom, standing before her, was a suave and well-mannered person. They enjoyed a nice and healthy professional friendship. He was married and Scarlett always wondered about his wife and thought she was a fortunate young lady to have such a hunky fellow returning home to her every night. Scarlett absolutely didn't fret being jam-packed into him. Behind her, and tragically not appearing to mind being pressed into her, was Ben. He was a bachelor with a reputation for womanizing in the workplace. He wasn't especially smooth. He was bound to strike out than hit a home run type of guy; however, it compensated for his absence of Romeo-abilities by hitting on anything with boobs. Scarlett could feel his hands on her hips. Typically, she would have made a whine; yet given how provocative she had kept herself throughout the morning, she didn't generally mind. Her panties were still cheerfully buzzing ceaselessly, and she was sandwiched between the two men, neither of whom were her husband. The conference began, yet her restless mind was exploring deeper and further into her lewd fantasy land of sexual joys.

Scarlett completely got animated by the buzzing in her panties. When the conference was over, she was certainly heading to the restroom to get herself off and calm down her sensual excitements once more. Be that as it may, just at that moment, Venus struck the chord of passion. The clit vibrator went from minimum buzz to full thunder and then off. Scarlett winced involuntarily and bumped upon Tom. "Oh no, so sorry," she murmured an apology. Then, the anal plug blasted off into motion. As that one was ceasing its movements, the g-spot vibrator kicked in and then again, the clitoral one. Again and again, the underwear pushed through the different toys. Scarlett desperately battled hard to look as exhausted as the rest of her colleagues, but waves after waves of passionate enthusiasm rocked through her body. The teasing torment proceeded for several minutes, but it felt like ages to Scarlett. Her breathing was getting heavier and her legs felt too weak to maintain her balance when, fortunately, the vibrations stopped.

Scarlett investigated the room with curious eyes to check whether anyone had seen or was observing her. She started to regain her strength as she concluded no one presumed what she was doing. At that moment, it began once more. This time each of the three vibrators sprang to life with more enthusiasm than ever before, although fortunately not at max speed. They were on at about half speed. "Incredible," Scarlett thought. Running this thing throughout the morning had destroyed her earthly senses. The speed started to pulse. The clit vibrator would cycle all over while the g-spot vibrator fluctuated in reverse action. Then, when one was moderate, the other was quick. Scarlett didn't realize she could program this exquisite function, yet she cherished it. The anal vibrator remained consistent for some time and then started flipping on and off in an interval of around five seconds. On the off chance that the underwear didn't stop, or the conference didn't end, Scarlett would have been exceptionally embarrassed at her sensual self-play. She realized she couldn't hold out any longer. She battled and she battled her inner evil spirit, but her ability to remain outwardly quiet was depleting her vitality. The idea of either fainting out in sensational pleasure or overwhelmingly orgasming in a room brimming with people started to consume her spirit. She could feel her will to resist the temptation of leaving her body and then nothing. The vibrations had ceased. She would lie to herself if she said her body hadn't betrayed her and desperately wished the panties had continued its stirring actions. In any case, her mind was grateful they had ceased their pulsations before her embarrassment could echo through the room.

Scarlett stopped; her thighs were moist with desperate cravings and she was certain the teasing underwear was drenched with juice as the conference wrapped up. As the room got vacant, the workers were beginning to gather up in small groups and started discussing the conference. Scarlett rushed back to her work area and grabbed her handbag and the remote for the vibrator. She nearly leaped on her feet and hurried to the restroom. As she was arriving at the doorway, she saw another lady from her cubicle heading toward the washroom as well. "Shit!" Scarlett thought. "What now?"

Just then her sex consumed deviant mind had a plan. One floor beneath Scarlett's office, there was a rented place. Actually, her company had leased the space to another company for some extra income and she was sure that the washrooms down that floor would be much more private. Scarlett redirected herself to the stairs and strolled down one floor. Throughout the entire way, her toys kept on pounding her rosebuds and anal cavity stimulating her almost to the extremities. The floor appeared to be deserted. Scarlett breathed a sigh of relief. Obviously, the couple of representatives left down here was still busy at lunch, or probably had gone out to enjoy a recess. It was just perfect.

As Scarlett entered the restroom, she quickly saw the handicapped stall was already booked. They had one lady employee who broke her leg and who worked on this floor, so it was most likely her. "I can hide in the corner stall until she leaves," Scarlett thought and plotted her idea. She moved into the corner stall and pulled out the remote. She spread her legs to take care of the underwear and tapped on tease mode. Her panties sprung to life, and she immediately felt her aroused body responding to another incredibly satisfying orgasm. Her ears were set on high alert to the stall on the opposite side and impatiently waited to hear a flush; indeed, it did happen just within thirty seconds. Scarlett heard the occupant moving around so she throttled up the speed of the vibrators to the next level. "Oh my God! This would be another big one," Scarlett thought and bit her lips. For a moment she could only hear her heart pounding like bass drums in her ear.

Scarlett heard the stall door squeaking to open and through the little space between her stall wall and the doorway, she saw a lady on crutches walking out.

"I will soon be alone," Scarlett thought. She heard the water running in the sink and the sound of the hand dryers running. At that moment, she heard the lady battling with her crutches to open the washroom door and then it was so gleefully silent. "Thank God," Scarlett sighed. She didn't waste any of her valuable time. She clicked the "Maximum Power" button on the remote and was overwhelmed by intense pulsations coursing all over her body. Lascivious thoughts conquered her mind and within moments, another massive pleasurable orgasm washed through her body. She endeavored hard to remain silent as she did in the upstairs restroom, yet the exciting constrictions gushing through her body pulled her clenched hand down and the sounds of ecstasy reverberated throughout the restroom.

Scarlett was shaking in the seat of the toilet as she experienced her overwhelming orgasm. She realized she had squirted again into the panties and she in fact loved it. The panties would be in a mess when she would take them off, or so she thought. However, the cleaning exertion was well justified, despite all the trouble. Scarlett shut the vibrators down and was ready to slide the panties off her overheated body when she suddenly heard something hit the vanity counter. Scarlett was petrified. "Was somebody listening to my moans and screams? Or was it just my imagination still seducing my mind?" Scarlett wondered as she gulped hard. She went quiet, not pulling down the underwear and keeping her ears and senses on high alert to trace the slightest of the sounds and the presence of an alien entity on her erotic realm.

Following several minutes, Scarlett surmised it was only her overactive senses. She prepared to slide the panties off when they were turned on once more. Again the teasing underwear started to cycle back and forth, again and again. Obviously, she cherished the stirring vibrations, yet she realized she needed to escape the restroom. She grabbed her remote and shut the panties' vibrators gradually. She then immediately slid out of them and pulled one of the batteries out of the waist band. Scarlett really strove hard to work the sticky and messy panties into her handbag. Once again, it wasn't a very well-planned idea to hide something devious and mischievous. Scarlett needed to wash them, yet she wasn't in the mood to take another risk and get caught. "I could wash the handbag later," Scarlett thought inwardly. When that rigorous assignment was done, she stood up and straightened her dress. She left the stall and headed to the sink when she was bewildered and intensely shocked that nearly made her petrified on the spot.

Standing at the sink and doing her cosmetics was a thirty-something lady. She was dressed sophisticatedly in an expensive-looking silk blouse and a skirt which streamed down over her knees. Scarlett didn't perceive her as a worker; however, she didn't know everybody on this floor so she thought her as an employee in some other office. She felt her cheeks burning and her heart pumped like that of an athlete after a marathon race. She couldn't talk. She just looked down at the floor and headed out of the restroom. She hurried to her car. Without the assistance of the panties to hold in her overflowing juices, her pussy fluid was starting to run down her inner thighs as the denim from her jeans scoured against her slit. Scarlett moved rapidly, apprehensive that she would explode again before she could arrive at her car. Fortunately, she didn't park her car too far away to reach. On the off chance that she had parked her car at the end of the parking lot, she would never have made it without orgasming again and it would have implied her jeans would bear the stains of her ecstasies, furthering her embarrassment. She just shivered at the terrible thought.

She sat in the vehicle and strove to calm her excitement. She started the motor and turned the AC system on high. Her nipples were hard as rocks and it wasn't because of the cold AC air. Her pussy was throbbing demanding further seductive consideration. There was no chance she could return to the workplace, not in her messy and disheveled condition. So Scarlett grabbed her juice coated mobile out of her handbag and called her immediate boss. Fortunately, her boss was out on a brief lunch and was on voice mail. So, Scarlett made up some horse shit phone message about having something at lunch that wasn't conducive to her stomach and getting ill. She was going to take the day off and return home.

Chapter 6

Then when Scarlett returned home, her mind was all the while reeling from the embarrassment of being caught red-handed while masturbating in the washroom at work by a stranger. Obviously, that led to another masturbation session, prompting another overwhelming climax and in the long run, her seductive assaults on her husband, Jacques, when he returned home. The following day, Scarlett sent an email describing the whole scene to her web sister of lewdness. That night, her unknown internet friend responded explaining to Scarlett that her story had so motivated her husband that he pounded her like never before and then revealed to her he had another brilliant idea.

The internet friend of hers didn't really brief the intricacies; however, Scarlett paused and thought rigorously. She sent an email to Bella getting some information about the unwavering quality of the panties' control unit and she replied no one at any point had an issue with it as just going wild. Bella reaffirmed she would ask the manufacturer about the product and Scarlett decided not to wear her teasing companion out in the open for some time.

Her virtual masturbation friend sent her a recap of her beloved husband's new strange idea. She informed Scarlett that quite a while before experimenting with toys, she and her husband swapped partners for a short time. His devious plan this time was to have her wear the teasing underwear and then hand over the remote to the couple down the road whom they swung with every once in a while. She disclosed to Scarlett how the wife particularly took to teasing her wildly until she asked the husband to fuck her with bestial wrath. Scarlett didn't have the foggiest idea what she was talking about or how she convinced her husband into swapping and all that. Scarlett had no idea what her secret internet friend looked like, yet the twisted fantasies of her based on her exquisite penmanship was hot as Scarlett crafted a kinky swapping scenario in her mind; the husband was with another woman while his wife achieved the peak of her excitement provoking her fuck buddy to ram her mercilessly in front of her husband. Scarlett was pounding her bald pussy with a rabbit vibrator envisioning herself helpless before a wild swapping scene, somewhat at the mercy of a sadistic dominant partner determined on preventing her from peaking while she got intensely aroused by witnessing the sex in front. It was exactly the same sex game in which Bella used her as a sex toy, the very first time when she wore the malicious panties, but that appeared to be more similar to experimentation. Scarlett didn't have a clue what was in store. This time she needed it seriously; she yearned for it desperately.

Scarlett didn't think Jacques was prepared to find out about her secret vibrator stimulated life, so she began to craft a wicked plan. The only individual she thought about that could deal with her fantasies was her mysterious internet friend, so Scarlett sent her an email and approached her for counsel. Her plan was to put the teasing underwear on and then some way or another bind her hands. Scarlett recollected the bondage cuffs Bella had utilized on her and that turned her on so much that she role-played with Clara behind everyone's back. Scarlett's secret internet companion recommended her to approach her home where she could tease her as much as she wanted, yet Scarlett was somewhat reluctant to explore her fantasies absolutely at the mercy of an unknown stranger, no matter how long they chatted over the internet or shared their illicit temptations. Scarlett offered another proposal instead; she would be in her living room where she could sit on the doorway patio and control the panties. The secret friend replied she'd need to come inside to release Scarlett. Scarlett didn't care for that thought. She revealed to her that she would need to consider it. Bella came to the rescue with a couple of cuffs having a timer locking system in case the regular cuffs would fail to perform their duties. Scarlett could set the time of her bondage and escape on her own. Her mysterious internet companion consented to the terms, and they scheduled a date for Thursday at 6 PM. Jacques would be working until 9 PM, so Scarlett decided two hours were sufficient for the cuffs. Scarlett's mysterious internet friend said she wouldn't be staying around that long; however, she could tease her for an hour or an hour and a half. She would then leave the panties on simmer so when the cuffs unrestrained Scarlett, she would be ready to complete the exciting task all by herself. It was an insane idea, yet Scarlett consented to it. She advised her internet friend to look for the blinds being shut on the living room window before moving toward the porch. She concurred under the given condition that Scarlett would not peek and notice her secretly. She said it was significantly more energizing because they had never met and the secrecies had a hidden seduction tempting the mind. Scarlett concurred and immediately began anticipating her next sensual adventure that was about to happen within a couple of days.

Scarlett ended up taking Thursday evening off and pampering herself at a neighborhood spa. For the rest of the world, she appeared to plan for an extraordinary date, which she was as it were. By 5:30 PM, Scarlett had been wearing the teasing panties and a shirt. She considered attaching the nipple pumps she had purchased soon after Bella had used it on her; however, she thought two hours were excessively long of a time for them. She had tried the cuffs a few times. Two hours was their maximum time limit, and they always got unlocked right on time. Scarlett walked around her bedroom wondering about whether she really had the guts to proceed with this. She checked the doorways. They were altogether bolted and dead locked. She calculated the dire consequences and scenarios of her scheduled bondage play, and she realized the worst-case scenario would be her cuffs wouldn't open and Jacques would discover about her deviant self. Obviously, at that moment, she would have to endeavor hard to make her explanations sensible and acceptable, but that would be it. He'd surely been the recipient of her revitalized libido.

By 5:55 PM, Scarlett had decided to proceed with the dangerously lewd plan. At 5:57 PM, she shut the blinds and at 5:59 PM, she locked her destiny with the cuffs attached to her wrists behind her back after sliding the blindfold on. She owned a very comfortable recliner positioned just beside the window and that was where she settled herself comfortably. She anticipated that the vibrators should turn on right away, yet they didn't. Five minutes passed by. Then, perhaps ten more minutes. Her expectation was developing continuously. At long last, at 6:15 PM, she heard a knock on the window and then the vibrators were turned on. Scarlett was already on the edge because of the remarkable and glorious sensual anticipation and was feeling better. She impatiently thought about how her mysterious internet friend, who by now was her teasing panties' controller, would realize how to prevent her from cumming. Scarlett later learned her secret panties' controller was sitting on her patio wearing her very own panties and strove to judge Scarlett's responses depending on what she was feeling.

When they exchanged emails reliving their experiences the following morning, they arrived at the conclusion that Scarlett's internet buddy had a lot higher teasing limit than hers. Or then again, perhaps it was the exotic sensualities of having a kinkier experience of submission and dominance and the thrill of not seeing anything, but just to feel. Be that as it may, Scarlett came at least six times before her mysterious internet buddy left her on tease mode and returned home to her beloved husband. The cuffs worked like a champ and Scarlett got away in the nick of time to passionately pleasure herself with the rabbit vibrator and then bathe and clean her toys before Jacques returned home. She was excessively exhausted to have any intercourse with him, yet since he was back to his freelancing work routine, he didn't appear to mind.

Their message exchanges after this event analyzed each pleasurable feeling and euphoric emotion from that night. At last, it was finalized that they needed to try the kinky experience once more. Scarlett was guaranteed by her secret accomplice that she could hold her on the edge much longer than their previous encounter and give her significantly more overpowering and ecstatic climaxes in the event that she could witness and hear how Scarlett was responding. Her secret internet buddy also revealed to her that her husband would be away the upcoming week. She would set aside a few minutes for Scarlett on the off chance that she needed to try the kinky experiment once more. Scarlett immediately concurred. Jacques would be working late on Wednesday and she was entitled to get an ordinary leave every month. Bella didn't have any bridal parties to showcase her products, so it would be incredibly awesome to experiment with the kink. They chose an early afternoon start time. In the last email exchange, Scarlett's secret internet friend disclosed to her, she was sending Scarlett a couple of more things to make the evening extraordinary. She guaranteed she could give Scarlett climaxes she had never experienced before. She likewise promised to wear her teasing underwear and let Scarlett take control after they were finished. Scarlett was informed there would be a box waiting at the door when she would wake up on Wednesday. Scarlett was desperate to grab it before Jacques discovered it. She was to wear what was in the crate and adhere to the guidelines inside. This seemed both ominous and thrilling. Scarlett continued getting messy in between her legs each time she wondered about it.

Wednesday morning when the alarm went off, Scarlett volunteered to make breakfast while Jacques showered.

Rather than going to the kitchen, she hit the front door and as promised there was a huge box marked SEX TOYS waiting eagerly for Scarlett. She hoped that it had not been there for long. She shrouded the crate in the cellar and afterward made soup and eggs for breakfast. They typically didn't have time and energy for a hot breakfast so Jacques was exceptionally keen and supportive of Scarlett's endeavors. When Jacques was eating, Scarlett went upstairs to dress for work. She wasn't going anyplace though, and he didn't have to know that. It was just a mere pretense. After he left, Scarlett hurried to the cellar and opened the crate. On the top, there was a note.

"My dearest, Scarlett,

It has been my exquisite pleasure to explore our sensualities and these incredible panties. Today I'm going to give you the ecstasies that you've never known. However, we need to do things my way. Apart from the panties, I need you to wear what is in the case."

76

Scarlett glanced in the crate and there was another sealed box.

"Try not to open the box until 11:30 AM. I need you to shower, shave your legs, underarms and pussy. I, then, need you to prepare and make yourself all attractive like you're dressing to tempt somebody on a date. I need you to make yourself feel unique for your exceptional day. At 11:30, I need you to put on what is in the crate and by 11:45, I need you to have your teasing panties on and be relaxing in your living room. Turn the seat around so you are looking out of the window. I'll be viewing the window, but you won't see me. Leave the back door opened. I will sit behind you on the couch and overwhelm your mind and senses. Don't stress and believe in me."

Scarlett was shaking and sat on the cellar floor as she read the note once more. Her pussy had drenched her cotton panties. She didn't have a clue what to do. She didn't have the foggiest idea whether she could proceed with this. An unknown and an absolute stranger would be in the living room, yet she couldn't see her and on the off chance that anyone went to the patio, they would see Scarlett. As usual, her brain changed to sexual fantasies autopilot and soon she was masturbating on the cellar floor. Simply her fingers, the note, and her lewd fantasies were enough to drag her to the zeniths of excitement. Time appeared to stop. Her fingers were still somewhere deep in her pussy, yet maybe they had their very own brain and Scarlett was unable to control them. She needed to realize what surrendering the control in dominance and submission role-play would feel like. She was desperate to realize how hard she could cum. The panties had assumed responsibility and control of her sexual existence and she needed to experience this.

Then, when Scarlett eventually had the enthusiastic strength, she willed herself off the floor and back to the kitchen for some espresso. She did as she had been commanded to do. She took a hot shower, encompassed by scented candles rather than the harsh vanity lights of her master bathroom. She shaved. She prepared herself. She took extra consideration with her make-up and she looked like an alluring temptress. Right at 11:30 AM, Scarlett opened the second box. There was another note.

"On the off chance that you are reading this, I believe you have already decided to proceed with your kink expedition. First and foremost, I need you to realize that if you would prefer not to proceed with the play today, I totally understand. I won't request that you do anything you would prefer not to do. If you want to stop at any point of time, just say the word 'watermelon' and I will stop. Then again, in case you want to proceed, I need you to adhere to the following directions totally."

Scarlett was shaking again and her pussy kept on leaking. She felt her heart and stomach doing somersaults in her throat.

"To begin with, put on the garments that are in the container. Your panties go on last and I believe you put new batteries in them."

As usual, Scarlett had dealt with that.

"Next put on the wrist cuffs. You can stroll down your stairs to the living room before putting on the high heels boots and strapping the short chain between them. You will likewise find a blindfold. Before you blindfold yourself and clasp your wrists together, in front, I need you to switch on your panties to teasing mode. Next, I need you to stride to your mailbox and leave your remote where I can fetch it. Then, toddle back again into the house, settle down comfortably on the seat, blindfold yourself, and bind your hands together behind your back. I'll understand you chose to proceed with our kink adventure if I see you outside. On the off chance that you changed your perspective, that is fine. In case that is the situation, I truly felt animated by our past encounters, yet this will be the last communication we will have."

Scarlett strove relentlessly to calm her restless nerves and then she reviewed the letter, twice. She investigated the crate. The contents were in fact pretty simple and straightforward. There was a leather bra. "I ought to have expected the nipple cut outs." Scarlett thought. It was fundamentally the same as the one Bella used on her. "Was Bella the same individual waiting patiently for me?" Scarlett swallowed hard. There was also a garter belt, black fish net stockings, and a couple of thigh-high leather boots with the most impossible high heels and two clasps designed to hold the short chain she found on the base of the crate.

As guaranteed there was likewise a blindfold and a couple of soft leather wrist cuffs. There was no timer arrangement. When Scarlett clipped the cuffs together, she was just going to be liberated by her secret friend or Jacques when he returned home in eight hours or something like that. Even though her mind was getting bombarded by all sorts of doubtful questions, she got dressed. She didn't require any lube to slide the g-spot vibrator into her pussy. Scarlett used some with the butt plug; however, in truth, she'd figured out how to slide it in effectively in the course of the most recent few months. Scarlett got the boots, the blindfold, and the remote and headed to the ground floor.

The clock in the living room rang 11:50. The hardest part was placing her remote in the letter box. Her outfit was horribly revealing, also her stone hard nipples were clearly exhibited. Scarlett turned the seat around to face the window and opened the blinds. Scarlett looked outside; however, she saw no vehicles or individuals. She realized her mysterious kink partner was viewing from some place. She realized she was out there. She couldn't delay the proceedings any further. She slid the boots onto her legs. The stockings aided and there was an exotic vibe to the leather sliding up her legs. Above all, the aromatic smell. Goodness the smell of the fine grained leather attacking her noses. She was at the now or never decision door. This was the last possibility for good judgment to supersede her bubbling desires. "Watermelon. Watermelon. Watermelon," she repeated to herself as she opened the front entryway.

She looked out of the yard searching for any of her neighbors or approaching vehicles. The chain and the heels would contrive to back her off. Scarlett couldn't run regardless of whether it implied getting captured. There was no traffic. That was the ideal opportunity. She tapped the remote to press three... The long, delicate, and unbearable tease. In a split second the panties woke up and similarly as fast she groaned. Utilizing small steps, she strolled down her front door and walkway to the letter box mounted on a post at the road. She had limited focus. A parade could have strutted by her home and she would not have seen it. She put the remote in the letter box and returned back to the house. A thirty second errand became two minutes because of the boots. She shut the entryway and locked it. Recollecting the guidance to open the indirect access, she moved as fast as conceivable to the kitchen to cross check the basic detail she was certain she had overlooked.

Back to the lounge room and into the seat. Blindfolded with hand behind her back. Her last vision was the clock on the wall showing 11:59am. Scarlett had done it. She had consented to put herself at the mercy of an outsider. A lady she didn't have any acquaintance with her name. Her pussy, ass, and clit were tingling with the erotic stimulations of a malevolent device which would show her no mercy or release until her secret accomplice showed up. "Would she show compassion for me and let me cum? Would it be the greatest climax of my life as she guaranteed? What payment would she request of me as I made certain to ask for my orgasmic bliss, both physically and psychologically?" Scarlett wondered breathlessly.

Tick, tock, the clock on the wall tolled twelve. "Where is she? Who is she? Besides, why the hell am I so wet considering her?" Scarlett thought over and over again.

How long had she been impatiently waiting? She heard the ring on her lounge room clock strike twelve soon after she had handcuffed her wrists behind her back. The vibrator on her clit and in her pussy and ass had been cheerfully buzzing ceaselessly at a speed unreasonably low for her to orgasm, yet sufficiently high to drive her excitement through the rooftop. A few times she thought she had heard her secret sweetheart open the back door; however, no one made their presence known or changed the speed on her remote controlled vibrating underwear. Time was stopping. Her brain was shattered with desire. The only thing that mattered to Scarlett was she wasn't there for an hour because that the clock had not ringed one.

Scarlett ended up imploring for sexual alleviation even though she didn't have the foggiest idea whether any other person was present in the room. On the off chance that somebody was in the house, they were remaining surprisingly calm, yet she couldn't control her feelings. At last, she broke down in tears as her most delicate spots ached with dire need. A need she couldn't meet without assistance. She heard the clock strike one. "Damn, it's just been 60 minutes," she wondered breathlessly. She had gone two hours prior, yet this time was unique. This time she was not depending on her timer handcuffs to release her. This time she needed to sit tight for help.

At long last, soon after the clock struck two, Scarlett heard the back door of her house opening. She, at that moment, heard the obvious sound of heels strolling over the kitchen floor. They seemed like stilettos. They were remarkably distinctive. The sound disappeared as she believed the lady arrived at the corridor mat or possibly she removed her shoes. Scarlett started to tense in sensual and terrifying anticipation expecting her mysterious friend's arrival in her controlled, unprotected, and overheated body. Her release, both metaphorically and actually would be impending.

Chapter 7

Scarlett detected her essence as she stood behind the seat. Their first physical contact was her hands stretching around the seat to twist and pinch the hardened stubs on her ample bosoms. Her apparently long fingernails scratched gradually against her touchy nipples. She envisioned her with long nails shining with bright red nail polish as she tormented her nipples fanning the flames of her fervent desire.

Her first sound was a groan. Her second physical contact was a subsequent blindfold being applied over the first. This one was a lot heavier and was bound much more tightly around her head. There was no possibility for even a peek from under the edge with this one. As speedy as she had showed up, her presence vanished.

Scarlett heard what she perceived as the lounge chair cushion compressing. Possibly she had plunked down. She, at that moment, heard a tick. From her experience, she realized that sound originated from the underwear remote. Her dull tease turned into a snappy explosion of vitality as the entirety of her delicate and sensitive spots got a thundering shock of vibration, delightful for around fifteen seconds. She was close. So close. And afterward the movement stopped. There was pin-drop silence in the room except from the sound of her pounding heart.

Scarlett heard the sound of a zipper. She realized it wasn't herself so her secret accomplice more likely than not been disrobing. She heard the buzz of a vibrator, yet it wasn't the one of hers. The sound got suppressed as it clearly discovered its way into the lady's pussy. The room was gradually filled with reverberating groans, just this time they were not from Scarlett. She needed to sit and patiently listen to the lady pleasuring herself while she could just sit and impatiently wait for her turn.

Again time stopped. Scarlett sat peacefully listening to her labored breathing and groans of delight until her secret partner, at long last, exploded. At the moment when the room was indeed quiet, Scarlett asked permission to cum. There was no answer. She desperately sought to know what her identity was. Again, there was no answer. She inquired as to whether she would at least turn on her panties regardless of whether they were at the teasing mode since anything was superior to nothing. She heard a tick, and the underwear began to cycle on and off between the three attachments. Scarlett detested this setting. It was more awful than teasing mode since it turned her on considerably more, yet as a matter of fact, she realized it wouldn't give her the much anticipated delight in the end.

Scarlett's expanded groans, be that as it may, made enough sound to shroud the echoes of the lady getting up and moving over to her. She didn't let out the slightest peep or touched her this time, yet Scarlett felt the plastic tip of a vibrator press against her lips. It wasn't turned on and she nipped at the tip with her tongue before it was squeezed into her mouth. She presently had each of the three of her openings filled and her clit humming, yet was still incapable to reach the zenith of her euphoria. The vibrator was held in her mouth while she relished the flavor of her mysterious sweetheart. Obviously fulfilled that Scarlett had cleaned her toy appropriately, the mysterious entity pulled it from her mouth. She, at that point, gave her nipples another pinch and tweak and was gone. Scarlett heard the squeak of their stairs as she kept on marinating in her own pleasure juices in the lounge room. "Why is she going upstairs? Why doesn't she simply allow me to come?" Scarlett wondered inwardly as goosebumps coursed all over her elegant skin and her heart pounded in her throat. The clock struck three while she still continued to wait impatiently.

Scarlett heard the stairs squeak again and afterward the panties were turned off. She felt her superb nails rake over her hardened nipples once again and afterward her secret accomplice was pulling her off the seat. She left her wrists handcuffed; however, Scarlett could tell she was unclipping her boots. Her mysterious friend, at that moment, started to slide the underwear down Scarlett's thighs and over the boots. Her legs were weak, yet with her assistance the panties slid over the boots and onto the floor. Scarlett felt the chain being reattached between the boots. Scarlett prayed as she trembled in fear and anticipation; she prayed she wasn't going to take another tour outside.

Scarlett didn't need to stress. She was directed to the stairs. She was guided up the stairs. Her secret sweetheart had one hand on her rear end, pressing it to enable her to maintain balance. Her other hand was on her lower back nudging her forward. Scarlett realized she was heading for the master bedroom and she was so damn right. Up they went until Scarlett was guided to the last entryway toward the end of the corridor. She was happy she had made the bed early today. Things being what they were, it didn't make a difference. Without any warning, Scarlett was pushed forward. As her legs hit the bed, she fell forward. Rather than her cushy sofa-bed, she crash landed on the much coarser material texture of the bondage bed she had demonstrated for Bella. As she lay bent over on the edge of the bed, she felt a sharp spank on her right butt cheek. Afterward, another one followed on the left butt cheek to make the count even. Scarlett, at that point, perceived her preferred vibrator, a rabbit with metal balls within it that turns and twists once being penetrated into her over animated pussy. She started to bump her hips backward onto the toy. Evidently, her absence of persistence was not acknowledged because the vibrator was removed and her butt was rewarded with two vicious spanks that surely had left imprints, or that was what Scarlett suspected.

Then, she felt her legs being raised as she was curled onto the bed and afterward onto her back. Scarlett recalled her first bondage bed climax because of Clara and wasn't frightened in any way. She felt her boots being unclipped before they were re-attached to the corners spreading her burning and hungry pussy open wide. She was lying on her back, yet was guided into a sitting position courtesy of two perfectly timed drags on her hardened and sensitive nipples. When she was positioned, her wrists were untied, and she was pushed down to her back. Now, her wrists were re-tied, and Scarlett was restrained spread eagle on the bondage bed. Indeed, she heard her rabbit vibrator turn on; however, rather than being penetrated in the pussy, her provocative, mysterious tormentor just positioned it up right along her pussy's external lips. Scarlett couldn't close her legs for better sensation. Its vibrations were hardly stimulating her pussy.

She could feel its buzz somewhat sufficiently, only to remind her that it was there, and the batteries were striving for an unfruitful result.

Scarlett felt a weight move as her secret sweetheart got off the bed. She attempted to think about what she was doing, yet proved unable. She, at that point, felt the edge of the bed moved again and afterward felt her leg being situated over her body. Without a word, hell her mysterious accomplice hadn't spoken yet, Scarlett felt a dribbling pussy slip over her mouth. She had never eaten a pussy before, and she unquestionably didn't have a choice about starting at this point. Her sweetheart waited a couple of seconds while she tentatively stuck out her tongue initially taking hardly any licks. Clearly impatient, she gripped her hair and started to forcibly ride her face. Scarlett was certain her sensual partner was getting a greater delight out of the friction of her nose against her clit and what pressure she could mount with her tongue than Scarlett's under-developed pussy eating abilities. "Is she over me for five minutes or ten? I don't have the foggiest idea," Scarlett wondered as time passed. However, in the end, her tormentor screeched in euphoric delight, a sign she took as a compliment.

Scarlett felt her get off the bed again eventually, felt the rabbit vibrator being pushed once again into her yearning pussy. She immediately groaned and started to remake her feeling searching for an ultimate explosive release. In any case, her sweetheart would have none of that. Before she could orgasm, she pulled the vibrator out. She heard her turn it off and afterward felt her reinsert it into her aching pussy. Scarlett, at that point, felt her moving back up to the top of the bed. She thought about whether she was going to make her devour her pussy once more. The appropriate response was yes and no.

Scarlett felt her lifting her head as another lash was pulled around. There was something lying on her jaw. She didn't have a clue what it was, yet it had a considerable amount of weight. She felt her again moving over her. It didn't take a lot of criminology work to understand that she had tied a dildo around her jaw as she mounted her face. Scarlett had seen these at Bella's home even though she had never inspected that personally at any of the sex parties. Her cunning tormentor ground her pussy over the strap-on dildo. Her tantalizing aroma pounced upon her nose as her juices spilled over the phallus and onto her mouth and nose. Scarlett was available in the room, yet her wicked tormentor didn't require her other than to give a strong foundation to her artificial cock.

Again and again, her secret pervert accomplice of sensual exploration beat her head into the pad as she rode the dildo. She clearly realized how to satisfy herself and, according to Scarlett's observation, exploded on three additional occasions while drifting over Scarlett's face. That was five body-shivering orgasms for her. Scarlett had been teased for at least three and a half hours was all the while begging for her first release. In the end, her tormentor was more likely than not worn out because Scarlett felt her stooping back up, popping the dildo free. There was the mandatory surge of air circulation into her gaping pussy exhibiting she had worked admirably screwing herself. Scarlett was envious.

Scarlett detected her tormentor inclining forward and by and by her pussy was smothered all over her face. Less on her mouth and more on her nose she was positioned this time as she smeared her face with her aroma. Each breath starting there on was loaded up with her aromatic smell. Her wicked accomplice evacuated the lashes holding the dildo. Like the vibrator previously, Scarlett had to wipe her juices off her toy before she got off the bed. As she was getting up, Scarlett felt her magnificent fingernails give a speedy scratch over her dismissed clit. Her cunning partner had realized how to make her groan and beg. That much was certain. Scarlett heard the rabbit vibrator turn on and felt it start to invade her, yet just for around two inches. "Damn, no climax up and coming from that!" Scarlett cursed her.

The vibrator was sufficiently far into her burning pussy to give her the shivers. Clearly her sinful tormentor was getting a charge out of teasing her. Scarlett didn't have a clue how long and how much more of the body-trembling temptations she could take; however, she had the awful inclination she was going to discover some more of the cruel teases. She heard the lady exploring her cabinet and afterward into her closet. She was looking through Scarlett's room and Scarlett implored she wasn't simply going to rob her and leave me. "How might I disclose this to the police?" Scarlett breathed hard. All things considered, she didn't have the foggiest idea what her identity was and what her name was, and what she resembled; even though she tied herself up for her secret sly partner and worshipped her pussy before she robbed her, visually impaired her, and left her with a vibrator in her yearning pussy. Scarlett could hardly admit to herself that she preferred being treated like some road-slide slut, leaving her with no option to mention about her adventures and misadventures.

After perhaps ten minutes, Scarlett felt the vibrator being pulled out of her pussy and turned off. Indeed, her devious sweetheart had her clean up the toy. Scarlett's juices tasted extremely pleasant to herself. She could sense that her secret partner was perched on the bed close to her head. Scarlett thought about whether she would need to worship her cunt once more. As usual, she was begging for a much anticipated orgasm. Scarlett even felt her standing up and afterward felt the weight between her legs.

Scarlett felt her mischievous partner blowing hot air across her clit. It felt delectably tempting. She, at that point, felt her cunning partner's forefinger slide into her sodden pussy as her tongue reached her clit. "At long last!" Scarlett thought. Through her intentional and measured ministrations, the devious partner carried her excitement to a fever pitch. Be that as it may, despite everything she would not let her cum. Scarlett was on the edge; however, she deliberately eased back or stopped her ministrations before Scarlett could explode. Battling against her bondage, Scarlett shouted. She groaned. She needed to break free just to complete the sensual activity all by herself. She had never been so turned on. After her last cycle of taking her to the edge, Scarlett felt her partner getting up. "Now what," Scarlett thought. "What else would she be able to do to me to tease me?"

Scarlett heard a ring from her watch. "Damn, is it four o'clock? I'd been on the edge for very nearly four hours." She wondered and screamed, "Fuck, I have to cum. Watermelon, fruits and vegetable salad, fuck you. Anything you desire to hear, I'll say! Give me relief! I'll suck your pussy again a short time later until you can't cum any longer! Fuck me! Smack me, whip me, do whatever you want, but please let me cum!"

Scarlett heard greater movement by the dresser and afterward sensed her back on the end of the bed. She was crazy prattling unintelligibly. She scarcely knew when the dildo again penetrated her. As her mind got up to speed with what her aroused body was feeling, Scarlett just murmured "Yessss!" as an enormous dildo filled her pussy. Her mischievous darling gradually pushed the dildo further and deeper into her drooling pussy and Scarlett's groans of sensual frustration became screams of ecstatic delight. At last, when Scarlett was more filled than she at any point had been previously, and her pussy was battling to extend enough to accommodate the alien intruder, she felt a little stub rub over her juicy pussy lips and a scratch at the underside of her throbbing clit. That was sufficient to push her right to the edge. She shouted for her wicked accomplice to take her like she'd never taken any other individual.

Scarlett felt the dildo starting to pull back. Her seductive tormentor was slow. She took as much time as was needed until just the tip was resting at the passage of her womanhood. At that moment, she felt the next stroke. Full, fuller, and to the fullest it went. She was jabbering again when the stub by and by clipped the edge of her throbbing clit. Her mischievous tormentor held the dildo there for a minute. Scarlett felt the weight on the bed move and felt the dildo whirl marginally in a roundabout movement. At that point, it dawned on her. She felt the sleeping mattress pressure shift somewhat as she pulled out. Her playful torturer was clearly wearing this enormous dildo and was fucking her like a man.

Not that Scarlett required any support; however, this revelation hit a nerve with her. Each stroke carried her closer to the revolutionary orgasm she knew was approaching. On the edge with each vigorous thrust, she battled to clutch her rational soundness as her climax developed in the depths of her clits. Her drenched pussy had extended enough to enable her secret sweetheart to build the rhythm and power of her powerful thrusts. Scarlett presently needed to prolong this euphoria; however, no matter how hard she attempted, she realized she couldn't last any longer. Scarlett was screaming obscenities at her cunning torturer trying to get her mind far from cumming to enable her body to develop a significantly tremendous release. "Fuck, fuck, fuck, yes, tear my pussy apart!" and "Don't stop. Please don't stop it," streamed uninhibitedly from her lips. Her voice was getting choked in her throat. She was shivering like a dry leaf in a snowstorm. She thought I even said, "I love you," yet she was so high above in cloud nine that nothing her body did was voluntary.

The straw that set her mind in an enraptured daze was the moment at which her passionate and cunning lover leaned down over Scarlett. Her arms and legs were positioned spread-eagled over her. Her hands gripped on her wrists just beneath the cuffs. Her bosoms were squashing into Scarlett's and she started to rape her mouth with her tongue and lips. Her excited torturer quit thrusting the dildo buried as far as possible in her drooling pussy and started pivoting her hips. The dildo started hitting new pressure points in her pussy Scarlett didn't know existed and the tremendous blast of pleasure happened.

Scarlett let out a yell into her passionate torturer's mouth as she was devoured by an enormous body shattering orgasm. As with Bella previously, her body trembled and shook and she lay underneath her unknown passionate darling. Her hips were bobbing and compelling the dildo to rise and fall, at least somewhat, although her devious lover was simply hanging on now. As Scarlett began to quiet, marginally, her cunning torturer restarted the ambush on her exposed body. She got again into a pushup position and continued shoving her pussy with her gigantic fuck stick. She held her position with one hand and brutally squeezed Scarlett's areolas. She slapped her cheek and afterward her succulent bosoms. Scarlett's whole body was devoured by ecstatic climax as waves and streams of enraptured joy coursed through her body. Again and again, her mischievous tormentor pounded the artificial cock into her and again and again, Scarlett orgasmed tremendously. Climaxes started to stream into each other so quick they became one steady discharge. After being prodded for four hours and begging to be permitted to orgasm, inevitably Scarlett needed to plead to be permitted to stop.

Fortunately, her tricksy accomplice was all the more obliging of this solicitation and quit thrusting and pulled her cock out of Scarlett with a revolting 'pop.' Scarlett was somewhat astonished she didn't pass out as she did with Bella, yet she wasn't astounded when she felt her playful partner moving and afterward felt the tip of the dildo pushing pass her luscious lips. Scarlett cleaned it affectionately, mewing like a cat with a saucer of milk. Indeed, even now, her mysterious sweetheart didn't utter a word. She felt her partner get up and afterward felt a bed sheet drawn over her. Again, she asked her what her identity was. Surely as now of, in their relationship, names were in order. Be that as it may, she didn't utter a word. Scarlett heard the sounds of another squishy pussy as her playful tormentor clearly was fingering herself while staring at her. Scarlett took pride heavily that her secret lover came rapidly. She, at that point, felt something extending over her head and covering her nose and mouth. It was a couple of cotton panties. They were likely Scarlett's, yet they certainly had been utilized to wipe up her secret friend's pussy juice. The taste and scent was familiar and delicious, sweet and exciting and each breath Scarlett took now helped her to remember her devious partner.

Scarlett listened to her strolling in the room. She attempted to consider how she would disclose her situation to Jacques when he would return home; however, fatigue soon conquered her and she nodded off. Scarlett slept the rest of the day unaware of anything around her. She, at long last, woke when she felt a sharp slap over her butt cheek. From the outset, she didn't have the foggiest idea where she was, nevertheless the astonishing and bewildering recollections of the day overflowed back to her. She was still in a bed, yet she wasn't spread eagled any longer. Her wrists were behind her back, this time in cuffs. She couldn't sense; however, she trusted they were her timer cuffs. Her boots were once again cuffed together; this time they were tied to one another without the advantage of the chain keeping her legs firmly together. Scarlett's calves and thighs were additionally lashed together, and she felt something lying on her swollen pussy and another belt around her hips holding whatever it was set up. She was still blindfolded. She flailed uncontrollably testing her restrains. As Scarlett was doing as such, she felt the now dry underwear being pulled back over her head. She quieted down and was remunerated with a profound passionate kiss which left her panting for air. Before she could speak, Scarlett felt another pair of underwear, clearly recently dirty by her secret sweetheart's pussy starting its voyage over her head to its resting place over her nose and mouth. These were much wetter than the first pair as she took a full breath to relish their hypnotic smell and taste.

Scarlett heard a tick and what she later realized was a Hitachi Wand starting to buzz on her clit, held tight by the hip tie. Her mischievous darling had fortunately picked the low setting. Scarlett didn't figure she could have survived a higher mode. She exploded violently again very quickly followed by a period of severe irritation and agony until her mind and violently abused clit could straighten out themselves and work to another tremendous climax. Scarlett forgot about counting her orgasms, teasing, irritation, torment, orgasm she had as she moved from side to side on the bed. At a certain point, she ended up on her stomach and started to bump the bed striving to drive the teasing wand harder against her hungry pussy. This didn't have the impact she wanted, so she battled to the edge of the bed and afterward tumbled off. The agony of smashing onto the floor was immediately supplanted by the delight of another body-trembling orgasm. Her bondage kept her from moving quickly; however, she figured out how to slither toward the restroom. Indeed, even being blinded by the blindfold, she was resolved to slither to the washroom where she believed she could arrive at the ledge and crush her pussy on it. She needed to scoot her direction like an inchworm as a result of her legs being squeezed together. Each time Scarlett stretched to push ahead, the ball of the wand hit the floor and squeezed all the more tightly against her clit and labia. Obviously, she cherished each minute and orgasmed twice all the more crawling over the floor.

Chapter 8

At last, Scarlett felt the cool washroom tile against her face. She rested for a minute; her new most loved toy was still giving her one more pleasurable climax. They were streaming like water now and the only thing she could consider was helping the toy carry out its responsibility. Recouping from her last powerful orgasm, Scarlett rose marginally to scoot another couple of inches when she felt a pull on the wand. "What the fuck?" Scarlett wondered as she moved over and over feeling the wand pulling the other way. At that point, it suddenly stopped. Her abused pussy was still violently throbbing against the ball of the Hitachi wand; however, no vibrations were satisfying her over-excited clit. "What was the deal?" She wondered breathlessly.

Scarlett lay on the floor, a stacking mess of spontaneously climaxed out framework. Her brain, at last, began to clear and recollecting how Bella would demonstrate the wand solved the riddle. The greatest preferred advantage to the wand, or its disadvantage for her situation, was that it wasn't battery worked. It is A/C controlled and connected to the wall. Clearly, she never needed to stress over her batteries going dead if somebody restrained her to it; however, on the off chance that she overlooked that and tugged the plug out of the wall, she was basically going to be screwed. Scarlett had a choice to make. She was at the threshold of the restroom entryway. Around three feet and some way or another getting to her feet and she could bump the ledge. Without the wand humming, in any case, she asked whether that deserved the exertion. Fifteen feet in the other way was the place the wand likely had been plugged in. Scarlett was speculating that she utilized the open outlet by the entryway and close to the bed. Fifteen feet was far, yet she desperately required the wand to be back on power.

The crawl was depleting. Inch by inch Scarlett advanced toward the entryway with the wand prodding her over-sensitive clit on each up and down cycle of her hips. Contemplating the magnificent vibrations kept her focused. She would not enable herself to consider what might occur in case she had utilized an alternate outlet and needed to look through the room. By and by time had stopped. Scarlett had no clue to what extent she had slept and now had no idea about to what extent her mission for control was taking. Jacques could be home any moment or it could even now be hours.

Scarlett was a perspiring mess when she made it to the wall. She was crushing her head around the floor covering scanning for the plug and fortunately, she discovered it. Now, she simply needed to get it connected to the wall. She wanted to attempt to connect it utilizing her teeth. It was exceedingly difficult for her. It would be terrible enough to disclose to Jacques why she was bound on the floor, yet in case she electrocuted herself, then that would be even more disastrous. No, she needed to utilize her hands. She gave careful consideration of where the plugging point was and afterward turned over on her side and attempted to discover the wire with her hands. After success with that errand, Scarlett squirmed over to the wall and began scanning for the wall socket. That undertaking was far more troublesome than the previous one. When Scarlett found the socket, she needed to make sense of how to twist her wrists to get the plug into the wall. She additionally needed to ensure the polarity plug was going the correct way.

This undertaking was disappointing. Scarlett was nearly to the point of tears, both in dissatisfaction for failing at the undertaking and deprived to recover the wand turned back on. Finally, Scarlett found the correct point and direction and she felt the plug slide into the wall socket. In a split second, her blissful wand sprung to life and almost immediately she felt her pleasure starting to develop once more. Scarlett figured the wand would rapidly take her over the edge; however, it didn't. For reasons unknown, her restless mind was searching for additional. Maybe it was the long crawl; however, her aroused mind was advising her body that she expected to turn the wand on high rather than low. "Be that as it may, how?" Scarlett wondered.

As Scarlett lay on the floor mulling over my alternatives, her excitement assembled and constructed, yet wouldn't go over the top. She had had enough sensual teasing for one day. She wasn't going to lay here floundering in her very own self indulgence and pussy juice until Jacques returned home. At last, in distress, Scarlett figured out how to squirm to her knees. She knew there was a bedside table on her right side. Possibly she could bump the corner and flip the power switch on. She attempted, yet her efforts were in vain. She had one more alternative in reach of the power line. The door handle. Scarlett struggled to her feet, yet she couldn't walk. What a sight—She more likely than not been hooping to the entryway and colliding with the wall. Scarlett slid along the entryway feeling her way for the handle. Her juices were running down her leg as she bumped the door handle attempting to both flip the switch and get the wand to apply for pressure against her clit. She succeeded in doing both. She was inching toward the zenith of another tremendous climax when the switch, at long last, kicked over to high. Scarlett winced at the unexpected multiplication of vibrations and fell backward on the floor as another massive climax consumed her. This time the torment didn't return and inside minutes, she was cumming once more. And afterward once more. And afterward, she heard a tick from behind her back. The cuffs were released automatically as per the time setting.

Scarlett immediately unfastened her wrists and afterward removed the blindfold. She kept on letting the wand do something amazing as she attempted to remove her boots. After a remarkable success, she proceeded onward to her calves and thighs. At long last, she was having the relieving choice to spread her legs and stretch. Scarlett needed to stop the vibrations of the wand; however, her desire wouldn't let her. She had been inching closer to another explosive orgasm. So throwing caution to the wind, Scarlett set down on the bed and began paying with her areolas. She was groaning pleasurably, "Yes mistress, fuck your sex slave," when her last overwhelming orgasm from the ordeal conquered her. Following a couple more minutes of rolling on the bed and writhing in extreme absolute delight, Scarlett turned off the wand and unstrapped it.

Scarlett lay on the bed attempting to revive and rise above the enraptured daze. She, at long last, had the thinking ahead to look at the alarm clock. It was 8:15. Eight or more long hours of torment, sensual teasing, and explosive climaxes had kept her occupied and ruined her completely. She took a profound, satisfied breath about what she had suffered and the powerful climaxes she had encountered. She had lost track. She never viewed herself as multi-orgasmic; however, she surmised she learned about herself something.

Lying in the post orgasmic enraptured daze, Scarlett was absentmindedly playing with her areolas when she heard the carport entryway open. "Crap! Jacques is home." She cursed herself. She leaped up and made a speedy scan of the room. There were toys, garments, and proof of her debauchery all over the place. Instantly, Scarlett was picking everything up and tossing it in the bottom cabinet drawer. She ran into the washroom and turned on the shower. She was going to hop in when she recollected the bondage mat on the bed. Sprinting back into the room, Scarlett first needed to decide how the lashes held it to the bed. When done, she immediately released it and afterward examined the room for a spot to conceal it. Scarlett was freezing; however, then it hit her. The bondage bed was rolled up and shifted under the bed as she heard the stairs creak and Jacques calling her name. Scarlett darted back to the restroom and hopped into the shower.

She immediately splashed her hair with cleanser as she heard him entering the room and worked it into foam. Jacques entered the washroom, and she acted shocked that she had not heard him. Fortunately, he was entirely exhausted from his day-long activity and in the wake of saying "howdy", he wandered back to the ground floor. It was then Scarlett thought of any proof that may be in the lounge room.

Scarlett washed off the cleanser and escaped the shower. As she glanced in the mirror, her well-used pussy was red and swollen, yet otherwise she gave no indications of sensual abuse. In the wake of toweling off, she returned into the room. It stunk of female sex. Scarlett trusted her feeling of smell was more receptive to the scent and that Jacques had some way or another missed it. After putting on her least attractive night wear, she opened the room window to let some air circulation in the room. As she was glancing out the window, she witnessed a vehicle down the block flashing its lights. And then, it pulled away from the curb and accelerated away. Scarlett couldn't make out a model of vehicle or any subtleties of the driver. "Was my mysterious sweetheart spying on me until I was safe?" Scarlett contemplated as she felt a warm shine over her body.

She realized she needed to confront Jacques and believed he would be too worn out to even think about realizing anything was not right. Luckily, he was daydreaming by the TV, so Scarlett plunked down on the sofa and went along with him. The two of them immediately nodded off in the lounge room. Scarlett woke to him shaking her delicately a couple of hours after the fact and guiding her to come upstairs with him.

Scarlett woke up the next morning sore and tired. She didn't have a sound sleep. Jacques was headed toward work and she was prepared to leave when she chose to browse her email. There was a message from her mysterious accomplice. Scarlett read it and reread it. Her hands found their way into her jeans. Her hungry pussy was wet once more.

Throughout the day at work, Scarlett's psyche replayed the encounters from the day preceding and persistently cycled back to the email she had gotten at the beginning of the day and how she ought to react to it. The email was basic. It was only two short sentences, actually. The first was an explanation that her mysterious darling made some extraordinary memories and would be at her home again same time after one week from now. It wasn't an inquiry whether Scarlett needed a return commitment. It was an explanation that she would be there. The second was a solicitation, or was it actually an order, to record her emotions about her experience and send them to her secret accomplice. Scarlett's pussy was drooling throughout the day pondering how this lady had assumed her to a position she had never been, the place her body shivered from her seductive touch and her powerful climaxes streamed like water. Scarlett yearned to feel that way once more.

Jacques was home that night, so Scarlett needed to hold up until he slept before composing her answer. Despite the fact that they had swore not to share individual data to one another, Scarlett couldn't satisfactorily portray her sentiments about the earlier day without doing as such. She thought her email ended up being around four pages in length and she needed to stop and jerk off twice while composing it. Each time she recalled being lashed to the bondage bed and pounded, she got wet.

The week crept by. Scarlett needed her so awful that she was encountering physical withdrawal torments as she watched her email represent new guidelines. At long last, the prior night they were to planning to meet, Scarlett got another message. Like before there would be another container on her doorstep by 6 am. By and by, she was to get ready herself and at 9:30am, essentially prior she noted, Scarlett was to open the case and adhere to the directions. She was on a tingling sensation throughout the night. She looked on the patio at 5:45 am and the crate was at that moment there. She could feel her mysterious accomplice's essence watching her as she recovered the case; however, she couldn't see anyone. Once again, Scarlett shrouded the case in the cellar and afterward made breakfast. She thought about whether her office would acknowledge that she had phoned in sick that day two weeks straight.

When Jacques was out the entryway, Scarlett immediately washed, shaved, and applied her make-up. She felt so filthy preparing for her "date" since she had never desired to cheat on Jacques, yet her pussy was controlling her life and she couldn't disapprove of it. Quickly at 9:30, Scarlett went to the cellar and opened the case. Shockingly, there wasn't much in it. Taking a quick look at the garments, she found a leather g-string. She additionally found a couple of high heels, very nearly 5" as per her speculation. There were additionally a lot of ankle cuffs and a red ball gag. On the base of the crate was an envelope which Scarlett believed contained her guidelines. Under the envelope, she found a couple of underwear. She grabbed them and carried them to her nose. Her fingertips demonstrated her that they were still wet. The freshness of the aroma disclosed to her that she had cummed in them just before closing the crate. Scarlett took a full breath appreciating their addictive fragrance. A wave of unquenchable desire fell over her. She paused for a minute to savor the euphoric inclination and afterward opened the envelope.

"Today will be straightforward. I need you to get the silver bullet vibrator I realize you have in your assortment. Ensure the batteries are new. On the off chance that you need to play with yourself a bit you can; however, I need you dressed and prepared by 10 am. Turn the vibrator on medium and slide it right into your pussy. After that, put on the g-string. I need you to cuff your ankles and afterward put on the wrist cuffs you got a week ago. Go to the lounge room and pull the blinds as far as possible up. That will be your sign that you have acknowledged my little arrangement.

I need you to go to your back yard. Leave the backdoor access opened. I need you to plunk down on one of the porch seats I saw a week ago. Your lower legs are to be restrained to the legs of the seat. At that point, after you connect the encased ball gag and the substantial leather blindfold from a week ago, I need you to cuff your wrists to the arm of the seat. On the off chance that you battle on your second wrist, I will acknowledge that. I'll deal with it when I show up. Yet regardless of whether you can't clip it in position, I need you to hold the rail as though it was. No playing with your delightful bosoms or pussy."

Chapter 9

Indeed Scarlett was being ordered to submit to a lady regardless she didn't have the foggiest idea who she was. By and by the throbbing in her hungry pussy implied she would comply. Scarlett took the crate and headed for the room. She surmised her secret dominatrix had given her consent to play with herself on the off chance that she wasn't sufficiently wet to embed the vibrator. "Did she have that one wrong?" Scarlett wondered. In case she had played with herself, she would have cummed on the spot. Her mysterious mistress hadn't prohibited that; however, as she had adapted a week ago with her and before that with Bella, not having a speedy simple cum could deliver profits in the long run. So Scarlett just adhered to the guidelines to turn on the vibrator, slide it home and rapidly pulled on the g-string to hold it in position. Understanding that would have been her lone vestment, made Scarlett feel doubly stripped and doubly scandalous. She adored it.

The heels would have been a test. Scarlett knew her legs and ass would look extraordinary while she was wearing them, yet she would hardly have the option to walk. Scarlett carried the shoes down the stairs alongside the thicker blindfold from a week ago and her new muffle. It wasn't even 9:45 when she opened the blinds. By 9:50, Scarlett was secured to the seat as instructed with the vibrator humming joyfully in her pussy and her eyes covered and her mouth secured. What's more, she waited. And, impatiently waited.

Without having the lounge clock tolling, Scarlett couldn't tell to what extent she had been waiting. The morning sun felt extraordinary on her skin. She had sunbathed topless previously and cherished the sentiment of liberty. Today, she had an alternate feeling. Weakness. Of the two, the last was considerably more animating. Scarlett had no clue how long she stayed there; however, in the end, she heard the clicking of her mysterious mistress's heels on the porch blocks. Consistently nearer the sound came until she heard a heavy bag or the like that hit the porch and afterward felt a gloved hand delicately stroke the side of her face. Scarlett promptly tilted her head in the hand's course. She felt the hand travel down her neck, over her succulent bosoms, down her stomach, over her drooling pussy, and afterward down her leg. The inclination was dazzling. Shockingly, it didn't last. When the hand finished its adventure, she heard the heels leaving and the back door open and close. Scarlett was distant from everyone else once more.

Again she was made to wait. Her skin was alive after her mistress's touch and she yearned to be touched once more. Indeed time stopped. Scarlett could do nothing, but wait impatiently. Only wait and have the vibrator tease and excite her over animated pussy. Only wait, and have the vibrator tease her hungry pussy and have her mind thinking frightful musings and fantasize about what her devious dominatrix would do to her. Furthermore, her restless mind could be extremely filthy.

It felt like it had been sixty minutes, yet it presumably was close to fifteen minutes when Scarlett heard the arrival of her mistress's high heels. It was a similar sound she heard a week ago, and she quickly remembered it has her. She had been desperately praying her mischievous dominatrix wouldn't prod her like she did a week ago. She implored her mistress would converse with her this week and disclose to her regarding her identity. She implored a great deal of things; however, for the most part she was grateful that her playful partner was there. Scarlett felt her gloved hand again starting to tease her. She attempted to express gratitude toward her through the gag. Her seductive dominatrix appeared to be gentler than a week ago as she petted her body, in spite of the fact that she was no less reluctant to tease her to the point of release and afterward back off. That was an alarming steadiness in their relationship.

Like the prior week, her deviant mistress carried Scarlett to the edge just to pull her back at last without sexual fulfillment. She was fortifying her submissive's preparation that she was in control and that in case Scarlett needed to cum, she expected to satisfy her. When her hands left her aroused body, Scarlett felt alone even though she realized her illicit partner was standing alongside her. She heard her rummaging through the bag and afterward felt a leash being attached to her neck. She likewise felt a slim chain being joined to the collar and then left to dangle against her juicy bosoms. Again, her devious partner left to leave Scarlett pondering this new advancement.

Scarlett's wait was not as long this time before she felt her playful mistress's hands start to disengage her bonds with the seat. As her hand got the leash, obviously she gave a hardened press to Scarlett's right bosom. A fast pull on the rope demonstrated she should rise. Standing up, Scarlett felt the leash lead her into her back yard. It was hard to stroll on the grass in her heels. She needed to stress over the heel sinking into the dirt. She additionally needed to worry about her neighbors. While her porch was genuinely isolated from prying eyes, the rest of the back yard wasn't. Scarlett hoped none of her neighbors were home from work sickness as she arrived at what she assessed was the center of the yard. A hand pushed on her shoulders demonstrating she should bow. As Scarlett arrived to her knees, the hand continued pushing exhibiting she should take position on all fours. "God how embarrassing it is." Scarlett wondered breathlessly. What's more, how stimulating it was!

Scarlett felt another pull on the rope and started to hurry along on her hands and knees like a canine. How additionally corrupting and embarrassing a position would her mistress be able to have picked? Scarlett made a circle around their entire yard before she felt the hard concrete of the porch underneath her hand. For the first time, her playful tormentor conversed with her.

"Sit. Stay," was all her command.

Two words. Her only recognizable proof. Scarlett didn't perceive the voice. Before this, she had been certain it was Bella, yet unmistakably it wasn't. She had even thought about that it might be Helena from the neighborhood. Be that as it may, the voice didn't match her either. Additionally, Helena didn't appear to be the dominant type. The more Scarlett had thought of her this week, the more her mistress had chosen she was bound to be in her situation than being the tormentor. She was bound to be collared than holding the leash. In any case, Scarlett diverged.

She heard the heels stroll back to the entryway once more. About a moment later, she heard the entryway opening and the mysterious lady strolling back toward her. Scarlett heard something put before her and felt the leash being grabbed. She felt the leash tugged and drawn toward her back as her mistress's hands unfastened her gag. Scarlett's blindfold remained firmly in position. She felt the leash by and by move to the front and a pull. She pushed ahead about a foot until she felt her dominant's hand on her head. Scarlett stopped and it pushed downward.

"Drink," was the single word sentence.

Now, Scarlett realized the amount all the more corrupting this could be. She brought down her head into the bowl and started to lap at the water. It tasted so great she didn't mind how she was getting it. Her mischievous mistress let her drink as much as she needed. At the point, when she pulled Scarlett's head up, the rope provoked her to pivot and head once more into the yard. She wasn't astounded when her deviant partner pulled her g-string down, pulled out the vibrator and stuck it in her mouth to clean it. She had been getting infatuated to like her taste. She was amazed that before her playful mistress pulled her g-spring back up, she requested her to pee. Scarlett tilted her head in a scrutinizing way toward her voice.

"This is your last possibility for some time. So, do it here or you will be rebuffed later."

That was the longest expression Scarlett had heard her mistress state yet and still it gave no insight regarding what her identity was. Clearly, she had never met her. She slapped her butt hard with her hand.

"I'm not kidding bitch. Do it!"

Scarlett needed to fight her tears as she stooped on all fours and pissed like a dog. A bitch hound in heat. This was not stimulating at all. Her face burned with mortification and without precedent for quite a while, she felt no excitement in her mistress's presence.

When she was done, Scarlett felt her deviant mistress pat her pussy with a paper towel. She, at that point, heard the murmur of the vibrator, on high this time, and immediately felt it reinserted into her pussy and held by the g-string. Her mischievous dominatrix, at that point, drove her back to the porch and again instructed her to stay. Against her better judgment, Scarlett's body quickly reacted to the intruder in a totally unsurprising manner.

She heard the entryway open and close as her playful partner left the yard. Scarlett was left with her creative mind running on top gear. She could undoubtedly remove the blindfold. The only thing halting her was her desire. By one way or another, Scarlett knew whether she did that, stopped the vibrator or even stood up, their kink game playing days would be finished. She wasn't prepared to risk that. She kept on waiting, positioned on all fours on her porch with the vibrator bringing her nearer and nearer to a volcanic climax she prayed she'd be permitted to get.

Scarlett heard the entryway creak once more. Her mistress was back. Her heels on the concrete affirmed that. She anticipated that her playful friend should take her inside and ideally back to her bed where she could ravage her once more. Yet, rather she went over the porch toward the path she perceived as the door. Scarlett needed to dissent. Doing this in the general protection of the back yard was a certain something; however, she was certain she couldn't escape discovery in the front. Be that as it may, Scarlett couldn't help it. She didn't need to state a word. She quietly pursued where the leash was taking her. She felt herself driven onto the grass of their home. She desperately prayed her neighbor wasn't home. Next, she felt the concrete of the carport. It would be ideal if her mistress would let this end. She wondered. Thankfully, Scarlett didn't hear any moving vehicles; however, that didn't mean no one was strolling through the area. At last, an upward pulling on her leash. She felt forward and her hand hit the side of a vehicle. An immediate quick movement and it felt the plank of flooring of an open entryway. Scarlett hurried into what she immediately perceived was a freight van. There was no floor covering or seats that obstructed her entrance. At least there would not be any windows either.

A smack to her left butt cheek as her mistress dropped the rope implying to turn left. Scarlett felt a thick coil spring mounted in the floor. Her hand pursued the spring, and she found a pony saddle. It didn't take a lot of reasoning to make sense of who it was for. She started to pride wholeheartedly that she recognized what her tormentor needed without waiting for guidance. Scarlett sat up and utilized two hands to explore the seat's position and afterward holding the edge, stood up. She moved by the seat and planned to swing her leg over it when her hand slid off the edge and through the center. She ceased when it hit a thick chamber. Holding it with her hand, Scarlett felt the veins and edges of a precisely shaped dildo. Anybody would have been terrified, yet rather she felt elation. She might not have known where she was going; however, at least she could get fucked in transit.

Once again Scarlett ran her hands around the seat to ensure she knew where the edges were and afterward she mounted it much like her adoration had mounted the jaw dildo on her face the prior week. It slid home effectively. She wasn't about the size of the strap-on dildo she had utilized a week ago. Scarlett was grinning and feeling pleased with herself when she felt her mistress snatch her left wrist. Rapidly, it was secured to a clasp on the roof. The equivalent was done to her right. Her mischievous partner left her feet free. In her heels, Scarlett could reach at the floor; however, in case she stood, the tip of the dildo still infiltrated her. Obviously, Scarlett wasn't discontent with that circumstance. She figured they were all set, yet before they left, another pair of dirtied underwear secured her noses. Her aroma still smelled perfect.

The side entryway was closed, and Scarlett heard her mistress in transition to the front of the van and the motor accelerating. She had no clue where they were driving. The streets were rough, and she could feel that. The low quality implied they were not approaching her private neighborhood. The city kept those avenues in great condition. She was speculating they were possibly downtown; however, in truth, the thing she was most focusing on were the sensations emanating from her yearning pussy as she kept on fucking herself on the seat. She was pleased the windows were up because she shouted in overwhelming climax time and again.

She would have been perfectly glad to have her mistress drive her around town for the rest of the day letting her cum her dolt head off, yet in the end, she felt the van go down a ramp. After a couple of sharp turns, it went down another slope and afterward a third before eventually stopping. Scarlett heard the motor turned off and detected her mistress moving into the rear of the van.

"Listen in darling. In case you want to proceed, you need to adhere to these directions intently. I will unfasten your bonds and leave the van. You are in third sub-basement of this building. It's not utilized for much any longer; however, it is observed by surveillance cameras. On the off chance that you need to proceed with our little game, wait for five minutes and afterward get dressed. There are garments in a crate behind you. The security watchman is a friend of mine. We won't experience any difficulty as long as you look ordinary strolling to the entryway; however, I can't get a stripped chick in. That doesn't look great in the video record. Try not to stress over the toys. I have more inside. Stroll to the entryway and head inside. It will be opened. Stroll a few doors down until you see a sign for Women's Locker Room. Meet me there. I doubt you will not meet anyone in transit, yet on the off chance that you do, simply walk like you live here and it won't make any difference. Do you get it?"

"Indeed," was my answer.

"Indeed, what?"

I thought for a minute. "Indeed, ma'am?"

"Close."

"Indeed, mistress?"

"Great. We'll deal with it. Five minutes. No more. In case you alter your perspective, simply stroll up the slopes to road level. There is cab stand in the corner."

With that the entryway opened and her mistress was gone disregarding her with her musings and her desire. Scarlett sat still on the dildo for possibly three more minutes. She wasn't generally considering any alternatives. She was going in. She realized that. Yet, her mind was still attempting to get around how she went from acquiring a modest vibrator to sitting pierced on this seat. The time had come to get dressed. The crate contained a couple of pants, a shirt and a couple of gym shoes. Not all that much, filthy, or animating and most likely the sort of garments that a laborer on this level would wear. It didn't take long to get dressed, and it didn't take long to walk the twenty-five feet to the entryway.

The entryway was heavy steel. The only markings were sub-basement three and deliveries. Scarlett surmised she was the delivery today. Pushing the entryway open took some effort, and it shut with a reverberating blast. She saw no one in the lobby. The building appeared to be empty. There was a sign pointing down a passage for deliveries and she saw a cargo lift. She strolled straight ahead as she had been told. She arrived at an entryway. It was a fence like you would discover in a secondary school recreation center. It was open and had been tied with a string so it wouldn't close. Scarlett proceeded ahead down the lobby. There was a wet, smelly scent, and almost no light. The lobby itself wasn't lit. The brightening originated from a single bulb close to the carport entryway.

Scarlett saw an entryway to her right side. It said practice room. There was a window in the entryway which she looked through. She couldn't see a lot of anything. There was a dim-red light, most likely from the exit sign; however, that was it. Through the hallway, Scarlett proceeded. She immediately arrived at a washroom on the left. There was a water fountain and two entryways. One said 'Men' and one said 'Women'. Hanging from the water fountain was another blindfold simply like the one she had left in the van. Scarlett clearly was in the perfect spot.

She never would have believed she had the strength and courage to act as she was acting, yet she didn't spare a moment to get the blindfold and tie it into place. She pushed the entryway open and strolled inside until she hit a tiled wall. The smell of mildew was stronger in this room. Scarlett heard the entryway shut and afterward the snap of a deadbolt. She stood still until she felt her mistress's hands on her shoulder. She guided her further into the openings of the locker room. Scarlett was envisioning in her mind what the locker room resembled in her gym center, albeit by one way or another she questioned if this was the same. The two sets of their heels were tapping on the tile floor and the idea of how delightful her savage paramour must look wearing those incredibly attractive sounding shoes made her knees weak. She sensed guided to turn left.

"Open the entryway."

Scarlett fumbled around, yet found a handle. This entryway was likewise heavy. She strolled over the threshold until the hands on her shoulders proclaimed she should stop.

"Strip. Don't take off blindfold and the shoes."

Scarlett heard her mistress leave and the entryway opened and closed once more. She thought about whether she was alone or if there was even a light on. It took more time to shed her garments than it had taken to put them on. She was shuddering and cold in the room, yet everything she could do was wait.

Luckily the entryway opened again rapidly. Scarlett heard her mistress's heels and afterward a heavy sack hammer on the floor. She stood waiting for instructions. She heard her playful partner opening the sack and afterward moved around her and the sound of tinkering with gear. Her mischievous accomplice, at that point, moved back to her and pushed on her shoulders. Scarlett promptly dropped to her knees and was immediately presented a wet pussy in her face. She didn't stop for a second as she pleasured her mistress orally. In spite of the fact that her wrists were not bound, she crossed her wrists behind her back. It just felt so natural and submissive. Her mistress's taste was flawless. Much preferable in the flesh over her underwear she enjoyed putting over her head. Scarlett lapped at her pussy until she peaked twice. Her face was covered with her mistress's juices as she denoted her domain by scouring herself on her forehead. Scarlett was her whore, and they both knew it.

"Do you need me to fuck you once more?"

"Indeed please," Scarlett reacted decisively.

"Who owns your pussy?"

"You, mistress."

"Will it always do what I state? Fuck who I tell it to fuck? Eat who I tell it to eat?"

"Indeed, mistress."

Her devious paramour was setting out the rules of their relationship.

"Having a slut like you around satisfies me. Would you like to please me?"

"Indeed, mistress. More than anything."

"I can be a brutal mistress, yet I am a reasonable one. I won't punish you except if you deserve it. Serve me well, and please me, and I will give you the delight that you crave so much. In any case, always remember, just like today, I cum first. I was not satisfied with how you balked when I ordered you to pee in your yard. I will give you a specific measure of tolerance since you are not appropriately trained at this point. Be that as it may, despite everything, I will punish you. Do you comprehend why I will punish you?"

"Because I resisted you?"

"Indeed, but there is more."

Scarlett needed to think for a minute. "Since I deserve it?"

"Truly you do, but continue."

Scarlett looked into her brain for the appropriate response. "Since you are my mistress?"

"No doubt about it."

"Since you are my mistress and need to prepare me to adhere to your guidelines?"

"Nearly there."

"Since you understand what is beneficial for me and what I need?" Scarlett was practically crying as she understood how much she cared about her mysterious darling. "Since I belong you and you have the right to be loved and have me pursue your orders without any doubt?"

"Excellent slave. At the point when I punish you, I do it because of affection, not despise. You will gain proficiency with the distinction. You defied me before and need to remember not to do that in future. Be that as it may, don't stress, I'll go easy on you today. Whenever you visit my 'office' you probably won't be so fortunate."

"Thank you, Mistress."

Scarlett felt the warm grasp of the leather cuffs being attached on her wrists and ankles. Her cunning courtesan, at that point, moved her against a cushioned cylinder somewhat about thigh high. She pushed her over bending her at the abdomen around it. She guided Scarlett to hold her position while she tied her feet spread wide over the base. On the opposite side her wrists were similarly connected. The spread of her legs left her pussy and butt head in plain view for her mistress. She could just expect that her promise to go easy on her wasn't a lie. She additionally believed her mistress's promise to fuck her would be satisfied.

She felt her devious mistress taping a riding crop over her posterior. Insufficient to hurt, it was sufficiently enough only to tell Scarlett where her secret partner was as she orbited her body.

"You are an incredibly excellent slave, Scarlett. Does your better half disclose to you how wonderful you are?"

"Not frequently enough, mistress."

"Pity. I wonder in case he might want red ass cheeks on you. I realize I do."

With that Scarlett heard the surge of air and felt the snap of leather over her can. She shouted out in torment as her nerves conveyed the thunderous explosion up her spinal cord to her brain.

"We're entirely well sound-proof down here, bitch. So don't stress over screaming. I rather like it."

Her mischievous paramour gave Scarlett nine additional smacks with the crop. She was beseeching her mistress to stop; however, her pussy was trickling its sauce down her legs. She could sense her mistress strolled before her and felt her gloved hand lifting her jaw line. She cautiously brushed away her submissive's tears before she felt her pussy once again discovering her face. Scarlett played out her obligations with zeal. She realized this was her place. Regardless of whether it was improvement in her oral serving technique or whether rebuffing her aroused her secret mistress, Scarlett was clueless; however, soon she was remunerated with a sweet spout of her delectable nectar as she held her head tight and peaked against her. Her mysterious dominant held her so tight that she couldn't inhale as she shuddered against her head. Her wails of delight were at least as boisterous as the screams of unbearable torment a couple of moments prior. This satisfied Scarlett.

As her mistress released Scarlett's head, she revealed to her she had earned a prize. She remained restrained in her bent over position while she heard her deviant mistress moving around the room. Scarlett tuned in as the sound of casters moving over the tile reverberated across the room. At that point, she heard a tick as she clearly locked the wheels in place. Scarlett wondered what kind of wicked gadget she was wheeling around her. As her psyche was attempting to decide what was going to occur, she felt her mischievous partner run her fingers over her drenched pussy. It felt so great she really wriggled her butt at her.

"Truly pet, show me how much you need me to touch you," she murmured.

Scarlett's subjugation didn't permit her much movement, yet she did what she could to ride her fingers and show her mistress her desperate longing. As wet as she had been previously, her juices were presently streaming considerably more plentifully. She realized her wicked dominatrix could never enable her to climax this way. It wasn't in her temperament. However, that didn't prevent Scarlett from attempting to catch her mistress's fingers at the perfect edge to take her over the top. Fulfilled that she was adequately stirred for whatever her mistress had arranged, Scarlett pulled her fingers out of her steaming grab. Obviously, she, at that point, made her lick them clean. Her secret tormentor giggled as she battled to stretch her tongue far enough as she continued pulling her fingers once again from her mouth. The flavor of her juice blended in with the smell of the leather gloves was intoxicating.

Scarlett detected her mistress strolling behind her again and afterward felt a rubber cushion being slid under her pussy. It probably had been a non-slip back because it stuck to the chamber. There was a hard stub that settled into the top folds of her pussy lips directly at the base of her clit. It didn't take a scientific genius to make sense of its objective. Scarlett could feel a wire running down from the cushion as it brushed against her leg. Her mischievous dominatrix pressed both her rear end together and constrained her to pivot her hips on the little stub.

"You have satisfied me today, slave Scarlett. You are delightfully submissive and you are rapidly learning your place. I was ready to rebuff you once more, but instead I am going to give you your reward. Today is our second time together. Before I acknowledge you into my harem of sex slaves, you should breeze successfully pass another test. In any case, for the time being, you can have a good time. I will be back soon."

The voice erupted from behind her. Scarlett heard the snap of a switch and the stub started to vibrate. She was profoundly satisfied to feel that the vibrations were stronger and ought to be sufficient to get her off. She, at that point, felt the head of a smooth dildo squeezing against her aching pussy. Obviously, it found little opposition due to her leaking juices. Scarlett heard her mysterious friend turning some sort of handle as she felt the invader dive further into the desirous pits of her womanhood. Evidently happy with her mistress's work, Scarlett heard the deviant woman click another switch, and the dildo started to pull out of her pussy and afterward thrust back in to the very same profundity it had been. Quickly, she understood what was going on. She had seen it in Bella's inventory. She heard the mechanical sound of the flywheel moving in ideal rhythm with the dildo's motion all through her pussy. She was bound

116

and being assaulted by a rape machine. Her kinky dominatrix balanced the speed. Somewhat quicker and she groaned in utmost delight. A little bit slower and she moaned in sexual disappointment.

"So what do you need, bitch? I have a few activities for about 30 minutes. I could leave this on quick with an incredible vibe and you'll be cumming in a matter of moments. Or then again, I could leave it on slow with the gentle vibe and teasing mode for you for the next thirty minutes. Well?"

Chapter 10

Scarlett knew the appropriate response she needed, yet she attempted to consider what her mysterious kinky partner needed. On the off chance that she let her secret partner tease her, she would realize she would be significantly more prepared to serve her upon her arrival. In any case, her mistress appeared to get off on when she acted like an all-out roadside slut. So, perhaps mentioning to her what she truly needed was better. At that point, it crossed her mind. There truly was just one right answer.

"Anything my mistress desires is the thing that I want. Quick, slow or even off, I will acknowledge your choice."

"An excellent answer, Pet. You are catching on quickly. For training purposes, I would leave it on the slow mode. However, as I said you have performed well today, so you have earned a reward. Let's see what destiny has in store for us, okay?"

Scarlett heard her mistress venturing into the bag once more.

"I realize you can't see this; however, what I am holding is a slave emblem. In case I acknowledge you into my slave family, you will be required to wear this consistently even when we are not together. It will serve to help you to remember who owns you; however, it isn't as obvious as a collar. I will unclip the necklace. On one side is engraved the word slave. On the other is engraved an image of a lady dangling from her wrists. I'm going to hurl it like a coin. Pick which side is slow and which is quick."

"I've constantly gotten delight when you tie me. The side with the lady is quick."

"Great. Here we go."

Scarlett didn't hear anything until the medal hit the floor. She heard it bob up and down and afterward perhaps move on its edge for a minute.

"Uh oh, it's attempting to escape. Hang on."

The wait was anguishing as Scarlett heard her mischievous accomplice stroll after the medal to decide her destiny. Her yearning pussy proceeded to juice along the length of the stationary dildo as her clit vibrated in compassion to the cushion. She was practically prepared to orgasm.

"Ok, here we go. I'll return in some time to check on you."

Scarlett heard the snap of the control and the dildo started to gradually thrust into her shuddering pussy. She heard another snap and the clit teaser backed off. "Damn!" She thought. This was most likely her arrangement from the earliest starting point. At that moment, concurrently she heard two additional snaps and both the dildo and vibrator sprung to life.

"Simply kidding slave. Have some good times."

Scarlett heard the entryway open and close as her devious fancy woman left her bound and groaning. She had her first enraptured climax within around two minutes of her turning on the fuck machine. Like their last gathering, her body was being molded to acknowledge numerous climaxes while bound. Again and again, Scarlett felt a tremendous orgasm tear through her. She realized normal sex could never profoundly fulfill her any longer. She was being instructed to want the kind of consideration just her devious accomplice could give her.

Scarlett was left on the chamber being screwed and vibrated by the machine for what appeared to be an unending length of time. She should have cum seven or eight times. She was certain there was a puddle of her juices on the floor. She was shouting in ecstatic pleasure over another peak when she heard the entryway open and afterward the machine clicked off. She was shaking as the vibrations and penetration halted.

"Gracious, thank you mistress. I love you."

Her fancy woman didn't let out the slightest peep. She felt the fuck machine being moved away and afterward felt her bonds being removed. She scoured her wrists to bring blood circulation once again flowing through them. She was walked out of the room, yet turned left rather than directly toward where she realized the entryway was found. Her deviant and kinky dominatrix guided her to stop, which she did. She heard a shower being turned on. She stood for at least a couple of minutes before being pushed forward under the flood of warm water.

"There is a bar of cleanser before you. Clean yourself well and turn the water off when you are finished."

Clearly her devious paramour would not like to get wet as she didn't accompanied her in the shower. Scarlett immediately washed off and afterward lathered up the cleanser to scour her body. She needed not to waste her time in the shower, yet return to her mistress as fast as could reasonably be expected. After another wash, Scarlett stopped the water. She felt a towel wrapping over her. This was not a modest Holiday Inn towel. It was thick, feathery, and lavish. Judging from the towel, she could have been in a luxurious and expensive spa, rather than a high-rise basement.

After she was dry, her wrists were again cuffed behind her back and her leash was by and by clipped to her collar.

"Time's slipping away. It's an ideal opportunity to get you home."

Scarlett pursued behind her secret mistress as she drove her out of the locker room. She had not enabled her to get dressed. Clearly, she was never again stressed over meeting anyone or the surveillance cameras. They strolled down the long corridor toward the parking area. Scarlett attempted to recall exactly how long the lobby was to measure how much further they had before she would be naked in the parking area. She figured they must be close when her special lady guided her into a right turn and up the stairs. She heard her mistress opening an entryway which she more likely than not strolled through.

"What do we have here, Natasha?" Scarlett heard a female voice say. Her playful mistress's name was Natasha.

"Only payment for letting me utilize the locker room. Same of course," Scarlett heard her dominatrix answer.

"Works for me as well."

Scarlett felt a pull on her leash as she heard a seat turning. She felt the security gatekeeper's hand on her shoulder as she was guided to the floor. She, at that point, felt a skirt brushing her brow as it was flipped over her. She wasn't wearing any underwear and obviously she had been foreseeing Scarlett's arrival since her pussy was already prepared for her tongue. Her pussy had a distinct and fairly foul and salty taste to it.

"That is right, bitch lady. Suck mom's pussy. I realized you were coming, so I didn't wash it throughout the previous three days. Work superbly and possibly I'll let your mistress bring you back for more. I have a major ole strap-on in the closet here which is perfect for your butt nugget."

The security woman kept up a constant flow of degrading remarks. Scarlett slurped up her every hole simply like she was drinking up her pussy juice. She imagined herself pierced on her dildo while spread around her desk. Her aroused body had arrived at the zenith of excitement by simply wondering about the devious comments and contemplating sex.

Scarlett found her excitement level becoming the all the more corrupting and grimy as the security woman conversed with her more and more. As she stooped on the floor of the security office, she was certain the tiles were messy. Scarlett realized they were cold to the touch. She was a naughty, dirty whore eating a slutty pussy, and she cherished it. The gatekeeper's hands were firmly grasping her hair controlling her head and in this way her tongue. She cherished it as well. Scarlett envisioned her wicked dominatrix viewing the progress, and he believed she was glad for her. Bent over, Scarlett knew her pussy and ass were uncovered. She ached for her Mistress, Mistress Natasha she currently knew, to touch her and get her off the cliffs once more.

The gatekeeper was certainly prepared for Scarlett's visit, yet she had great control of her sensual excitements since it took a long time and loads of tiresome exertion on Scarlett's part to bring her off. After she exploded uncontrollably, Scarlett felt her deviant mistress pull on her leash driving her to stand up. She didn't get a thank you as they left the workplace and strolled over into the carport. Her mischievous dominatrix didn't let out the slightest peep until Scarlett was moving to go into the van.

"Penelope valued your endeavors, Scarlett. In case you decide to see me once more, tributing and pleasing the security woman will be a piece of your obligations. It's a tax I pay for access to the locker room. Do you get it?"

"Truly, Mistress Natasha."

"I thought about whether you got that. Indeed, my name is Natasha, yet I want to be referred to as Mistress N. Now, would you like to ride home on the seat with the dildo in the back of my car or will I simply cuff you on the seat in the back?"

That was most likely the silliest inquiry Scarlett had heard in quite a while. The ride home appeared to be longer and bumpier than the ride there. "Was my dominatrix taking an alternate course or was her pussy only sore from the fuck machine and her butt still sensitive from the riding crop?" Scarlett couldn't have cared less. She was profoundly satisfied once more, bobbing on the seat and crying in orgasmic climax each couple of minutes. At the point when the van, at long last, halted and she was walked naked up her front walkway, Scarlett didn't give it a second thought whether anyone was spying. From the front, she was commanded to slither through the grass to the back yard. As though her deviant mistress was back tracking her steps, she took Scarlett for a turn around the yard and afterward again commanded her to pee. It had been hours since they were in this position. This time, Scarlett didn't hesitate for a second. She just inclined forward and let go a stream directly on the yard. She was then coordinated to crawl into the house. The leash drove the way and soon she was back in her spacious bedroom.

Mistress Natasha situated Scarlett on her knees, and one again, she orally pleasured her brilliant pussy. Her taste was much fresher and exotic than Penelope's and she had cherished completely as her mistress rode her face and took her pleasure. From that point, Scarlett was situated on her bed and her wrist cuffs were supplanted by the clock cuffs bound through the headboard. This time her mistress didn't lock her legs or utilize any deliberately set toys to torment her. She affectionately pulled a cover over her outstretched body and revealed to her that she had two hours to take a nap and around three hours before Jacques returned home. Scarlett valued her concern that she would not need to hurry this time and nodded off to rest.

Scarlett anticipated that an email should be hanging tight for her the following morning, yet there wasn't one. She didn't know whether she ought to be so strong as to send one. All things considered, she was not accountable for this relationship. A few days passed by and she thought about whether she had accomplished something inappropriately. Scarlett was on a tingling sensation holding on to get a notification from her seductive mistress. At last, on the following Friday she reached Scarlett. Just it wasn't the means by which she anticipated.

Waiting for her on her work area at office was a beige manila envelope. There was no arrival address, yet the penmanship of her name coordinated with her mistress's first letter she wrote to her was enough for Scarlett to rationalize everything. Her cubicle mates had not landed at work, yet so she promptly opened the envelope. Inside were a note and a DVD. The DVD had a manually written mark. Slave Scarlett. Her heart sank. Clearly, she would have been the topic of the video. Scarlett started to peruse the letter. Her hands were shaking, her fingers were numb, and she felt a tingling sensation in between her legs.

"My gorgeous Scarlett. I am anticipating your third and last tryout for my harem. Enclosed in the envelope, you will discover a recap of our last session. I'm certain you will discover it as invigorating as I did. I expect an email from you after you watch it. Your last tryout will be next Thursday. You will be spending the night with me so concoct any reason you need to your better half. You can that you never drink too much, but you got tipsy with the young ladies after work and you had too much to drive home. So you're crashing at a colleague's home. In any case, you can concoct anything you desire. I realize he always expects your company at night on the bed, so it may be the toughest challenge, yet I'm certain you can do it."

Simply seeing her penmanship had Scarlett's inner parts going to jelly.

"Your email basically needs to state 'Yes' or 'No.' There is no requirement for any extra words. In case you state 'Yes', you will get guidelines by the end of business Thursday. On the off chance that you choose 'No', I won't get in touch with you once more. The DVD is the main copy. It is all yours to keep as a souvenir. I anticipate your answer by early afternoon."

"Shit. Early afternoon. How could I watch the DVD before at that time?"Scarlett thought inwardly. Individuals were filling into the workplace as of now. There was no chance she could watch it here. Be that as it may, it didn't generally make a difference. She definitely comprehended what the appropriate response would be. She emailed her mistress at 7:56 am. It simply said "Yes."

Her tension and expectation was building. Thursday, she would, at long last, meet her provocative mistress, even though she had been serving her for a considerable length of time in namelessness. Scarlett now presumed that her mistress worked at her office. The envelope left around her work desk with the DVD of their last session didn't have a return address and their office assistant had not enrolled any deliveries by a courier. Scarlett went through a few days systematically scanning through her office attempting to figure out what her mistress's identity was. The security watchwoman called her Natasha; however, they didn't have any employee named Natasha working in the office. Possibly the security guard had utilized her middle name or possibly it was simply to distract Scarlett; however, she discovered nothing related to a 'Natasha' in their office.

There was likewise a clue on the DVD. In her private minutes at home, Scarlett had viewed the DVD until it was copied into her animated psyche. One thing that struck her was the camera was not generally on a tripod. Now and again, it changed position or zoomed in. She started to shake when she understood that implied she had not been alone with her deviant mistress. For at least some portion of their erotic time together, another person was with them. Another anonymous individual was recording her depravity. Even though the camera administrator had been mindful so as not to show her seductive mistress's face, there was one shot of her nailing Scarlett from behind which demonstrated a couple of interlocking female images with a couple of handcuffs hanging down from them tattooed on the small of her back. She attempted wandering around their office and discretely keeping an eye on her associates at the restroom sink planning to get a glimpse at the generally secured work of art, the tattoo, covered up underneath a shirt. Again Scarlett failed to find out her actual identity.

She, at long last, needed to fall back on speculating about her secret mistress based on her height. She knew that when she was on her knees, her wicked mistress's pussy was level with her mouth. Her devious mistress had the ideal height to eat her pussy, possibly. Scarlett realized her mistress generally wore heels with her. She could just assume that they were at least three inches tall. So she needed to assess where every lady's pussy in the workplace would be given those conditions. Her secret mistress additionally had the most wonderful penmanship. Most documents in their office were typed on the computer, yet there was an archive of documents to inspect as some of them had signatures.

Chapter 11

Essentially, Scarlett made herself insane attempting to make sense of who Mistress Natasha was without any success. She, in every case, simply ended up wet, aroused and no closer to finding her actual identity. She would simply need to wait impatiently until Thursday, just three days away. Time slithered. Scarlett got no messages or notes from her so called mistress, Natasha. She was on a tingling sensation. She needed to jerk off five or six times each day to keep her head on straight. On Wednesday, she was horny enough when she woke up to wear the remote-controlled panties to office once more. The last time they had glitches, and she nearly got caught red-handed pleasuring herself was during the video conference. She got trapped in the women's restroom. The experience mortified Scarlett;

however, the animating recollections excited her enough to attempt once more. As she was sitting at her cubicle encompassed by her colleagues, joyfully yet quietly humming ceaselessly with her remote-controlled panties, Scarlett understood another piece of information about her secret mistress and why she must be someone from the office. She had never had her underwear exhibit some glitches or since and Bella guaranteed she'd never heard or leaned anything such as this, yet imagine a scenario in which someone in the workplace either took Scarlett's remote or had their own during the video conference. Maybe someone was playing with her even when she was in the conference room. The idea was sufficient to send Scarlett hurrying to the restroom to soothe the tension and release the anticipation that had developed in her crotch. Luckily, this time she wasn't caught red-handed.

Thursday unfolded. Today was the day. Scarlett couldn't settle on what to wear. She expected her seductive mistress would provide her any garments she required. Hell, she would most likely simply end up stripped. So Scarlett wore her typical traditionalist business suit to make it easygoing. She made some hard memories focusing on her work. She knew someone in the workplace was going to approach her, and as the day progressed, Scarlett ended up incapacitated in the office. In her mind, she estimated with the likelihood that every lady in her office was her dominatrix. She looked as the clock gradually moved during the hour somewhere in the range of 4:00 pm and 5:00 pm. The day's end consistently appeared to be longer; however, this hour appeared to last an unending length of time. The workplace began emptying itself, yet at the same time, there was no message. Scarlett was getting edgy. At 4:55, their secretary stopped by her work cubicle.

"This just came for you," she said grabbing a FedEx box. "The conveyance guy said they were running late today and apologized for not being here prior."

Scarlett assured the receptionist that it was fine. As she left, Scarlett gave the case a shake. It was light and seemed like just a few things were inside. She timidly checked out the workplace. There were a few people still there, but most everybody had left for home by five. A few ladies she had chosen in the top of her "mistress pool" were still in their workplaces. "Is it accurate to say that they were holding on to perceive how I responded to the substance in the container? When might they approach me?" Scarlett swallowed hard.

Her hands were shaking as she tore open the seal on the crate. There was the normal letter, a couple of shoes, and a collar with a lot of nipple clamps joined to a ring in the front. Her wet pussy immediately turned into a blazing flood as Scarlett got the letter.

"My dearest Scarlett. I trust you have been anticipating this evening. I need you to go out and get some supper. I need you fit as fiddle and back to the workplace by 6:15. From 6:15 to 6:50, I need you to sit at your work area cubicle and consider what it will mean for you to serve me tonight and into the future. Try not to move from your work area and don't jerk off no matter how desperate and compelling your lust-filled urge is. I foresee the workplace will be vacant by 6:30. At 6:50, I need you to strip off those unflattering garments you are wearing and stuff them in your work desk cabinet. Put on the collar, nipple clamps, and the shoes and afterward walk down the stairs to the women's restroom. In the handicapped stall, you will discover further guidelines." The letter was printed, yet marked Mistress Natasha in the handwriting that made Scarlett feeble.

She took a full breath and set the note back in the crate and the case in her cabinet. She had an hour to eat. It didn't take that long, so she went through twenty minutes strolling around outside the office building attempting to calm down her agitated nerves. As demanded, Scarlett was back at her work area several minutes ahead of schedule. The workplace appeared to be vacant, yet she could feel her mistress's eyes on her. In her psyche, her cunning mistress must be watching her and observing her compliance. Scarlett's thirty-five minutes were spent in reflection on their relationship had developed and bonded. The expectation was killing Scarlett. She was having goosebumps and her heart was in her throat. She was happy the workplace was vacant ahead of schedule. There didn't appear to be anyone around as Scarlett started stripping at 6:50. She was set up for her mischievous dominatrix to pop out of her hiding place just like a lioness from her liar and assume responsibility of her conquest; however, it didn't occur. Scarlett had a sense of security in her office as she strolled naked through the corridors to arrive at the stairs. She realized the lifts had cameras, and she trusted the stairs were devoid of any security cameras.

Scarlett was shivering as she streaked through the office building. She would have been mortified on the off chance that she had been caught red-handed, yet as it might have been, she was simply thrilled. She didn't waste time and realized she had made it to the restroom before seven. The entire area seemed void. Possibly she was waiting in the stall. Scarlett pushed the enormous entryway open on the handicapped stall, yet all she discovered was a video camera on a tripod and two dildos. There was likewise a note on the tripod.

"Congrats. You've made it this far. To demonstrate your compliance and dependability, I trust the only thing appeared on this tape are you coming in naked. I need you to sit on the latrine and fuck yourself. I'm certain you've needed to do that for quite a long time. So here is your opportunity. Utilize one of the dildos on each of your opening and fuck yourself until you orgasm. There's no hurry, so live it up. I'll know whether you're faking, so don't. After you are done, I need you to carry the camera and the dildos to my office. It is on this very floor. I'm certain you can discover it. The correct method to enter my office is on your hands and knees. Arrange the camera outside my entryway to catch your entrance. I'll have more guidelines when you arrive."

A rational individual could never be adhering to these guidelines. But Scarlett grabbed the dildos. The large one effectively slid into her pussy. She could see herself in the screen of the video camera. She looked completely trashy as she sat back on the latrine and spread her legs for the world, well at least to her Mistress Natasha's camera, to see. After a couple of scrumptiously squishy strokes in her pussy, she got the smaller dildo and started sucking it. Subsequent to figuring out how to cherish butt-centric penetration from the remote-controlled underwear, the smaller dildo returned home in her butt-hole without a lot of exertion. Scarlett inclined toward her side and lifted her leg against the stall wall so that the camera could get a better perspective of the two holes being pleasured. There was no compelling reason to counterfeit any sensational satisfaction as her body released the sensual vitality which had been repressed throughout the day. Scarlett attempted to give coy looks to the camera, yet she didn't think she was effective. After only a couple of moments, her desire conquered her and I exploded tremendously. Losing control of her legs, Scarlett kicked the tripod. She was appreciative that it didn't fall over, but she was certain the focal point caught a fascinating sight as the force of her climax truly knocked her out of the focus frame.

Scarlett grabbed the camera and for the record, expressed thanks to her mischievous dominatrix. As she quieted down, Scarlett all of a sudden had the acknowledgment that she needed to discover Mistress Natasha's office. Be that as it may, strolling naked through the building carrying a camcorder was unquestionably not her concept of a decent time. Still, Scarlett couldn't delay. She was certain the camera had a time keeper so her mistress would know. She got the camera and her note and strolled into the corridor and afterward into the elevator lounge. The floor numbers on one of the lifts was changing. She wasn't the only one in the building. Scarlett immediately made arrangements to cover up in the washroom if the lift stopped at her floor, yet it passed her. She inhaled a sigh of deep relief and set out on her errand to discover her paramour's office. Things being what they are, it was simpler than she suspected it would be.

Alongside the lift was a floor registry. Scarlett had just checked everybody in her organization, yet she had failed to consider different organizations operating in the building. Checking the directory, und6er the heading of "Building Management," she found a tag for Miss S. McCarthy. There were no 'Natasha' recorded, yet she recalled her mysterious mistress instructing her to refer to her as Miss S. So Scarlett decided this must be the place. She strolled a few doors down in opposite direction from her workplace and the restrooms. There was an entryway without a window that said "Building Management" that coordinated the number on the registry. She arranged the camera and opened the entryway. She dropped to her knees and slithered into the workplace. Gazing upward, there was no one there. Scarlett stood up and recovered the camera and set it inside the workplace. There was a lobby with a few offices. They all looked dark aside from the last one where she could see light from under the entryway.

The crawl down the passage made Scarlett feel like she was sealing her destiny. She desperately prayed she was in the right spot or she would never live this down and would need to leave her place of employment. The entryway was closed, so Scarlett knocked the door at. She heard a familiar voice instructing her to enter. She turned the handle and pushed the entryway open at the base wiggling her rear end for the camera as she entered Miss S. McCarthy's office.

"Your humble slave is reporting for duty, Mistress N." Scarlett started.

"Welcome slave Scarlett. Happy you could make it today around evening time."

Scarlett kept her eyes on the floor before her as Mistress N. stood and strolled from behind her work area. Her legs and feet were exactly as Scarlett had envisioned them in her agitated psyche. Her 4" stilettos conditioned her wonderful calves. Scarlett pursued her legs up as far as she could and her daring mind provoked her to do without getting consent. At the point when Scarlett's eyes arrived at the hem of her mini-skirt around five inches above the knee, she dropped her look back to the floor.

"Stand and look at me Scarlett."

Scarlett stood up and recognized Mistress N. right away. She was the lady who had found Scarlett jerking off in the restroom. She just had a look at Mistress N. through her shame-filled eyes the last time. In any case, now as she savored her excellence, she was in absolute wonderment. Mistress N. was most likely fifteen years older than her, yet she was dazzling. She was dressed provocatively in a perfectly sized exclusively custom fitted business suit. Scarlett watched in bewilderment as Mistress N. advanced toward her and took her face in her grasp. She gave her a soulful, passionate, and certainly wet, profound kiss.

"We will have a ton of fun tonight, pet."

Miss S. revealed to Scarlett that they were going out for beverages and dancing. She unfastened a hanging bag and pulled out a dark semi-formal dress. She likewise pulled out a translucent g-string and a little box, which Scarlett perceived as a Ben-Wa ball holder. Scarlett required no grease to embed the balls into her seething pussy. The panties, slim as they were, felt like she was wearing nothing by any stretch of the imagination. "At least, they would hold the balls in," Scarlett figured. The dress was in reality more unobtrusive than she would have speculated. It secured her succulent bosoms and reached down a few inches over her knees. She wasn't insane that her playful mistress had not decided to give a bra to the outfit, yet things being as they were, it wasn't really awful.

They headed first floor together in the lift. Scarlett was jerking as the balls did something amazing when she began strolling. Natasha drove which left Scarlett liberated to squirm in the front seat. They headed to a lavish and reputed night club. She was shocked that they didn't go to a lesbian or S&M lounge, yet she knew not to scrutinize her thoughtful dominatrix. They found a parking spot in the club's lot. Before they got out of their car, Mistress N. had begun to hike up Scarlett's dress. She, at that point, squeezed the sides of the g-string and pulled on the top until the sides disappeared between her slave's pussy lips. Scarlett felt herself streaming around the sides of the g-string and realized her pussy lips would now be incredibly teased by those panties much in the way the balls were teasing her inner parts. She pursued Mistress N. into the club. It was practically 8:00 pm.

There were a couple of individuals dancing and a couple of more people relaxing at the bar, but the spot was quite moderate. Scarlett assumed it was early, and that Thursday was certifiably not a major night out. Natasha and she found a stall in a faintly lit corner where they had the option to taste two or three glasses of wine and talk for almost an hour prior to initiate the proceedings and the club turned the music up. By then a series of folks, some attractive, some not, started hitting on them. With a very much rehearsed wave of the hand, Miss Natasha sent them all away until a nerdy looking school type kid drew nearer. Scarlett didn't have the foggiest idea whether Natasha had compassion for him since he was unmistakably out of their group or in case it was an aspect of her ground breaking strategy; however, she proposed (Scarlett acknowledged it as an order) that she must hit the dance floor with him.

On the off chance that you've never danced while loaded down with Ben-Wa balls, you are absolutely clueless about what you're missing. Between the balls and the g-string wadded up in her crotch, the dancing motion was arousing Scarlett. Before the end of the tune, she doubted herself if she could make it back to their corner without cumming. Luckily, a soft melodious song went ahead, and Scarlett had the option to wrap her arms over her nerdy partner in sparkling shield to steady herself and calm down her racing heart beat. She held him tight. He didn't know how to manage his hands, even though she secretly and desperately wished for him to press her ass or grope her bosoms. Scarlett figured out how to trap his knee between her legs when the melodious tune ended bumping him in an entirely pleasurable manner.

Her nerdy hero, at long last, understood that Scarlett was essentially stroking off against him. He had a grin from ear to ear. At the point when the melodious tune ended, the DJ declared he was taking a break. Scarlett was sad. Her accomplice turned out to be a lot bolder and inquired as to whether he could take her home. She disclosed to him that she was with someone and didn't believe that was such a smart thought. They strolled back to the table, and he shocked Scarlett when he gave a similar proposal to Natasha. Clearly, he thought in case he hit out with Scarlett, then perhaps Natasha would state yes. Scarlett was a little stressed that Natasha might state yes for her since she picked the club for some hideous reason; however she didn't. She instructed Scarlett to sit down and inquired if he would be so kind to buy them another round.

The nerdy hero calmly inquired if he wasn't their type, for what reason would he be interested to buy them drinks? Natasha inquired as to whether he had realized Scarlett was attempting to cum on his leg. The nerdy legend said obviously he had. Natasha revealed to him that her friend was horny because her significant other wasn't meeting up to and fulfilling her needs. That obviously was a falsehood. By then, Natasha was the one not fulfilling up Scarlett's needs, yet it was an innocent exaggeration that the nerd could without any trouble accepted. Natasha, at that point, proposed to let him watch Scarlett cum in return for two additional glasses of wine. Really fast, he was at the bar as Scarlett was glaring at Natasha with blazing knives from her eyes.

"Goodness please Scarlett. I realize you need it. It will be fun when you are going make his night."

Scarlett wasn't in a situation to argue as the nerd came back with beverages in his grasp and slid into the corner alongside her.

"Scarlett," Natasha started. "This decent noble man has presented to us a drink. I think it is time you reimbursed him."

Scarlett hesitantly spread her legs under the table laying one on his leg and one on her wicked mistress. She was gazing at his face the entire time and she expected Natasha was gazing at her. When she touched her burning pussy, all the musings of bondage vanished like a puff of smoke. She felt wet and messy as she started fingering her throbbing clit and sliding her fingers all over her sodden slit. Scarlett could sense he was hypnotized as into her presentation as was herself. There was no requirement for her to counterfeit the zenith of her excitement. The main question she had was whether she would be too noisy when she orgasmed. She tackled this issue by burying her head on his bicep as she shouted out loud in euphoric delight into his arm. She was certain her devious paramour was intensely satisfied by her exhibition and she was confident that the nerd got his money's worth.

Chapter 12

After Scarlett climaxed tremendously, he once again offered to take them home when her mistress revealed to him they both appreciated and preferred the company of ladies and sent him away. He left with a grin all over and a bulge in his pants. He was $10 lighter, yet obviously, a lot more glad that he anticipated his night to be. Scarlett watched him disappear in the general direction of the rest rooms. She could bet she could think about what he did straightaway.

Natasha and Scarlett sat and tasted their new glasses of wine while Scarlett calmed down her agitated nerves. Other men had seen her presentation. From their seats, the bar, and from different stalls, Scarlett observed men holding folded bills clearly offering cash for a repeated provocative performance. Scarlett thought about whether her mischievous dominatrix brought her along to save money on wine. Scarlett was going to ask Natasha about it when she saw her manager Leilani and her better half stroll in. What was all the more stunning was she saw her cubicle colleague Brooklynn with them. This wasn't the 'Brooklynn' she knew, notwithstanding. At work, Brooklynn was the introvert one in our four people workgroup. She was exceptionally preservationist, always wearing professional dresses, yet not especially uncovering or provocative garments. She never wore heels and infrequently discussed her personal life. The Brooklynn that Scarlett presently observed was totally unique. She was dressed to the nines out of a smooth dress cut high up her thigh and deep down her chest. Her hair, generally tied up in a tight bun was down around her shoulders and styled for a night out on the town. Practically most stunning was the pair of fuck me siphons on her feet. Who even realized she had legs not to mention a conditioned set that run as far as possible up to an extremely tight ass. In truth, Scarlett nearly didn't recognize her. Scarlett was practically flabbergasted because the most stunning part was Leilani's better half had his arm around Brooklynn's abdomen. It wasn't just a friendly hug just like 'I'm giving you a friendly squeeze sort of embrace'. They were strolling affectionately hand in hand into the club.

Leilani obviously wasn't oblivious to the circumstance. She had turned and stared at the pair and wasn't frantic. "What was happening here?" Scarlett wondered as she promptly sank down into the stall.

"What's up Scarlett?" Natasha inquired.

"My manager just strolled in. I can't have her see me here."

"Why not? You're not accomplishing anything wrong."

"Truly? So grinding myself on a stranger and afterward jerking off for him is typical?" Scarlett reacted.

"It probably won't be ordinary, yet there is nothing amiss with being here."

"Would we be able to go now before she sees us? Please?" Scarlett practically begged.

"Well since you asked decently, we surely can. Be that as it may, you will owe me one for this."

Scarlett previously owed her mischievous mistress everything this night. She could never deny a request from her so she wasn't too stressed over what her mistress's demanding announcement might involve. "Fine, but how about we please escape from here."

They discretely advanced toward the entryway. When Scarlett was past an angle where she could have looked at her manager, she rushed to the passageway. Natasha was following at a progressively relaxed pace and made up for lost time to her slave in the parking area. Scarlett was grinning. Natasha was most certainly not.

"Never do that again, slave. You should remain behind your mistress and walk at my pace. You will be punished when we return to the office."

Scarlett looked down at the ground after understanding her mistake. The drive back to the workplace hushed up. She hoped she had not blown the last meeting. They took the lift back up to Natasha's floor and strolled into her office.

"I've been wondering about a proper discipline for you. Strip."

Scarlett quickly pulled off the dress and the g-string. She had figured out how to leave the heels on so she did leave the heels on. As she pulled the g-string off, the balls slid out of her sodden pussy and made a banging sound as they followed gravity hitting the floor.

"Sufficiently wet, whore?" Natasha provoked.

Scarlett's cheeks burned and she reddened, at that point bent over and got the balls. She cleaned them with her tongue like she cleaned all her dominatrix's toys and afterward given them back to Natasha. She placed them back in their case and opened one of her desk drawers and dropped them in. Natasha likewise took the opportunity to haul out a collar and a leash. "At least I had not blown the last meeting totally," Scarlett wondered inwardly. In the wake of clipping her obedient slave in, Natasha pulled on the leash and they headed toward the entryway. Her legs started to weaken as they arrived at the elevator bank. She pursued Natasha meekly into the lift and she picked her slave's floor. "Where were we going?" Scarlett swallowed hard.

As the building administrator, Natasha had a pass key to every one of the organizations operating in the complex and Scarlett, before long, ended up strolling through her office entrance, at that point, her cubicle, afterward the conference room, and lastly to her supervisor's office. Natasha opened the entryway and guided her obedient slave inside. There was an image of Leilani and her significant other on the work area.

"I needed to converse with your manager and check whether she could smell how messy you were at the club. You're presumably invulnerable to your splendid fragrance by this point, yet I guarantee you that charming nerd kid realized you were eager for advancement. Since you denied me the delight of giving you a little public embarrassment, I think we'll leave Leilani a little present for tomorrow."

Scarlett didn't have a clue what Natasha was discussing, and she didn't think she needed to know either. Natasha plunked down in Leilani's luxuriously designated leather workstation seat and motioned her submissive slave over her lap. They began with a vivacious hand spanking, so Scarlett would remember her place in their relationship. Her bottom was set ablaze; however, with each slap, a wave of sensual delight surged up through her pussy and directly into her mind. Scarlett's was granulating her groin on her playful dominatrix's much like she had on her poor nerdy dance partner. She was certain in case Natasha had allowed her, she could have cum just from the vigorous spanking; however, her mischievous mistress had different thoughts.

Natasha motioned for Scarlett to sit on the huge oak work desk. Scarlett was certain her sweat-soaked ass and drooling pussy marked a serious impression on Leilani's month-to-month planning booklet on the top of her work desk. She spread her legs without being told. She was hoping her innovatively playful paramour would soon give her some sensual relief from her agitating excitement. Natasha did, yet not in the way in which Scarlett was anticipating. Grabbing her manager's telephone receiver, she commanded her to jerk off with it. She needed her slave's captivating aroma on the mouthpiece. So tomorrow first thing her supervisor would get a stunning surprise. Scarlett was pretty netted out at the idea, yet she additionally expected to orgasm and grabbed the extemporized toy and started scouring it against her drenched slit.

Natasha gave a shout out to Scarlett as she got into the inconsiderate provocative demonstration. She unclipped the telephone cord, so her dutiful slave could embed the handset deep into her pussy. Scarlett hoped her gushing fluid wouldn't destroy the microphone, yet she wasn't going to stop. She was drawing nearer and closer to the zenith of her thrilling euphoria when Natasha slapped her hand and commanded her to heel. She opened her eyes with sickening dread and let go of the telephone. Natasha pulled the shimmering receiver out of her slave's juicy pussy and plugged the cord back in. She looked in awe as her devious mistress deliberately set the receiver back to the telephone cradle without wiping the abundance juice off. She, at that point, stood up and motioned for her slave to do likewise. Scarlett bounced off the work desk to stand beside her. The top sheet of paper on the monthly planning document stuck to her rear end, and she needed to strip it back. There was an ideal butt print on it.

"Now, I need you to rub your little pink pussy everywhere throughout the seat. Spread your splendid fragrance around. Stink it up awesomely great."

After the telephone receiver, this errand appeared to be practically comical. Scarlett stood on the seat of the leather chair and as Natasha steadied it, she scoured herself everywhere throughout the leather headrest. Reaching the lower back of the seat proved increasingly tricky. She needed to sit on the seat and wrap her legs around the arm rests and around the back to reach. Natasha wasn't satisfied with her dedicated slave's endeavors. So she shoved two fingers inside her leaking cunt and in the wake of squirming them around to her undying appreciation, she pulled them out and wiped them everywhere throughout the seat. She repeated this tenacious procedure a few times until she was satisfied and her slave was a gasping mess. Scarlett implored her to enable her to cum. She said, "You could, slave. But not here."

She instructed her to slither like the bitch hound she was and guided her again into the lobby. Natasha bolted Leilani's entryway. She'd never realize anyone was there when she landed at the workplace the following day. Natasha led, and Scarlett pursued as they made it back to the cubicle where her sultry slave worked.

"Have you ever been fucked on your work area?"

"No, Mistress N."

"Well, I guess this is the perfect time for it."

That was the way by which it came to be that at 10:00 pm on a Thursday night. Scarlett ended up bent over on her work desk while another lady finger-fucked her to an explosive climax. It was so brilliant. Scarlett knew her work area and the majority of her cubicle mates would now realize the similar invigorating aroma of her sex like her manager's office and she couldn't have cared less. She rode her wicked dominatrix's fingers as she grinded her clit into the edge of the work desk and cried like a sex-crazed monster. Incredibly, her seductive mistress allowed her to peak, even though Scarlett thought she would stop her on the edge once more. At the point when they were done, she dropped to the floor, got to her dominant mistress's ankles and kissed her feet while expressing gratitude toward her again and again for allowing her to orgasm.

"We've just started, pet. You have to call your husband and remind him you are not returning back home tonight."

Scarlett had completely disregarded Jacques. Her animated psyche had been occupied, after all. She decided from her cell. Jacques didn't appear to be astonished. He sounded drowsy. He expressed gratitude toward her for calling and told her to make some great memories. Scarlett was relieved that he believed her, trusted her enough, and that she didn't need to make up a greater story about her hideous party than a senior colleague's farewell party. As she hung up the telephone, Natasha pulled on the leash once more. Scarlett was permitted to walk this time. Natasha revealed to her two steps behind and one to the left side; always, two steps behind and either to the left or to the right side. They strolled back to the lobby, and Natasha relocked her slave's office entryway. Scarlett realized they were going back to her mistress's office. But, she was wrong.

Rather, they strolled around the corner and down a lobby. This side had the men's washroom. Scarlett thought about whether her playful mistress would have her leave a present for the men in her workplace as well; however, they strolled past the restroom stopping at the cargo lift. She got a terrible inclination in the pit of her stomach as they paused. The lift showed up. It was certainly a service elevator devoid of the advanced adorning touches of the different lifts in her office building; however, it had the extra destination buttons, which promptly got her attention. Past the lobby button where different lifts landed was B1, B2, and B3. Sub-basement cellars three. Her playful mistress's other office. Scarlett understood as they descended that their last session occurred straightforwardly in this building and she knew where they were going.

This lift was much slower than the passenger lifts which gave Scarlett more opportunity to think, stress, recall, and even dream a bit. Gradually they slipped into the guts of the basement. As the entryways opened, she promptly perceived the faintly lit, moist, and mildew covered lobby. Leaving the lift, she saw the entryway was closed going to the old locker rooms. Natasha never turned; rather she was guiding her obedient slave directly to the security office. Penelope was not on obligation. Another watchwoman, Trisha was. She obviously had expected them and communicated that Penelope had raved about Scarlett's oral abilities. She said she was prepared for "her bribe" and spread her legs for Scarlett. Like Penelope before her, their experience was businesslike. Clearly, her tongue was paying the entrance fees to the locker room. After Trisha was completely satisfied, three tremendous climaxes later, she gave a key to Natasha. Going down the lobby, Scarlett felt alive as they strolled into the darkness. At least it was an unknown darkness to Scarlett. She was clueless what was in store.

Chapter 13

This time Scarlett was permitted to see the room. As she had imagined in her aroused mind, the locker room had for some time been neglected and truly wasn't appropriate for use. The tiles were mildew-covered even though it seemed every one of the apparatuses were useful. The previous storeroom which had been changed over to a make-shift dungeon was cleaner. The paint was a couple of years old, yet still decent. There were sufficient subjugations and S&M gears to host a genuine party. Scarlett pondered exactly what Mistress Natasha had coming up for her. As it turned out, she could speculate very little. Natasha let her go to the washroom, and afterward, she restrained her to the twin size bed in the corner of the room. After that she tied on the jaw-line dildo and rode her slave's pretty face until she shouted in stirring delight. It was almost 11:00 PM when she orgasmed. Natasha, at that point, pulled a frilly cover over her body and disclosed to her slave that she was returning home. Scarlett began to twist in her restrains. She would not like to be left alone there. Natasha let Scarlett know that there was nothing to worry because Trisha would take care of her and that she would see her in the early morning. Natasha turned the lights off on her way out. It was tranquil. The only sounds Scarlett could hear were her heart pounding in her chest and her breathing.

Left without incitement and no real way to get herself off, Scarlet, in the end, nodded off. In reality, she slept well overall. She couldn't recollect awakening during that night time until she felt pressure on her head. She woke to the dim restroom light sparkling around the open entryway of her room. Rising and falling over her face was the succulent pussy of another lady. She couldn't look her face. Everything she could observe was pussy and succulent boobs. She had a watchwoman's shirt on. So Scarlett assumed it was Penelope. She didn't talk though. She just took her pleasure until she was intensely fulfilled and afterward set her skirt back on and exited the entryway. A couple of moments later Trisha came in. The scene was repeated. She dropped her skirt, fucked her face, orgasmed as she trembled vigorously, and then left. Scarlett was feeling as if she was a fucking sex tot and nothing more. Rather than getting dressed and leaving, be that as it may, Trisha untied her restrains.

"I'm taking a break now. You have to go to the washroom and shower. You stink like a whorehouse."

Scarlett would not like to question Trisha, but at least some portion of that smell was from her and her security accomplice. Still, Scarlett was glad to be free, so she did as she was asked to do. The shower tiles were truly frightful, yet the water pressure was great and the temperature was warm. The shower felt extraordinary, and Scarlett spent somewhat longer than she would normally do in her shower just to rejuvenate herself. She had her eyes shut standing under the gushing and refreshing stream of water letting her body return to a soothing calmness when she heard Trisha's roar.

"Enough whore. I need to return home. Get back in here."

Scarlett snapped back to the present time and stopped the water. She toweled off and strolled again into the locker room when she had learned about Trisha's and Penelope's utmost enjoyment as they used her. Scarlett was hoping Trisha had some garments for her to wear, so she could either head home or up to her work. She couldn't determine what time it was, nevertheless she suspected the shift change was most likely either 6:00 or 7:00 am. As she strolled into the locker room, Trisha was patting the cylinder she probably had been restrained to, the last time she was here.

"I realize you preferred this last time, bitch. I witnessed a video of you as you climaxed before your mistress's fuck machine. I'm certain you will appreciate it as much as you did the last time."

Scarlett got an opportunity to inspect the apparatus this time. It resembled a short aerobatic pommel horse. She was speculating that was the item that overturned her life completely because she was used and abused on it by Natasha for her pleasure, even when she didn't know her real identity. From that point forward it had been adjusted to include restraint snares, the clit vibrators, and a couple of things she evidently had not been acquainted with yet. Scarlett didn't spare a moment to bend herself over the pony by and by. She hoped that Penelope would hook her back to the fuck machine. On the off chance that she needed to sit tight for Mistress Natasha, at least she could appreciate it.

When Scarlett was bound, Trisha stood before her, bent over and pushed her butt-hole in her face. "Tongue my black eye, you filthy white slut. You white whores constantly like tasting black ass, don't you?"

Scarlett couldn't represent every single white young lady, yet she realized she found both the black security personals excited her intensely. The two of them appeared to be dominant and powerful which was extremely tempting for her corrupted mind. Trisha ground her butts into her face scouring her foul tasting opening all over Scarlett's mouth and nose. She scoured her face for a couple of moments until she felt bored playing this game. Scarlett realized Trisha would have her eat her once more, yet she started to leave. Clearly the smell of her butts was going to stay with her for some time.

Scarlett heard Trisha rummaging one of the cupboards. She came back with two things. One was a huge butt plug with a long hair tail. The other was her ever present blindfold.

"I always preferred the appearance of this tail. I've never let someone pierce something of this size deep inside my ass previously, yet I'm certain you can take it."

Scarlett begged Trisha not to stick that huge butt plug in her, yet all her efforts were in vain. At least she lubed it up sufficiently before she started shoving and twisting it into her rectum. It was a lot bigger than the butt plug from the vibrating panties. Scarlett had generally thought those were entirely huge and the dildo she had utilized the last evening in the washroom wasn't matching up to this size. This thing felt like it was tearing her into halves. Scarlett snorted and grunted attempting to adjust her animated psyche off the excruciating violation, yet Trisha would not take no for an answer and continued shoving until Scarlett's body, at last, yielded and the phallus covered itself deep in her butt cavity. She could feel the hairs from her new tail brushing against her voluptuous ass cheeks and thighs. She couldn't see it, yet she was certain her tail displayed a serious sight when they filled her completely and the only thing she would see was herself being bent over the pommel horse with a tail hanging out of her butts.

Trisha moved back Scarlett me a tied the blindfold in place. Anything that would occur next, she would be without any indications. She could tell her current playful tormentor was strolling past her when she felt a sharp smack on her ample butt cheeks.

"Simply loosen up, bitch. Your mistresses will be here soon."

Scarlett heard her snickering as she exited and afterward heard the flip of the light switch and the closing of the entryway.

"Mistress? Did I hear her right? Did she truly emphasize the plural form of the word?" Scarlett had her heart in her throat as she thought back about the words.

She was left alone in obscurity. She was naked, cold, and tied bent over the pommel horse. Everything she could do was to just wait impatiently and think. Well she could likewise feel her juices streaming down her thigh. Luckily, she didn't need to wait for long. After just around fifteen minutes, Scarlett indeed heard the entryway opening. She felt a soft hand measuring and cupping her butts and meandering up her back.

"Good morning pet," Scarlett heard her mischievous mistress Natasha state. "How could you rest the last evening?"

She started to reply; however, she ceased when she felt her finger start to infiltrate her wetness.

"I can tell you are still delighted with our little game plan," she cooed as her finger kept on investigating her slave's pussy.

"Almost certainly you are thinking about what will occur. Let me explain. I belong to a group of dominatrices who trade ideas and thoughts and once in a while, slaves. We each have a stable of ladies ready to commit to our commands and wishes. The numbers change, yet we each normally keep from one to four slaves at some random time. A few of us are strictly lesbian; a few of us share with our husbands."

Scarlett was attempting to concentrate on what her cunning mistress was letting her know; however, it was troublesome as she kept on controlling her sex.

"Since we do swap slaves every now and then, we as a pack consented to decide on adding anyone to the gathering. Today you will meet three additional mistresses and potentially some of the slaves. While you would belong to me, you should serve them undeniably or without any question if our relationship is to work. The room you are in is my private haven. I just bring my slaves here and just share them with Penelope and Trisha. Consequently, your meetings with different mistresses won't be here. Anyway, I do have a great deal of work to do today. So they will be in this building."

On the off chance that Scarlett had not been bound to the pommel horse, she assumed her knees would have buckled.

"You can still pull out from this game if you want. I'm certain this wasn't exactly what you anticipated today. In case you decide to proceed, we'll need to call your manager and reveal to her you're sick or something urgent popped up in your schedule. You ought to most likely call your husband as well. Tell him you're tired or hung over from the last night's party, but would need to report to your office. So you would be home in the evening. So, would you like to proceed?"

"Yes. Mistress N," Scarlett answered right away.

"Great. We should prepare you."

Mistress Natasha unfastened Scarlett and pulled off her blindfold. She blinked a few times as her eyes changed in accordance to the light. Natasha was wearing tight fitting mocha coffee darker dress. The length was underneath her knee and she had put on shoes with a modest one-inch heel. She looked proficient, very simple, definitely not a wild mistress who now controlled Scarlett's sexual coexistence.

Natasha stared at her obedient slave's tail and scolded Trisha for embedding it into Scarlett. "I like this tail for certain slaves, yet you were not readied for it. I am sorry. In case you are acknowledged into the group, I will ensure you get enough anal training so that utilizing these toys would be a pleasurable encounter. I have not chosen in case I'm going to horse train you yet. So let's simply forget about this for the time being."

Natasha gradually pulled the anal intruder from her slave's anal cavity. Scarlett felt more degraded than she had ever felt in her life. She was certain her rear end could never be the same again.

Natasha had Scarlett shower and fix her hair and cosmetics. She instructed her to dress herself up to impress the other mistresses. She was nearly done when she moved toward Scarlett from behind and began tapping baby powder all over her body. "Trust me," she assured her.

Natasha led her submissive once more into her dungeon and commanded her to sit on a little stool. Scarlett stared at the stool hoping to see a dildo standing up or something, yet now and then, a stool was only a stool. Mistress Natasha then opened a container and pulled an odd looking dress out.

"We like to dress up with our slaves. Today you will be a Batgirl. Not like the 'Yvonne Craig' on the TV soap, be that as it may, you will be the one who gets teased not the teaser. Like you however, she did consistently appear to like being tied up."

Mistress Natasha grasped a purple latex catsuit. Scarlett had never observed a wonderful item such as this from such closeness. It was both terrifying and energizing simultaneously. Natasha started to unfurl the suit and helped her obedient submissive to slid her legs into it. Her slave had never worn anything so tight-fitting and choking previously. Scarlett now comprehended the requirement for the powder. It was a challenge even with her intelligent mistress's assistance to get her legs into the suit. She could just expect the torso would be to a greater challenge and it was. Scarlett needed to bend over and pull her arms in to enable enough leeway in the suit to get in on her body. At the point when she stood back up, it tightened blowing her mind. There was an embedded bra which cuddled

151

around her juicy bosoms. Mistress Natasha then slid a couple of red go-go boots onto her slave's feet. They appeared as though a bizarre decision, yet Scarlett weren't going to dissent. There was a strap at the top of the shoes which her dominatrix fixed and afterward secured with a little paddle lock. The boots were not falling off until she was prepared for them to fall off.

Scarlett's hands were shrouded in latex gloves framed in the catsuit itself, even though her dominatrix wanted to put soft red sleeves over her wrists. At last, a red latex hood was pulled over her head. Her hair streamed under the edge of the hood. Mistress Natasha prodded her hair, so it was adjusted around her head and not amassing unevenly. The hood had built in plastic ears at the top and small cuts at the eyes and over her ears. Her nose was covered in a plastic nose piece inside the veil; however, the gaps were sufficiently large to permit typical breathing. The mouth gap was fairly enormous. Her whole lip territory and part of her cheeks pushed through the gap and were clearly exhibited, or all the more precisely accessible, for her dominatrix's pleasure.

Scarlett stared at the remarkable transformation in the mirror. The suit fitted her like a second skin. Each tempting curve of her seductive body was highlighted. The built in bra looked like something Madonna or Lady Gaga would wear. She didn't think there was a lot of her holding up the strong cone-shaped bosoms which pushed disgustingly out of the front of the suit high above her chest. The boots were a challenge to stroll in. Scarlett had started to get acquainted with strolling in heels as high, yet the snugness of the suit made moving her legs troublesome and left her temperamental. As they left the locker room and down the corridor, Scarlett started to feel an elation and warmth wash over her aroused body. Trisha was their first stop to hear her point of view regarding her outfit. Scarlett wasn't amazed to hear it was great. She was completely prepared to shower her oral tributes on her womanhood once more, but instead Mistress Natasha guided her back to the corridor.

As they sat tight for the cargo lift, Mistress Natasha clipped two extra bits of latex over the eye cuts. Clearly, she didn't want her submissive slave to know where they were going. Scarlett attempted to count the floors on the lift. She couldn't be certain, yet she thought they halted one story below Natasha's office and two stories beneath hers. She was hustled out of the lift.

"This floor is empty. The occupant moved out a couple of months back. It will be ideal for your meetings."

Scarlett was led through the workplace. She attempted to picture how her office was spread out to decide where she was. She immediately surrendered as they turned where her office didn't have turns and she understood the design and layout of the floor was extraordinary. They arrived at their goal and Natasha put her slave in an office seat. "How about we make those calls," she said.

First, they called Jacques, and Scarlett let him know everything was alright. He posed a couple of inquiries about what she did the last evening at the farewell party and she needed to think rapidly a couple of lies on her feet. She informed him concerning visiting some the club with Leilani, her significant other, and Brooklynn and another friend Natasha who managed and administered the office building. Jacques appeared to buy his mischievous wife's version of the story; yet Scarlett was extremely happy to be done with the discussion. She despised lying and didn't consider herself to be an excellent liar. Next, she called Leilani. Fortunately, she got her voice message. Evidently, it was still early. At Natasha's proposal, Scarlett revealed to Leilani that she was experiencing some car problems and that she would be available in the office the next day. Clearly, her calls were not a dull affair.

Scarlett was now free for an additional couple of hours before she would busy herself. Mistress Natasha took her arm demonstrating the time had come to stand once more. Scarlett felt her rubbing her hands all over her suit. She didn't have a lot of sensation within, but she could sense she was getting a charge out of the material experience. Natasha, at that point, grasped her slave's hand and pulled it forward. Scarlett felt a table. Presumably, a conference table deserted from the past inhabitant. As her mistress pulled her hand along the edge, she felt a tie. Natasha, at that point, pulled her hand onto the top of the table and Scarlett felt the delicate cushioning. She promptly perceived the bondage bed.

Dominatrix Natasha started to help her slave onto the table. It was difficult because Scarlett couldn't twist her legs so much. With her hands on the table, her mistress needed to put both her hands on her butt and essentially pushed her up onto the table. Scarlett ended up on her hands and knees, a latex feline in doggie position. She started to push toward the center of the table, yet a sharp smack on her voluptuous ass guiding her to stop. The impression of the spank was significantly more pronounced than when her seductive mistress was basically touching her. Maybe it was the position fixing the suit significantly more that enabled the punishing wave to proliferate over a greater amount of her body. Maybe it was her excitement. Maybe Scarlett truly couldn't have cared less about the explanation, yet it felt better and went directly to her animated pussy.

Scarlett quit moving and sat tight for her mistress's best course of action. She felt a zipper encased in the groin of the catsuit being opened. The strain in the base of the suit released offering access to her burning pussy and ass. It was still tight, yet at least, Scarlett could inhale somewhat easily. Her playful mistress gave her another swat, and she kept creeping to the center of the table where she moved her onto her back and tied her onto the subjugation bed. As Scarlett was speculated, she wasn't utilizing the Velcro lashes. She was going to be stuck there until she would be freed. Her wicked mistress fingered her once more. Scarlett had no doubt she would be satisfied with the degree of smoothness she would discover. She felt her mistress's hands snaking up to her voluptuous bosoms. Even when she had been adjusted into the catsuit, Scarlett had not observed the nipple access panels. They were practically similar to a Ziploc sack closure as Mistress Natasha deftly opened the region of the suit directly over her hard nipples enabling them to jump out. This further relaxed the suit. It was currently more comfortable.

Scarlett expected she would be prodded now. Nothing in her experience with Mistress Natasha persuaded her to believe she would be getting off very soon. In any case, the very demonstration of being teased mischievously and playfully had become an enormous turn-on because she realized her inevitable sensual release would be mind-blowing. Mistress Natasha didn't disappoint her slave. Scarlett felt the clingy electrical pad of remote-controlled underwear being joined to both her areolas. She truly didn't care for the electric play, yet she was in no spot to whine. Scarlett, at that point, felt another pad being appended to her clit. "Shit, the clit teaser was fun, but electric play on the pussy? Not great," Scarlett wondered. Her naughty mistress worked rapidly and proficiently to wire her up and afterward zipped the suit back. It was a battle to get the pussy zipper shut, but the areola Ziplocs shut decently effectively.

"I have certain errands to complete, bitch. Different paramours ought to be arriving here shortly. Please them like you want to please me and you'll be fine. I've let them know not to mark you, yet I can't assure that you won't be rebuffed for being the filthy slut that you are. Have a lot of fun. I'll be back by early afternoon."

Her profane language and portrayal of Scarlett didn't bother her. The time of her guaranteed return was the one that disturbed her. Early afternoon. It sounded practically like a capital punishment as the first shock of power hitting her nipples and clit. Leilani had not answered her telephone. She used to arrive in the workplace by 8am. That implies Scarlett had at least four hours up here. As a second shock of electricity hit her areolas, she could just implore her new mysterious women would show benevolence toward her. A brief span later, a milder shock hit her clit. At that point, a more stronger one than the previous ones hit only her left areola. Obviously, the electric controller had a random component to it. This was going to be a long morning.

Scarlett was clueless how long she lay on the table alone with her erotic contemplations and the stinging nibbles of power tormenting her areolas and clit. The gentler ones, which the controller appeared to favor, were keeping her stirred. They were, or her body chose they were because she required them to be, very invigorating. In any case, each ten shocks or so, a powerful electric shock would shake her body. These were not stimulating and were very excruciating. Particularly when the controller chose to hit her clit with a shock, any delight that had been building depleted out of her body. Obviously, the insidious machine would reset to bring down voltages and start ramping her back up. After a few cycles like this, Scarlett understood that the quantity of low intensity hits was expanding in each cycle. From a powerful pop toward the start for each three delicate ones to once every five, at that point each ten, and now every twenty, the electrical toy started to tease Scarlett. Her body was turning out to be increasingly excited while her animated psyche battled to estimate when the following hard shock would occur. She felt like her body was deceiving her. She shouldn't appreciate this treatment. Be that as it may, Scarlett knew better. What she termed a powerful shock thirty minutes prior now appeared to be gentle, and was a turn-on. On the off chance that she could hang on sufficiently long so the interim of delicate electrical kisses for sufficiently long, she might really have the option to cum.

Scarlett lay on the table twisting in her restraints as she sunk further and more profound into the corruption of her enraptured bliss. Her lone musings were on the triangle of pleasure and torment under her cat-suit and how much longer she would need to get off. She was drawing nearer each cycle and realized her peak would be soon. She simply needed to make it a little longer. Somewhat more. A couple of more cycles. Somewhat more. At that point, she heard the entryway open.

Chapter 14

Scarlett heard heels on the hardwood floor. They were not her mistress's sound. The heels were distinctive just like the length of the walk. She nearly couldn't believe her ears had become alert according to her condition when she was blindfolded that she could realize who was approaching her from the very little data. She heard her stroll over to the table. She was standing by the controls for the electric cushions. "What was she going to do?" Scarlett wondered. She heard the tapping of her fingers on the crate and afterward felt the change...

Scarlett heard the snap of the electric control box and felt every one of the three electric cushions spring to lie with a delicate charge. Her body strained and her back angled upward toward her mysterious advocate. As it adjusted to the shivering sensations, her body relaxed back onto the subjugation bed and a groan got away from her mouth. She felt a hand running itself over her latex clad body as if to check her immovability. Scarlett was appreciative that her tormentor was enabling the shivering to proceed and hoped the visual structure she was showing satisfied her enough to allow her to cum.

Her mysterious teaser's hands arrived at her head and Scarlett could detect that she was standing at the narrow end of the table. She felt her anonymous playful mistress pressing both hands onto her cheeks, supporting her head, and afterward pushing down her shoulders, and over her bosoms. The proceeding with electric charges were driving her closer to the edge as Scarlett now felt two additional sets of hands starting to run up her legs. She was being stroked all over the place and she withered on the bed as much as her bonds would permit. She attempted to picture what she should resemble which just blazed the fire between her legs. She started to whine as the incitement over ran her body's control mechanisms. Again and again, the hands made their adventures up and down her legs, simply brushing the edges of her pussy, and down and up her head to her succulent bosoms.

These new ladies were viable by the way they were invigorating her. Scarlett certain they had done this previously. Their touch was totally different from Mistress Natasha. Not really better, yet extraordinary. Scarlett recollected what her teasing mistress had disclosed to her that she would try out for three extra dominants today and they might carry their slaves with them. Scarlett thought about whether each one of these three ladies was dominatrices or if there was a blend of dominants and submissive touches taking a control of her body. Of course, her absence of sight because of the blindfold prompted an expanded familiarity with the sounds around her. Regrettably, aside from an incidental heel click and her groaning, the room was silent. One of the ladies, the lady at her head, wore a particular intoxicating scent. Scarlett didn't perceive the aroma, yet she knew whether she smelled it once more, she would perceive the wearer. She attempted to indentify the ladies working her legs so she might have the option to perceive her later; however she gave no trace of identity.

They proceeded with their sensual massaging of her body for at least ten minutes. Scarlett was gasping in dire need and almost standing on the cliffs of her excitement; however she couldn't exactly go over the edge. In the long run, the electric cushions were stopped and removed. With the zipper down and her pussy uncovered, her new mysterious mistresses enchanting fragrance was currently overpowered by the excitement smell radiating from her suit. Scarlett felt a finger plunge into her pussy. It met no obstruction as her abundant sex fluids had greased up her totally. The finger pulled away, and she heard someone go "Ummm!" She, at that point, felt another finger enter and leave her sex and from the opposite side of the table another exhilarating sound reverberated.

Scarlett asked for them to restore their fingers into her burning pussy and to get her off, yet they didn't say anything. Obviously, they were resolved to keep up their obscurity similarly as Mistress Natasha had accomplished for such a long time. Scarlett heard the zipper of a skirt or dress being pulled down and felt someone getting on the table with her. She wasn't shocked at all when an extremely wet pussy slipped onto her yearning lips. As Mistress Natasha had trained her, 'the mistress consistently cums first', so Scarlett immediately got down to business. Again the pride owner of this succulent pussy was a lot gentler than Mistress Natasha. She held Scarlett's head, yet didn't pull it upward by her hair, or crushed it or smeared it into her pussy. She was possibly more aroused because it didn't take a lot of work for Scarlett to make her explode vigorously on her mouth. Scarlett assumed that on the off chance they were playing with a newly restrained beauty like hers, they couldn't control their arousal. The mysterious lady generously covered Scarlett's face with her juices. Now, alongside her lavish perfume, Scarlett would have a second method to distinguish her. She moved off the table, and Scarlett readied herself to serve and please following lady.

Be that as it may, a surprising thing occurred. Rather than feeling another dominant lady moving over her head, she felt a warm tongue start to lap at her animated pussy. The mysterious lady was in tight to her seething love opening taking in all the juice that she could give. She had Scarlett climb the notorious walls of pleasurable excitement in a moment or two. Scarlett begged her teaser not to stop and to take her to the zenith of excitement. As she was appreciating and cherishing her tormentor's oral abilities, Scarlett heard a snort and afterward felt her head bob against her yearning pussy. The woman's tongue lapped against her throbbing clit in an exciting manner and afterward she felt her head bounce back away from her body. At that point, she heard the secret woman screech, "Fuck me my beloved mistress!"

That woman had ended the quietness the three ladies had kept up. Scarlett had been focusing on her utmost delight, so she didn't generally process the voice efficiently. But, she realized it sounded somewhat familiar. She heard a sharp smack on her bottom, clearly because of her sudden outburst of fervor. Scarlett currently imagined a delightful slave young lady bent over the table. She was orally tributing Scarlett's pussy while her devious mistress took her from behind. From the power, the obedient submissive was bobbing her head into her groin. Scarlett could just accept that the woman's playful mistress was utilizing a strap-on dildo to pound her slave.

This revelation filled in as all the motivation her restless mind anticipated to take her over the edge and give the mysterious lady's mouth her tasteful cum. Scarlett battled against her restrains as her body attempted to arch and twist while the tremendous peak tore through her. Within moments, the discreet lady orally who was servicing Scarlett's pussy also reached her enraptured zenith as her mistress kept on pounding her from behind. When she had quieted down, Scarlett felt her moving far away from the table. Nearly as fast, Scarlett's mouth was presented the strap-on dildo which had abused the lady. She surmised the two dominatrices shared their feeling for toy cleaning techniques as the immense plastic cock was squeezed into her gaping mouth. While Scarlett was blowing the monstrous plastic cock, she felt another tongue starting to lick her sodden external lips. She was sensitive subsequent to having just cum, so the skilled tongue had no issue starting to invigorate her body to another orgasmic peak.

Like her sister in bondage, Scarlett imagined this slave orally tributing her pussy while she cleaned her mistress's strap-on. Minutes after the silicone dick was pulled from her mouth, Scarlett indeed felt a head hammering into her pelvis and she realized the submissive girl's authoritative mistress had mounted her. Their coupling lasted longer this time, but ended just in an exhilarating fashion. Both the mysterious slave and Scarlett experienced another body-trembling orgasmic delight. Afterward Scarlett got the chance to taste her secret partner's flavor as she cleaned the dildo. She now had three types of pussy to focus on memory and one expensive perfume. The short voice personality was a distant memory. Every one of the three ladies gave Scarlett a kiss, and she heard the entryway opening and close. Two mistresses were pleased, two to go.

Scarlett lay on the table for some time. Her abused pussy was jerking in the post orgasmic sparkle of two brilliant orgasmic peaks. She thought she nodded off for some time since she woke to the pinch of another feminine hand. This time, Scarlett felt two sets of hands investigating her seductive body, even though they appeared to be mindful so as not to get excessively near her aching pussy or areolas. As Scarlett thought about what debasing act she might need to perform for these two, she felt somebody climbing up the table. Scarlett adjusted her servile tongue to carry out its responsibility; however, as opposed to sitting on her, the devious lady settled alongside her with her butt settled close to Scarlett's armpit. Scarlett heard the sounds of a lady delightfully pleasuring another lady and sensed she was getting devoured. The lady made no attempt to contact Scarlett, other than her lower back contacting the catsuit. Obviously, whoever was eating her out was gifted dependent on the sounds the mysterious woman started to make lying beside Scarlett. Scarlett had to lie vulnerably and unsatisfied, sexually frustrated as the lady delighted in three climaxes at the tongue of her playmate. Scarlett figured out how to refrain from begging. She realized it wouldn't do any great in their game at any cost, but she filed away in her mind each and every sound the mysterious slave made. There were no words, yet her shouts of enraptured happiness had a much characterized rhythm and timbre. Scarlett realized she could identify them on the off chance that she at least heard them once more.

At long last, the slave had her fulfillment. Scarlett anticipated that she should share a portion of her flavorsome juices with me, yet she didn't. Rather as she bounced off the table, Scarlett felt the other lady jumping on. She thought about whether their scene would be rehashed, yet immediately made sense of that wouldn't be the situation as she felt her legs straddling her head. In contrast to her last accomplice, this one was looking down the table with her rear end situated right on her nose and her pussy already dribbling into her hungry mouth. Scarlett stuck out her tongue to start what she realized the mysterious play partner needed when she felt her lean down over her body and bury her own tongue in her seething nectar pot. Scarlett could just envision the expression on her mistresses' faces as the slave and she 69-ed for her and their pleasure. She immediately got the message that the gathering's slaves were going to delight her today on condition that their mistresses were pleasured first. Scarlett had never done a 69 and thought that it was exceptionally energizing. From what she could tell her slave accomplice was getting a charge out of it as well. Her mistress gave them a lot of time to work each other into an exhilarating rupture and they exploded into orgasmic bliss together. It was practically sweet because there had been no spanking, pounding, teasing, toys or debasing acts. Aside from Scarlett being bound to the table and blindfolded, it was practically normal.

When they were done, Scarlett anticipated that the ladies should make a speedy exit. Before they left, be that as it may, she felt a little vibrating egg being inserted into her drenched vagina and the zipper being pulled back up. The damn thing wasn't exceptionally incredible. She surmised mistress number four simply needed her on the rocks before her appearance.

By and by, Scarlett was left to glimmer in her very own fascinating juices as her restless mind dashed through every one of the conceivable outcomes and permutations of accomplices and exercises her new circumstance could involve. She made a decent attempt to persuade her mind to take her over the edge, yet she couldn't arrive at a tremendous climax just from the restricted vibrations of the egg. She turned out to be increasingly disappointed and sexually frustrated. "Had it been thirty minutes? An entire hour?" She couldn't tell. Without a doubt it was nearly time for Mistress Natasha to return. These ladies had trapped her aroused psyche, body, and soul. She desperately prayed she had measured up to the expectations and would be acknowledged into their gathering. She couldn't stand to think about the other alternative and what she might do in case they dismissed her. At last, Scarlett heard the entryway opening once more.

"Hi pet," Scarlett heard Mistress Natasha state. "You've done well up until this point. Just a single additional challenge for you today."

"Thank you Mistress N. I've unquestionably cherished today's activities up until this point."

"Truly, I'm certain you have, based on the reports I've gotten. I'm here with another companion and her slave. Like the previous ones they won't talk, yet I guarantee you that you do know them. Something our gathering truly appreciates is gangbangs. Indeed, even the mistresses appreciate them every once in a while, albeit principally we lean toward choosing a slave and screwing her into subjugation."

That sounded enjoyable to Scarlett. She listened eagerly. It was everything she could do.

"Here's the game plan. You are going to service my companion while her slave tributes my sex orally. In case you work superbly, she and I will fuck your pussy and ass while you eat out the slave. On the off chance that you don't perform admirably, the meeting is finished and you won't join our gathering. That, however I'll take you back to the ground floor and rebuff you like you've never been rebuffed for spoiling our time. Get it?"

"Indeed, Mistress N. I won't let you down."

"I realize you won't, pet."

Scarlett felt her bonds being evacuated and at someone's direction, she sat up. She felt a hand take hers and was guided off the table. She gradually strolled as she was led by the hand over the room where she was directed to bow down. Her hands were bound behind her back and her head was maneuvered down into an eagerly anticipating pussy. Evidently, there was some office seats additionally left behind because she could feel the cushioned edge of the seat on her chest as she devoured, slurped, and affectionately tribute the delicious pussy before her. Scarlett could tell it had been shaved as she imagined a youthful mistress enjoying her submission. She could hear the sounds of her mistress getting pleasured alongside hers. Her mistress was most likely sitting in a similar seat. She envisioned the two authoritarian mistresses holding court as they were being pleasured by their obedient slaves. She couldn't think about a spot she would preferably be rather than at her feet with her pussy in her mouth.

Mistress Natasha was the first to cum, but Scarlett's new seductive mistress was directly behind her. She started to push her hips upward as she reached her pinnacle of excitement forcing Scarlett's head back. Scarlett needed to battle for adjustment. She needed to be certain that as a slave, she didn't stop until she was commanded to do as such. It was an uproarious, messy climax, and Scarlett took pride that she was responsible for it. A while later and to the astonishment of no one, Mistress Natasha declared it was the ideal opportunity for Scarlett to get fucked. Scarlett had been anticipating this for a considerable length of time and she chuckled with extreme joy.

Scarlett was stood up and felt the passionate embrace of the other slave. At the point when she kissed her, she could taste her mistress on her luscious lips. Scarlett realized her slave partner could also taste her mistress on hers, which truly turned her on. Her hands were still handcuffed behind her back so she couldn't guard herself from her desperate craving to touch herself as they made out. She suspected that their owners were getting ready; however she was concentrating on the mouth before her. At long last, Scarlett heard her Mistress Natasha proclaiming, "Enough," and assumed responsibility for the circumstance. She unclipped her wrists, and Scarlett was moved back to where the seats were found. Perhaps, Mistress Natasha plunked down because Scarlett felt her pulling her in reverse while she guided her to relax. Scarlett arrived on Natasha's lap, the two of them looking directly at one another; the only difference being Scarlett being blindfolded. She felt the dildo Natasha had tied to her hips poke in between her legs.

"This one is penetrating your ass."

Scarlett could feel the liberal amount of lube sliding off the dildo onto her leg. She attempted to sit up enough to mount the cock; however, she battled with the position. She felt a hand starting to stroke her clit and direct the toy to its new home, her anal cavity. The bulbous tip found the passage to her sacred hole, and she started to squirm to enable it to penetrate. When the first inch or so was firmly situated, Scarlett felt hands on her shoulders driving her down. Like a shot, she sank onto its massive length. Expressing gratitude toward God, she was delighted that it was relatively little. Quickly, Scarlett detected somebody moving before her and afterward a lot bigger strap-on was prodding the passageway to her pussy. There was no requirement for any extra lube as her natural sex juices coated the intruder enabling her to slide the plastic cock deep into her belly in one strong thrust.

Scarlett was speared between these two influential ladies. Her caring mistress was taking her anal cavity. She wasn't moving a lot. Her new unknown mistress was driving her cock into her sodden pussy as though her life relied upon it. Each vigorous thrust was sufficiently powerful enough to move her rear end off her deviant mistress's dildo making her fuck herself. Mistress Natasha deftly reached over her chest and unzipped the nipple clamps. Scarlett was attempting to hold herself up with her arms underneath her on the arms of the seat and adjust her balance while she was getting fucked more enthusiastically than she at any point had in her life. Mistress Natasha, mindful of how aroused Scarlett got from the nipple play, was deftly stimulating her hardened stubs driving her sensual energy ever more elevated.

While Scarlett was being fucked, she heard the obvious squish of a lady fingering herself to the remarkable sight. She didn't know where the other slave had gone; however, she could clearly hear her stroking off. Before long, the other slave's groans blended in with hers. Scarlett realized her submissive partner was getting off watching her get skewered by her mistress and she was getting off envisioning what the other girl resembled fingering herself. The passionate sounds of feminine love were reverberating through the empty office as their sweat-soaked bodies moved as one to a destined orgasmic peak. Nothing was going to stop Scarlett now. Both her playful mistresses could pull out as of now and no threat of spanking would have prevented her hands from completing what they had begun.

Luckily, it didn't end up like that. First to cum was the jerking off slave. With a scream, she peaked terribly. Scarlett wished she could have seen her slave partner; however, the power of her orgasmic climax must have motivated her mistress because, even though Scarlett would not have hoped it was conceivable, her mistress began thrusting her much harder. Now her dominatrix let go of her nipples and gripped her voluptuous butt cheeks. With the strength she didn't know her mistress possessed, she gripped her rear end and began lifting it all over her strap-on. The two ladies immediately found a tormenting rhythm with one of their cock shoving Scarlett while the other withdrew and afterward rapidly slammed in. Scarlett had tossed her hips forward to coordinate her secret mistress's vigorous poundings and then hammer her butt down on Mistress Natasha to maximize her infiltration. Scarlett didn't have a clue whether this session was being recorded, yet she furtively hoped it was because she needed to see herself getting fucked so hard. In case this was the sort of fucking the Mistress Club practiced, Scarlett desperately needed to enroll in the club and she realized she would effectively have a place.

As anyone can envision, they couldn't keep this pace up long. Scarlett was rapidly arriving at the edge of the excitement when from before her, she heard a bestial moan and afterward a shout of euphoric joy as the secret mistress orgasmed and came hard. Scarlett would later found out that her mistress's strap-on had a little dildo within and that she had been screwing herself while she reamed her. At the time, all she knew was someone, not exactly a foot before her was in the throes of a invigorating climax and that set her off. Scarlett was counting stars as she experience a powerful orgasm. She lost all control as her bodily capacities went on autopilot. Her mistress gripped her hips and pulled her down on her dildo and held her tight. In advance, the orgasming secret lady clearly fell in reverse as she was cumming as the dildo in her pussy popped free similarly as Scarlett started to cum. Mistress Natasha held Scarlett tight as her climax tore through me. Scarlett was certain she would have fallen on the floor if her strap-on had not acted like a bicycle kick stand to help me. When it was done, Scarlett was drooped on her lap incapable to move.

Once again Scarlett must have passed out. She woke on the bondage bed. Her eye cuts were open, and she was not bound to the table. The room was vacant; however, it smelled of energetic sex. Scarlett had no clue what time it was. She waited. Her legs were still somewhat weak, yet she immediately recovered her stance. Scarlett looked out the entryway to ensure the floor was truly vacant. Aside from some crates and a periodic seat, file organizer or desk, there was nothing.

She had no telephone to call Mistress Natasha and no craving to stroll through the open passages to her office, so she returned into the conference room to wait for her. Her restless mind replayed the most recent twenty-four hours, and she felt better.

Mistress Natasha strolled in with a bag containing new garments for Scarlett. For reasons unknown, Scarlett anticipated that she should dress her up like a whore, yet they were proficient and superbly appropriate for the workplace. She even had a standard bra and panties. No nipple slits, butt plugs, or vibrators. Scarlett felt oddly vacant. She additionally had a towel which she allowed Scarlett to use to wipe down her perspiration. But obviously, a shower before dressing was impossible. Scarlett surmised Mistress Natasha needed her to feel like she was ridden hard and released wet and horny, regardless of whether she didn't look that way.

It was 12:45 when Scarlett completed the process of dressing. Mistress Natasha clarified that she figured Scarlett did incredible during the tryout, yet would need to check with the other three dominatrices before she could accept her into the gathering. Scarlett disclosed to her that she would be demotivated in case she didn't meet up to their anticipation. She embraced Scarlett and let her know not to stress. They left the workplace hand in hand and proceeded to the lift. They went up to Natasha's floor where she gave Scarlett an enthusiastic kiss before disappearing into her office. Scarlett walked toward her office. She truly preferred not to be returning to work. She nearly wished somebody at her office had ended up being her new mystery mistress, so she could serve her during the rest of the day.

Scarlett sat in her workplace cubicle with her three colleagues doing whatever it took on her part not to show that her life had been transformed. She experienced difficulty looking at Brooklynn without flinching after seeing her with Leilani and her significant other at the club the prior night. The afternoon delayed and again she thought that it was hard to focus on her work. At 4:45 PM Leilani summoned her into her office. As she left their cubicle, she thought she heard chuckling and laughing, yet perhaps it was only her creative mind.

Chapter 15

Leilani simply needed to discuss about Scarlett's vehicle and needed to ensure everything was going okay. She said Scarlett appeared to be distracted for the current week and she was concerned. Scarlett disclosed to her manager that she simply had a plenty of dealings at the forefront of her thoughts this week and her car breaking down was the last straw. Leilani encouraged her saying that things would show signs of improvement and to keep a firm upper lip. Scarlett looked down at her monthly scheduling document and she could swear that she at least could observe her rear end impression from the previous evening once more. It was most likely her restless mind messing around with her. They talked for around ten minutes. Scarlett was planning to leave when her telephone rang. After accepting the call, Leilani excused herself to rush to the CEO's office to manage some crisis. "I'll be seeing you next week," she shouted at Scarlett as she exited the entryway. Alone in her office, Scarlett needed to know something. She strolled over to her seat and squeezed her face against the top of the backrest. She took a full breath. Truly, she could even now smell herself. Her fascinating fragrance wasn't strong as it was the previous night, but possibly she was the one in particular who could smell it. Scarlett was certain Leilani must have smelled it as well. She permitted herself a nervous and proud smile and exited the room.

Driving home, Scarlett had annoying questions that she had not performed admirably in her challenges for inclusion in the BDSM group. She realized she didn't have anything to rationalize that feeling together, but she stressed nonetheless. Scarlett, at that point, started to consider Jacques. Regardless of whether her hideous tale about spending the night with a companion held up, in the long run, he would discover that she started meeting and servicing four dominatrices. As upsetting as these musings were, her pussy was getting wet once more. When she returned home, she realized she would be assaulting Jacques whenever she could.

The weekend went with no message from Mistress Natasha. Scarlett made an effort not to stress. She fucked Jacques Friday night, Saturday, and Sunday. It was practically similar to bygone eras, the early days of their marriage. What wasn't similar to the old times was each time they were out of the house and Scarlett saw an alluring lady, she considered what it would resemble bowing under them devouring their pussy. She went through the weekend in a condition of consistent excitement. She decided to head into the workplace early Monday in order to meet Natasha before work. If she was lucky, she could her in the locker room. Natasha brought her up to her office. Scarlett strolled two steps behind her and one step to her left side. She appeared to be satisfied that her pet obeyed and remembered without being told.

Once in the protection of her office, Natasha commanded Scarlett to get on her knees and she hiked up her skirt in return. She had Scarlett servicing for a decent twenty minutes before she pushed her slave away and fixed her skirt. She had not cum yet, which the obedient slave accepted as a personal failure.

"Try not to stress over that I didn't cum. Return back during your lunch break. You can complete your task at that point."

Scarlett looked at the clock on Natasha's desk cabinet and saw it was 8:02 AM, so she excused herself and hustled out of the entryway. A gorgeous, youthful receptionist was in the front office. She grinned at Scarlett as she left. "Did she know why I was there?" Scarlett swallowed hard. From the corner of her eye, Scarlett saw her stand up and stroll a few doors down toward Natasha's office. "Is it accurate to say that she was going to complete what I had started?" Her restless mind was bombarding her with questions, but she didn't have the opportunity to stress. She didn't wait for the lift to show up. Instead, she hurried up the stairs and into her office.

She devoted her morning to making up for lost time at work by completing the pending tasks she had blown off from the last week. At 11:45 AM, she received an instant message on her cell phone. All it said was "early afternoon." It was from Mistress Natasha. Precisely around early afternoon, Scarlett landed back at her mistress's workplace. The secretary accompanied her back to Natasha and afterward said she was going to lunch. She inquired as to whether Natasha would need something. Natasha just looked at Scarlett dead in the eyes without flinching and said "No, I'm great."

In Scarlett's mind everything now had a twofold sexual importance. She was certain the young receptionist knew precisely why she was there and thought about whether Natasha had her at her mercy much as she was. Scarlett didn't have long to stress over it. Natasha requested her to strip, which she did immediately. She, at that point, went through the following forty-five minutes licking, slurping, and lapping her tongue at the pit of her womanhood. This time Mistress Natasha did cum and on numerous occasions indeed. Scarlett was aching in desperate need when Natasha revealed to her that she was done for the day. Scarlett didn't have the foggiest idea whether she would be permitted to pleasure her mistress as she stood at attention before her large oak desk. She stayed there with a mollified look all over. It was presently 12:50 PM and she should have been returning to her workplace.

"I conversed with different mistresses. They were altogether satisfied with your dedicated endeavors. Well three were satisfied and one of them thought you required significantly more training to polish your work. In any case, you're in."

Scarlett applauded with satisfaction and her proud grin beamed from ear to ear.

"I need you to return to work. I'm occupied for the rest of the day, yet I need you here at 7:30 AM again tomorrow morning. Actually, your new starting time is 7:30 AM, at least half an hour earlier than your pussy eating training before work. Sooner or later, different mistresses in our gathering may get in touch with you for a personal appreciation. I anticipate that you should serve them as you serve me. As the newest member of our group, you are low lady on the chain of command. The ranking goes me, the other three dominatrices, at that point, the six different slaves, and lastly you. You are not expected to serve different slaves with the exception of under the particular direction of a mistress; however, when there is a humble undertaking to do and we're in a gathering, expect that you will grab the terrible jobs first. Do you get it?"

"Truly, mistress."

"Great. Now off you go and I'll see you tomorrow first thing."

Scarlett left the workplace. Indeed the receptionist was sitting at her workstation. The scoff she gave Scarlett compelled her to believe she knew precisely why she was there. Scarlett spent the evening with her mistress's succulent pussy at the forefront of her restless thoughts and her flavorsome taste in her mouth. Scarlett was in paradise. She worked tenaciously attempting to focus on her pending tasks. At 5:00 pm, she was still working dedicatedly as the workplace was purging out. She knew Jacques wouldn't be home until at least seven, so she decided to work somewhat late to make up for her absence in the office during the last couple of weeks. At 5:30, she realized she was the only individual left in the workplace. Fascinating memories of what happened the last time she was the only individual in the office overwhelmed her agitated psyche and she needed to take a psychological break because she felt a wave of sensual excitement streaming over her body.

Scarlett was in her very own fantasies when Leilani's entryway opened. She didn't realize her manager was still here. She appeared as amazed to see her staff as Scarlett was to see her. She had put on something else and now had an unzipped semi-formal dress and stockings on. She seemed as if she was setting off to a club. She was likewise grasping a couple of exceptionally high heels.

"Meeting Thomas for supper out this evening," Leilani shouted as she took off apparently for the washroom.

"Sure you are. You and your significant other meeting Brooklynn again," Scarlett thought. She attempted to focus back on work, but the memories of Thomas with his arm around Brooklynn's waist flashed back into her restless mind animating her. "Possibly, the time had come to return home." Scarlett wondered again. As she was packing up, Leilani wavered over into the workplace. She was wearing the shoes, yet her dress was still unzipped. She headed into her office and afterward called Scarlett in. She turned her back toward her employee and requested that Scarlett should zip her up.

"Do you like to dance? You and Jacques should hang around with Thomas and me at some point."

"Sure," Scarlett lied. Jacques loathed dancing, and she wasn't that attracted to Thomas.

"I must get moving. Would you be able to bolt up the office?"

"Don't worry about it. I was simply wrapping up some work."

"Amazing."

As Scarlett was going to stroll back to her work area, she saw Leilani pull a perfume bottle out of her work desk cabinet. Scarlett continued moving, yet she heard her manager spraying a mist into the air and over her dress. Scarlett imagined Leilani strolled through the mist of perfume sprayed into the air. Scarlett sat down at her work desk and pretended to be working, yet all she was doing was wondering about Leilani and Brooklynn. "This is bad. I shouldn't fantasize about colleagues," Scarlett thought inwardly. Leilani left her office resembling a million dollars exotic girl. She had changed her hair in the restroom and was dressed to the nines. She strolled by Scarlett's cubicle and wished her an amazing weekend. She stepped out of the office and was gone, but the splendid aroma from her scent lingered palpably. Scarlett realized that fascinating aroma. She had smelled it previously. "Oh my good God! Leilani was one of the dominants!" Scarlett was left with a gaping wide mouth.

That acknowledgment hit her like a huge amount of bricks and in a split second, over flooded her pussy. Scarlett reclined in her seat. How was this conceivable? She must be the person controlling the panties that game changing day of her video conference. How would she be able to not make herself known? Possibly, she was the one not certain about Scarlett. The aching need in her pussy must be tended to. As Scarlett continued smelling that addictive fragrance, it brought back such a large number of recollections in her mind. Coupled with the stimulated state that Mistress Natasha had left her during the early afternoon, it set her cunt on fire. She needed to scratch her tingle. Scarlett got up to go to the washroom. Since she didn't know Leilani was still in the workplace, she couldn't take the risk of another colleague jumping out of his or her chamber or cubicle while she would be busy fingering herself in her workstation. For reasons unknown, she looked at Brooklynn's cubicle. On the wall, there was an image of her with Leilani and Thomas. Scarlett had seen that image on numerous occasions. It was shot in a business meeting in Vegas. She had never seen that both Leilani and Thomas had their arms wrapped around Brooklynn who stood between them. She had never thought of it as anything other than a posed picture, yet as she took a closer and investigating look at it intently, more so with the past twenty-four hour experience and memories fucking her imaginations, she realized perhaps the image meant more than that. The embrace looked like a possession. "Bloody hell! Brooklynn must be Leilani's slave. Hell, she is most likely the lady I had 69-ed with during the early hours of the day and who jerked off while

Natasha and Leilani fucked me," Scarlett felt her throat drying up. Her legs weakened. She needed to plunk down.

Scarlett went ahead ignoring the potential risks. Her cold, trembling fingers found her clit and her sodden slit as she sat in Brooklynn's seat and gazed at her image with Leilani. Their status had not so much been affirmed, yet to her savage desire, the circumstantial proof was all that anyone could need for a conviction. Scarlett had exclusive focus gazing at their image as her fingers flew over her throbbing clit and immediately carried herself to an extremely fulfilling orgasmic peak. Scarlett was enticed as she soiled Brooklynn's seat like she had done to Leilani's; however, she reconsidered it. She ended up getting highly stimulated by that thought that the next office day, possibly her colleague might have the chance to smell something exquisite in her cubicle.

Scarlett stuffed up her things and headed home. She was somewhat older and certainly somewhat smarter than when she went out that morning. She was additionally anticipating getting down to business the following day.

In transit home, her cell phone rang. It was Bella. She had not talked a lot to her over the recent weeks. Her party and sex toy business was backing off, even though she said her web business was going strong, so she was doing fine. She disclosed to Scarlett that she was hosting a gigantic fetish gathering that was simply reserved for Friday night and inquired as to whether Scarlett could work. Scarlett replied that she would need to check with Jacques. Bella said no issue and inquired if she could confirm that to her by tomorrow, then that would be incredible. She said Clara was planned to attend the gathering and that she was coming over tomorrow evening for some very late outfit modifications. Bella questioned if Scarlett could go along with them as she had some new outfits for her to try out and needed to ensure everything was OK before the show. Scarlett confirmed her that she would check with Jacques today around evening time and call her tomorrow.

Chapter 16

The following day, Scarlett landed at the workplace at 7:30 AM and went directly to her Mistress's office. Natasha was on the telephone and she waved her into her office. After Scarlett shut the entryway, she dropped to her knees and crawled to her work desk. With a straightforward gesture, Natasha guided Scarlett behind her work desk and between her legs. She was wearing a short skirt. Scarlett wasn't astounded to discover that her playful mistress wasn't wearing any underwear or that her pussy was smooth fully expecting her service. Natasha kept on chatting on the telephone as her dutiful slave cherished the delicacy of her pussy. It seemed like she was making party arrangements and Scarlett thought about whether she would be invited. Natasha didn't appear to be in a rush for her slave to make her cum. She didn't pressure her slave's head into her groin or guide her with regards to the fierceness her slave should exhibit to complete the fascinating service. Scarlett lazily continued on ahead and around twenty minutes after the fact her mistress rewarded her dedicated efforts by feeding the juices of her sex. It was certifiably not a tremendous climax; however, Natasha appeared to be satisfied. She instructed her slave to go to her office, but to be back at 12:30 PM for a second engagement. As Scarlett left her mistress's office, she saw that her assistant had shown up. As usual, she gave Scarlett a threatening look. Scarlett rushed past her and upstairs to her office. She was done with Natasha for a couple of hours. "Would this be the day when Leilani assumes control of me?" Scarlett thought breathlessly.

Everybody recorded their attendance into the office as if it were an ordinary day. For everybody, except Scarlett it most likely was. Obviously this was her new normal so she assumed it was an ordinary day. She didn't have any contact with Leilani that morning. By early afternoon, she was thinking about whether possibly she had dreamed about her manager excessively. Perhaps, it was a coincidence Leilani wore that sort of scent. At 12:30 PM, Scarlett headed downstairs and once again serviced her dominatrix, Mistress Natasha. She didn't touch her slave which was frustrating. Her secretary wasn't at her work desk when Scarlett showed up; fortunately, she still wasn't there when Scarlett left. Throughout the evening, Scarlett wandered off in fantasy land about being taken to the locker room by her mistress and her manager. A few times, her cubicle colleagues captured her in her own little fantasy world as they were conversing with her and she paid any attention to their words. Scarlett was happy when 5:00 PM rolled around and she could leave her office. She was to somewhat astonished that her mistress didn't summon her for a post work orgasmic pleasure and servicing. Leaving the workplace, Scarlett decided not to consider it. Thus, she headed straight for Bella's residence.

Bella welcomed Scarlett with a major friendly embrace. She informed her that Clara was running a little late. That made Scarlett's savage submissive reception antennas go up. "How advantageous!" She wondered inwardly. They were alone in Bella's house. Bella could make her passionate advances toward Scarlett. By that time, Scarlett had begun fantasizing that any lady could be one of her four mistresses. Surely, she thought about her primary dominatrix, Mistress Natasha, and she unequivocally presumed her manager Leilani was number two. The third, even though still anonymous, had a particular tattoo. Bella didn't have that tattoo; however unmistakably took part in giving the toys which carried Scarlett through this fascinating transformation. She, and particularly Clara, realized that Scarlett cherished being restrained at any toy party. Hence, Scarlett had her as a prime suspect in her list.

She pursued Bella down the stairs to her storm cellar office. Bella clarified that one of her best fetish customers was going to have a get-together that Friday. Verifiably, this unknown lady's parties produced the most income from any exhibition in any business calendar. So Bella constantly attempted to work out something extraordinary. This year, rather than the customary leather gear, Bella wanted to exhibit an unexpected closure of the fashion show. She said she needed Clara and Scarlett to demonstrate the standard lingerie alongside the typical cuffs, collars, corsets, and leashes. For the grand finale, however, Bella needed both of her business partners to assemble everything and show up as mistress and slave. After that revelation, Scarlett thought that they were arriving at some common grounds.

Bella proceeded, "I don't know if I had told you before, but Clara is a submissive."

No, she had not disclosed to Scarlett that. In fact, because of what Clara did to Scarlett when she was bound to the table in a BDSM party, provoked her to believe that she pegged for a Dom. Scarlett must have looked befuddled.

"Clara likes to be ordered around. I'll dress you up as her mistress and you should lead her around the party as your slave."

As a matter of fact, Scarlett would have wanted to have Clara lead her around the room as her slave, yet she consented to do as Bella proposed. She heard strides on the stairs and Clara descended into the basement room. Bella immediately explained how she needed to end the show and Clara unquestionably concurred while giving Scarlett a coy look simultaneously. Bella advised Clara to strip which she managed without any remark. Bella then started dressing her up in her slave outfit.

Portraying the outfit was troublesome. Bella said she was going for the Arabian Prince and his group of harem young lady looks. Everything Scarlett could envision was if Barbara Eden from 'I Dream of Jeannie' were a sex slave, "What might she resemble?" Clara put on a small bra and miniscule g-string. Bella then gave her a fine fishnet pantaloon with strips cut up on both sides which literally did nothing to cover her legs and just served to entice somebody to devour her seductive curves. The cuffs of the trousers had worked in lash which Bella secured tightly. Scarlett likewise saw a ring introduced to tie an ill-bred slave later. The top of the trousers had a comparable contraption embedded. Bella fixed the abdomen around Clara giving another bondage point. Bella had Clara strolled around the room. The texture in the trousers streamed with the air movement produced by her strolling. The cuts up the trouser legs moved to and fro giving tantalizing looks at her legs and afterward concealing them from sight. Scarlett couldn't take her eyes off Clara.

"It would appear that the impact I needed is working, eh Clara?" Bella teased. Clara concurred. Scarlett was embarrassed at being caught red-handed devouring Clara's attractive looks.

The top of Clara's outfit was of a frilly material, yet it stopped at a tight elastic band which curled just underneath her ample bosoms. The arms had cuts like the trousers and reached at her wrists. Likewise with the base of the trousers, a tight strap with rings was fitted at the top of both her wrists and at the neckline. Clara moved her arms, and the material appeared to glide. By and by, Scarlett couldn't quit looking at her.

"That is not terrible, Clara. I think you've demonstrated that this outfit will catch the party attendees' consideration."

She, at that point, snapped her fingers before Scarlett's face which took her back to the real world.

"I am worried about how that bra fits at the top. How about we take that off?"

Scarlett looked as Bella stripped the top up over Clara's bosoms. Clara then unclasped the bra and Bella pulled the top down. Clara's areolas jabbed through the fishnet. She was clearly having a good time. Bella backed up to inspect her handicraft, while Clara appreciated herself in a mirror. Nothing would look terrible on Clara. Her young athletic body could wear anything and this outfit was no special case.

After satisfying herself with Clara's ensemble, Bella directed her attention toward Scarlett. She instructed her to strip, which she did energetically. Scarlett wished her outfit would have been like

Clara's; however tragically it was substantially less uncovering. As a matter of fact, it was straightforwardly boring. Bella dressed Scarlett like some sort of Arabian Sultan. She had a long streaming robe which secured her body totally and even wrapped around the top of her head. Scarlett stared at Bella in dismay. Certainly, this wasn't what she expected to wear at the party.

Bella gripped a leash of one of her work areas and slipped it onto Clara's collar. She gave Scarlett the opposite end and had her lead her "slave" around the basement while she viewed. It was a totally unnatural situation for Scarlett to be in. It didn't feel right, not just because of what she was wearing, but also because Scarlett desired to be the one led. Bella although was satisfied that the pair of outfits fit what she needed. Clara appeared to be glad, even though Scarlett felt compelled to voice her disappointment.

"Try not to stress, Scarlett. The host has an entire collection of harem theme in her home. She had a few slave girls of her own, so Clara's outfit will fit right in and so will be yours."

Scarlett didn't generally trust her; however, what would she be able to do. Bella took a couple of notes for certain adjustments to her robe while Clara got dressed and returned home. She, at that point, had Scarlett dressed. Scarlett intentionally took as much time as necessary pulling on her garments. She needed to offer Bella a chance to assume control of her, but it didn't occur.

Scarlett had not gotten any sexual fulfillment today, and she was beginning to get frustrated about it. She left Bella's house in sexual disappointment. It happened the second time today. First, her dominatrix had not called her to her office at the end of today's work. Second neither Bella nor Clara had taken her or touched her that night. Life as a submissive was befuddling. "How might they have opposed my charms when I was stripped naked and accessible to them?" Scarlett thought inwardly.

The next day at work was a lot of like the day preceding. Scarlett ate her mistress's pussy for breakfast and lunch, albeit fortunately, her mistress allowed her the joy of sitting on her work desk, spreading her legs, and stroking off for her pleasure. Natasha's secretary's grin was more knowing than irritating when Scarlett left. Leilani was wearing a similar scent when she left the workplace that night. Brooklynn was dressed more pleasantly than expected and Scarlett thought about whether they were going out together. It appeared every one of her contemplations and particularly how she considered others presently rotated around sex. That night as she lay in bed unable to rest, she considered the ladies she assumed had helped Natasha enslave her and inquired whether she was anticipating her carnal wants on them or whether they were truly in the scene.

Friday morning began as normally as possible. Scarlett was under her mistress's work area at 7:30 AM sharp. She was nestled into a ball in the foot well of the work area, her head buried in Natasha's pussy obediently performing her servile morning rituals, when she heard the entryway open and the secretary strolled in. Scarlett sensed she definitely recognized what Scarlett did in this office. Thus, Scarlett didn't stop. Moreover, neither did Natasha. She and her secretary talked as if nothing was strange while Scarlett kept on servicing her. She heard the entryway close again and afterward tried harder enthusiastically to make her mistress cum. Scarlett was rewarded with a mouthful of her delicious nectar and the utmost fulfillment of a task completed successfully and performed dutifully. At the point when she slithered out from under the work area of Natasha, she was astonished to see the face of the secretary.

Her dominatrix introduced her as Theresa. She was stripped naked. Scarlett was in sheer shock, but still she was clueless of what to do.

"Theresa is the one you 69-ed with during your challenges. She's been earnestly pleading for me to orchestrate an encore. She's been a decent little slave this week, so I revealed to her today that she would get her prize."

Natasha commanded Scarlett to strip and lie on her back on her couch. At long last, Scarlett would get some action in her mistress's office. Theresa, at that point, lay over her and they started to pleasure and service each another, passionately. It was as sublime as the first run through and since Scarlett could see her, it was significantly more enjoyable and animating than before. Mistress Natasha permitted them proceed until they both orgasmed in an enraptured bliss. It was a vastly improved approach to begin the day as Scarlett made the stride back upstairs and Theresa settled at her reception counter.

The rest of the morning, Scarlett's excitement fabricated and built up gradually. She was anticipating the toy party today around evening time and was considerably more thrilled to a return engagement with her Mistress Natasha and Theresa at lunch. Tragically, when she went down the stairs around early afternoon, Theresa let her know that Natasha needed to leave because of some sort of crisis. Theresa looked disappointed as well. Scarlett considered how frequently during the day Mistress Natasha benefited herself of Theresa's charms and her oral services and how regularly Theresa was exceptionally satisfied. She was in dire need of some urgent fulfillment and enthusiastically offered her tongue ministrations to Theresa under condition that she would reciprocate; however she turned her offer down. She admitted that Mistress Natasha had left strict rules for her not to engage in any sexual relations with anyone until she returned. Scarlett was terribly irritated and frustrated, obviously, yet she comprehended.

She left the workplace feeling both disappointed and horny. At that point, she saw the cargo lift. She stopped. Theresa had been commanded to be abstinent, yet Scarlett was not. Looking back, perhaps this wasn't the best choice; however, she brought the lift down to the locker room security office. Penelope was on duty. She didn't appear to be amazed to see Scarlett. Scarlett had overlooked the lift surveillance cameras.

"So your mistress left you frustrated today, huh, slave bitch?" Penelope roared. Everything Scarlett could do was nodding her approval. Her head was down in submission to the ebony dominatrix queen and in surrender of her free will. She was still constrained by her savage and unfulfilled desires.

"Tell me bitch. What do you need?"

"I have to cum. I'll do anything you desire, but please make me cum."

"First of all, how about we check whether that pretty tongue of yours has adapted any new tricks since our last meeting."

Penelope stood up and removed her trousers. Scarlett had learned some new tricks at the tutelage of her dominatrix and Penelope appeared to appreciate the implementation. In record time compared to their last meeting, she made her new mistress experience an orgasmic peak. All the while, Penelope kept on calling Scarlett with every filthy names and slangs known in the dictionary. Scarlett accepted the boisterous verbal attack as a commendation to her breath-taking oral abilities and stood up while licking her flavor off her lips. Her own pussy was trickling, and she was anticipating whatever incitement Penelope would provide. She pulled her trousers up and ordered Scarlett to leave.

Scarlett stammered in shocking dismay, "But what about my desires?"

"Do you believe I'm going to touch that filthy slutty pussy? I don't know where it's been, do I? Return upstairs to your washroom. You're great at fingering yourself there."

Scarlett was annoyed. "How could she use me and deny me?" She made a pouty look expressing her irritation. At the moment, Scarlett didn't notice and realize the connection between Penelope's inhumane activities and that of Mistress Natasha's who fundamentally did likewise that day. Penelope wasn't her dominatrix so fuck her. That was the last time she was going to ask for some favor from her.

Scarlett raged out of her office to the sound of boisterous chuckling. She took the lift back up to her workplace. She was still raging with anger. Getting off the lift, she stared at the washroom entryway. She was all tempted to step inside. She needed to head inside. She was ready to head inside. Be that as it may, she didn't. She could control her desires. She assured herself. "I'm not governed by my pussy and my dire need to cum. I can defeat eat this terrible urge," She babbled to herself inwardly, desperately trying to pull herself up.

She returned into her office. It appeared everybody was still at lunch and her cubicle region was abandoned. Scarlett took her seat at her work area to blow out the resentment. She was, at long last, quieting down when she heard Leilani's entryway open. Sneaking over the cubicle wall, she saw Brooklynn strolling out of the entryway. She was fastening the top bottoms on her pullover. Scarlett immediately sat down in her seat and pretended to be working. As Brooklynn was rounding the corner into their cubicle work area, she bounced back in bewilderment.

"Goodness, I'm sorry Scarlett. I didn't know you returned from lunch."

I took a gander at her. Her face was flush and her lips were coated. I realized that look. I had it each morning.

"That is alright, Brooklynn. I just got back."

Indeed, Scarlett just returned from licking the security watchwoman and was attempting to get control over her wild desires. The picture of Brooklynn on her knees before Leilani surely wasn't going to help her unrestrained libido. Her stirred-up excitement was fuming. There was no disregarding it or attempting to make it to leave with delightful contemplations. It craved for utmost fulfillment, and it required that now. Scarlett pardoned herself. "I have to go to the restroom, Brooklynn. Something I had at lunch didn't comply with my stomach."

Scarlett basically dashed out of her cubicle office. Hurrying past Leilani's entryway, she utilized her fringe vision sufficiently only to see Leilani sitting at her work desk. She couldn't see her legs; however, in her mind, she could see her wearing a short skirt with Brooklynn servicing her pussy. Scarlett needed to leave. Once out the entryway, she hit the stairwell. The lift took excessively long. Down one flight, she went and into the management office. Theresa attempted to stop her; however, she jumped directly past her. With Theresa was in pursuit, she attempted to open Natasha's entryway, yet it was bolted. As she jerked the door knob in a futile attempt to wiggle the lock, Theresa's hand gripped hers.

"You can't go in there."

"Why not? Would she be in there with another girl, a slave?"

As the words left her mouth, Scarlett already lamented bursting into the workplace. It was not her place to interrogate how, when, or why her mistress decided to utilize her.

"No, she's as yet not here. However, I'm not permitted into her office when she's not there."

"I'm not requesting that you go into the workplace. I just truly need a spot to cum that doesn't have a surveillance camera."

"Are you serious?"

"I'm dead serious. Penelope wouldn't satisfy me and my manager just fucked colleague. I'm terribly horny and I'm going insane."

Theresa saw Scarlett like she comprehended.

"Let me get the key."

Scarlett, at long last, could have a couple of relaxed breath as Theresa returned to her workstation. She returned back to Scarlett with a key ring and opened Natasha's door. "Just be fast, OK?"

Scarlett needed to inform her that there was no chance this was going to take long. Moreover, her mid-day break just had around ten minutes left. Strolling into her mistress's office, Scarlett remembered stepping into Leilani's office with a similar reason quite recently. She inspected Natasha's telephone. It worked once to get her off. It would work once more. In any case, even as occupied as her brain was by her overall desperate urge to cum, Scarlett had the reasonable idea that she shouldn't repeat the trick. She checked out the workplace and found what she urgently required. On the top of Natasha's cabinet were two or three bottles of water. They were the 500 ml size. This was great. At least, she let herself know.

Scarlett slid out of her underwear and got the nearest bottle. She plunked down in Natasha's seat and propped her spread legs out around her work desk. She was, at that point, wet and her foreplay had been mental throughout the day. She immediately put the bottle top in her mouth to give it a quick salivation and then inserted it down to her pussy. She was a little amazed at how effectively it slid in and surprisingly upbeat about how great it felt. Scarlett shut her eyes and let the sensations wash all over her body as she gradually fucked herself with the plastic bottle. Waves of enraptured joy washed over her. It didn't take long. Again, she envisioned Brooklynn before her manager, Leilani. Scarlett, at that point, thought of Theresa and herself pleasuring their mistress, Mistress Natasha. At last, she imagined about Clara. It wasn't the slave girl Clara, however. It was Mistress Clara overwhelming her as she laid bound spread-eagled underneath her. This time rather than dry bumping her, she was wearing a terrifying looking strap-on and taking what she needed from her powerless body.

The last picture of Clara's wild red hair dancing about her head as she stressed to fuck her harder set off Scarlett's tremendous orgasmic peak. She wailed in fascinating joy and her pussy snapped hard against the jug. Her left fingers were moving over her clit while her right hand shoved the container all through her fuck hole. Scarlett shouted out in euphoria as a brilliant blaze of excitement attacked her intuitive mind. At that point, there was another thundering jolt all over her body. She opened her eyes to see Theresa standing before the work desk with a pocket-sized digital camera. Getting captured did nothing to lessen her vibrations of ecstatic delight. In case anything it did was to expand her enthusiasm. Again her pussy clipped down on the container as another wave of electric pleasure slammed over her body. Theresa continued snapping pictures, and Scarlett continued cumming.

At long last, she quieted down. Scarlett was late returning to the workplace, yet despite everything, I expected to sit and recuperate for a couple of moments. Theresa took the bottle from her hand.

"I must remember not to drink any water in this office," Theresa kidded.

Scarlett looked as Theresa set it back on the cabinet. The label was drenched, yet that would dry. She thought about whether her flavor would stay on the container after it was uncapped.

"You are in a tough situation when Mistress sees these photos," Theresa proposed.

Scarlett couldn't have cared less. Natasha could beat her or whip her. That was a little price to pay for that significant cum. At the point when Scarlett offered that rationalization to Theresa, she really concurred with her. She saw Theresa peering toward the jugs as she advanced out of the workplace. Scarlett didn't think back. She was now determined to get upstairs.

Chapter 16

Her cubicle colleagues had all returned from lunch or for Brooklynn's situation, back from Leilani's pussy. No one said anything regarding Scarlett being fifteen minutes late or looking as flushed as Brooklynn had before. The remainder of the day flew by. Having a monstrous climax for lunch can get that going. Likewise anticipating a night of sensual activities could likewise help. Scarlett was still longing for being put under Bella's tutelage tonight or submitting to Clara; however, regardless of whether that didn't occur, simply exhibiting the garments would have her turned on for herself and Jacques when she would return home.

About 3:45 PM, Scarlett saw Brooklynn receive a telephone call and afterward head into Leilani's office. Sure they could have been examining the promotional offers they had been chipping away at, but that ought to have implied a group meeting. All things considered, Brooklynn was back on her knees. Regardless of whether such wasn't actuality, in her dreamland, Brooklynn was bent over on Leilani's lap and was getting spanked. The familiar tingle was back in her pussy and she advanced back to the restroom. As she strolled in, Scarlett originally stared at the roof. There was a little camera pointed away from the stalls down and checking around and sink zones. In case Penelope was watching, she would know where Scarlett was.

Next Scarlett checked the stalls down. Fortunately, she had the spot to herself. Slipping into the first stall, dragging her skirt down, and her hand slipped in her underwear in a record time. Now, she envisioned Theresa repeating her bottle-orgasm execution and Brooklynn blowing Leilani's better half while she got fucked by her manager, Leilani. Evidently, her body was figuring out how to cum faster, an awesome thing, as it just took a couple of moments of clitoral incitement and envisioning her colleagues fucking in various positions and situations to get herself off. Scarlett didn't cum so tremendously and pleasurably as she did in Natasha's office, yet it was sufficient to bring some relief until this evening. As she stood by the sink cleaning up, a brilliant thought crossed her mind. After she dried her hands, she pulled out an additional toilet paper roll out of the dispenser. She got a pen from her satchel and started to wrap on the toilet paper when she heard the entryway open. In strolled Brooklynn with an extremely deliberate stride. On the off chance that she saw Scarlett, she would have wished a proper greeting; however, she went directly into a stall. Scarlett heard Brooklynn sitting down, yet she didn't hear her peeing. "Does she show I'm here?" She wondered.

Corrupted evil musings flashed through her thoughts. Scarlett knew why Brooklynn was there and was almost certain she had sensed someone presence in the stall. So, Brooklynn wouldn't begin until she heard her other accomplice leave. Scarlett realized Brooklynn wouldn't begin her self-pleasure until the washroom was vacant. She held up the sign she had written to the camera. It said "Fuck you Penelope!" She, at that point, dropped the sign and pulled up her pullover and bra flashing her tits to the camera. Actually, this was a poorly conceived notion since she didn't have the foggiest idea who else watched those tapes; however, she was still pissed at Penelope. She discarded the toilet paper and tried to make an uproarious exit from the restroom. At the point when she shut the entryway, she held it so it restored a little slower than expected. That brought a most roaring squeak from the pivot. It likewise enabled Scarlett to keep it an inch open so she could listen. She had no reason why she was doing this on the off chance that any other person went to the restroom right, at that point. She guessed she could disclose to them she was carefully listening to Brooklynn jerking off. The obvious sounds of fingers sloshing in a wet pussy began nearly when the entryway was shut.

Scarlett's very own pussy was beginning to shiver and tingle as she listened to Brooklynn pleasure herself. She sat tight for a minute when another malicious idea entered her thoughts. She noisily pushed open the entryway, strolling into the washroom and went in the stall next to Brooklynn. She was effectively listening when the sound of the entryway closing calmed the washroom. She didn't hear anything from the stall beside her. Scarlett knew for a fact that Scarlett was battling her urges right at that moment. Her desperate need to cum was fighting with her severe longing not to get captured. Scarlett had the option to pee and pretend her genuine reason behind being there. In an attack of envy, she thought about standing in the stall and attempting to outlive her. She even had the idea of jerking off again to check whether Brooklynn would go along with her. Be that as it may, at last, Scarlett had her snicker, flushed the toilet, washed her hands, and left. Again, she shut the entryway cautiously and strove to hear on the off chance that Brooklynn restarted her pleasurable fulfillment. At the point when she heard that her colleague did, she opened the entryway, and let it swing shut. At least, she would give Brooklynn something to consider wondering about whether another person had entered the washroom.

Back at her cubicle, Scarlett hoped that Brooklynn would soon return. She was pretending to work, yet she was truly looking for her colleague so she could see the guilty look all over. She thought about whether Brooklynn would express anything or attempt to come up with a rationalization. Obviously, Brooklynn didn't. She returned a couple of moments later and plunked down without offering any remarks. Scarlett stayed there with an egotistical fulfillment of knowing the two of them had mischievously and satisfactorily pleasured themselves minutes before in a same washroom. She likewise realized what had, or at least who had, put her in such a dire situation, in which she expected to pleasure herself. Scarlett pondered precisely what Leilani had done to drive Brooklynn's wild cravings sufficiently high enough to risk getting captured to fulfill her desires. She had her creative mind; however, she needed facts to check and confirm.

Shockingly nothing else occurred before the end of the work day. Brooklynn appeared to get down working moving forward without any more interruptions. Obviously, her finger was sufficient for her. Scarlett was still delightfully anticipating the toy party. Bella, Clara and she had decided to ride together, so Scarlett went to Bella's home. She was terribly busy packing the sample cases and garments into her van when Scarlett showed up. Bella gave her a major friendly embrace. Maybe it was Scarlett's heightened sexual desires, but she could have sworn Bella held her somewhat more and more tightly than she would under normal circumstances. Clara showed up minutes after the incident and got a similar passionate embrace, yet Scarlett didn't see anything strange. She should simply be horny once more.

When the van was stuffed, they took off. Bella was driving and Clara was sitting in the front seat. Scarlett was on a seat right in the back with the sample crates on the floor in front of her. It struck Scarlett as odd why she wasn't driving herself. Luckily, the travel time was short and they before long, landed at a spaciously decorated mansion in one of the lavish neighborhoods. They each grabbed a sample crate and set out toward the entryway. Bella rang the doorbell and soon after the substantial oak entryway swung open. Bella and Clara strolled in. As Scarlett crossed the threshold, she got a significant stun. Holding the entryway was Thomas, Leilani's husband. "What …The… Mother… Fucking Fuck?" She wondered. Scarlett, at that point, saw Leilani leaving the kitchen toward the lounge room. She was cleaning her hands on a drying towel.

"The snacks are almost ready. Everyone ought to be here within thirty minutes."

Leilani held back when she saw Scarlett.

"Well…Well… Hi Scarlett. This is an unexpected amazement. I didn't have any idea you worked with Bella."

Scarlett recalled back that Bella disclosed to her this would have been an extraordinary gathering for one the greatest clients and multiple lucrative deals. She abruptly became extremely intrigued by what sort of things Leilani and her companions purchased.

"Hello Leilani. The astonishment is all mine, in fact! I didn't realize we were arriving at your home."

Scarlett needed to ask where Brooklynn was since she was certain she would visit the gathering; however she reconsidered it. Their relationship was an office mystery, so it was better that she didn't spill the beans on what she discovered about them.

"Well don't simply remain there everybody. Enter."

Leilani led them into the lounge where she was busy arranging for the party. After they put the cases down Clara and Scarlett came back to the van and got the garments. At the point when they strolled back in, Bella and Leilani had all the earmarks of being somewhere down in a private discussion. Scarlett inquired as to whether Clara had ever been at a party here previously and she said no. Thomas had vanished to the basement, his "man cave" as Leilani depicted it. "He'll be gone until the gathering is over," Leilani laughed.

They were escorted to a visitor room where they could change their ensembles. Scarlett additionally noticed a second visitor room where a heap of towels and a container of hand sanitizer were situated beside the bedside table. She conjectured that Leilani anticipated more than one of her visitors to have a hands-on exhibition. Bella stepped into the room and advised Clara and Scarlett to put on their first pieces of lingerie as the visitors would be here soon. Scarlett had never gotten over the devious rush of stripping down and dressing seductively for a room filled with strangers. Tonight, she additionally got the excitement of watching Clara do likewise. As they readied themselves for their introduction, Scarlett really wanted to believe that tonight must be the night that Leilani would reveal her true self in front of everybody. She was certain she would be ravaged before the end of the fascinating night.

Individuals began streaming in for the gathering. Bella had Clara and Scarlett dressed in French maid's outfits and they were commanded to serve a lot of wine as per the demands and requests of the ladies. Obviously, Leilani and Bella needed everybody free before they truly began. After about thirty minutes, Bella murmured something in Clara's ear. She nodded and headed out to their dressing room. Without any formal guidance, Scarlett continued serving the beverages and snacks while Bella proceeded with her sales pitch to sell as many of her products as she could. Scarlett saw several ladies disappearing into the guest room, both alone and in couples. Clearly the wine was helping the attempt to sell something. Clara returned wearing her first noteworthy and seductive outfit of the night. As she strutted around the room, Scarlett saw a few ladies take certain liberty to touch her in ways not acknowledged at different gatherings. Still, neither she nor Bella endeavored to address the wrong touches. Scarlett looked as one lady, claiming to examine the fit over Clara's ample butts, ran her hand directly between her legs. She saw Clara moan and knew precisely what she was feeling.

Bella then sent Scarlett back to change. As she was leaving the room in one of her loved trim teddies, the cellar entryway flung open nearly smacking her in the face. Thomas dashed through the entryway not understanding he nearly clipped Scarlett. She paused as fast as she could and was still on her pussyfoots as he shut the entryway and saw her.

"Oh no, I'm sorry," Thomas said. While his lips were stating sorry, his eyes were unquestionably busy investigating her. He gave Scarlett a look from head to toe and afterward back up once more. He didn't attempt to conceal that he was doing it.

"Decent. Bella consistently has the best models."

With that he turned and started strolling to the parlor. There he revealed to Leilani he was going out and wished everybody a goodbye. He disappeared through another entryway, which Scarlett thought was the carport. She made her entry into the lounge room. Everyone's eyes were on her as she made her first entrance through the party as a model rather than a servant. The lady who had been fondling Clara gave a similar move at her. She inquired whether the base of the teddy fit effectively and in the process ran her hand up and down Scarlett's slit and up the crack of her butts. Scarlett needed to take a full breath to refrain from shouting out. She paraded around the room, yet she was certain the teddy truly didn't fit now since the groin was stuck up the cut of butt cheeks, thanks to the lady's meandering hands. No one referenced her dresses' glitch. She got the feeling about how the night would proceed.

Bella, in reality, was ordering an extraordinary number of items. Clara and Scarlett kept flaunting their seductive feminine assets just as our own. The party attendees dynamically took more freedoms "checking the product" and Scarlett, because she was getting intensely turned on by the pawing. She looked at Clara who showed off an expression of having a great time, the same amount of as they seemed to be. Bella had directed the attempt to close the deal onto the fetish gear. Scarlett accepted the bondage bed would, before long, be showing up, and she was completely prepared to demonstrate.

Before that could occur, in any case, Leilani reported they were going to take a break. She needed to serve more wine and Bella said that her assistants required time to get in their last outfits. Clara and Scarlett strolled to the room and stripped out of our outfits. Clara discovered her outfit of harem girls; however, Scarlett couldn't find the Arab Slave Trader ensemble she was supposed to wear. Luckily, Bella arrived into the room. At the point when she disclosed to Bella that she couldn't find her outfit, she answered that because she had altered her perspective. She said that something had been annoying her about what Scarlett looked like in the dress. She said that she sense Scarlett's uneasiness and unhappiness with leading Clara around the room and chose the entire idea wasn't getting down to business. Scarlett investigated Clara who was caught up with putting on her dress and then looked at Bella with a confounded expression.

"I preferred how Clara's ensemble looked. She's as yet going to be the group of harem girl. I have something different for you."

Scarlett was frightened and captivated by what Bella had thought about. Her pussy had been wet throughout the night and she would have exited to the party bare if that would have given her some sensual relief. Bella pulled out a little bag Scarlett had not seen when they stacked the garments in the car. From inside, Bella brought forth a couple of short leather boots with a high stiletto heel. They reached over her ankles with the essential locking instrument to keep them on her feet and D-rings within and outside to hold it in place for the wearer if necessary. Alright, to hold Scarlett set up ideally. She had her sit on the bed while she put them on her feet. Bella was stooping before Scarlett with a fascinating view of her sodden pussy, a reality that didn't escape her as she envisioned herself bowing before her.

After the boots, Bella had Scarlett slip on a leather coat. The sleeves were cut practically like Clara's harem girls outfit in that the sleeves were progressively similar to pieces of leather encircling in a locking cuff again with two D-rings. The base of the coat snapped tight against her midriff. There were four buttons running from simply over her navel to simply beneath her bosoms. The top neckline of the coat snapped tight around her neck. Again, there was a D-connector. The center of the coat flared out in a diamond-shape that uncovered a wide zone of her ample bosoms. Essentially, from her areolas, they were uncovered. The coat must have been exclusively customized because it fit Scarlett perfectly and gave her succulent bosoms simply enough support and internal tilt for the most exposure. The coat flare trapped her nipples in place, unexposed, yet secured scarcely and held her tightly. Scarlett was certain it could be convinced to uncover a greater amount of her chest, but the way, in which it was fitted now, Scarlett would be at least marginally contained. Scarlett thought about what bottom Bella needed to coordinate this mind-blowing coat. She possibly could have guessed and unquestionably ought to have comprehended what was coming... the remote-controlled vibrating panties.

Scarlett offered no resistance as Bella slid the underwear up her legs. Her will to oppose had long vaporized from her mind. She had no uncertainty that Bella planned to exhibit the maximum potential of her most costly item to this horde of horny ladies who had just indicated they were in a purchasing mood. Scarlett saw the underwear didn't have the g-spot vibrator embedded. That was either something to be thankful for or an awful thing relying upon how everyone looked at it. She realized that it would spare her some embarrassment in case she didn't squirt in the exhibition. Rather than the slim bent vibrator, an enormous thick one had supplanted it. The equivalent was valid for the anal stimulation. While not as large as the pussy vibrator, it was altogether thicker and longer than the one Scarlett normally utilized. Bella pushed her face down on the bed and started lubing up her rear end with her finger. Scarlett didn't grumble, and she didn't bitch. She simply lay there and let her partner do what she knew was coming. She ended up stuffed like she had been in Natasha's subjugation nest when she got her first double penetration. Just this time, the fucking wouldn't stop until the batteries wore out alongside the additional stirring of the clit vibrating pad. Scarlett, in fact would not have been ready to take the panties off until Bella gave her the key.

Happy with the positioning of the three panties toys, Bella enabled Scarlett to get back on her feet. Each step was an ecstatic adventure as the vibrators moved within her. They were not by any means turned on yet, and right now, Scarlett was feeling the splendid impacts. The last step before their revelation was a leash for both their collars. With that Bella led her two slaves once again into the parlor. Clara was strolling with her head up taking pride wholeheartedly in both her outfit and her position. Scarlett attempted to pursue her lead, but with each step her knees got more fragile as she fucked herself and scoured her clit on the plastic stub.

At the point when they arrived at the center of the room, Bella gave Clara's chain to Leilani who continued to gradually walk her around the room flaunting the brilliant ensemble. The room was swirling with sexual vitality as each lady in participation was locked to the perfect redhead parading her stuff. Scarlett nearly felt ignored standing in the center of the room.

When Clara had completed her course, Leilani plunked down and pulled Clara onto her lap. Most likely Leilani was getting a charge out of the role of slave trader. Scarlett could just hope she would do likewise for her soon. Bella seemed prepared to start her show. Without any difficulty and a carabineer, Scarlett's wrists were soon clipped behind her back. As she expected, her luscious bosoms swelled out of the front of the coat. Her hard nipples presently strained to stay contained by the lapel. She realized what was coming, and she was mortified by how awful her body needed this.

Bella pulled out the remote and started to clarify its highlights. She turned on each of the three vibes at full power and right away Scarlett's knees buckled and she crumbled on the floor. The quality of the vibrations astonished her. They appeared to be substantially more extraordinary than the pair Scarlett already had. Maybe they were another model. Bella stopped the vibes as fast as possible.

"As should be obvious, at full power, the underwear can be a quite difficult to deal with. I suggest lower settings and particularly the teasing settings as you get acquainted with their power and operation."

Bella handed the remote to the lady sitting to her left side who analyzed it completely. Scarlett battled to her feet, challenged more from the shoes and cuffs and not from the now torpid vibes when she saw her point the remote. "For what reason do ladies think it is an enchantment wand to focus on me?" Scarlett wondered as the lady pressed a button. This time just the clit buzzer turned on at a truly sustainable and pleasurable pace. Scarlett grinned at the lady who at that point clicked another button which breathed life into the butt plug. Her grin changed to a glower as her ass got stimulated. She was certain the lady could peruse the strained quality and exhilaration in her face. She grinned obviously fulfilled and turned the two vibes off. The lady, at that point, gave the remote to the lady sitting beside her. Every lady thusly enjoyed prodding Scarlett to the point of sensual peak before turning it off. As Clara and Scarlett moved around the room, the greater part of the consideration had moved from the Harem girl lingerie to the pitilessly teased Scarlett. She was quickly moving toward the zenith of her pleasurable excitement where she couldn't take any more. The last lady finally had the remote. It was Leilani. She immediately pushed various buttons on the remote and the ass, pussy, and clit cycle that Scarlett had felt in the workplace; it made her recall the bewildering memories of her happy past. Leilani grinned at her as Scarlett affirmed that it must be Leilani controlling her in the conference room. She got up and strolled over to Scarlett. She pushed the remote down into her cleavage demonstrating no progressions to this program which would make Scarlett crazy within seconds. She, at that point, murmured in her ear.

"I've had my eyes on you for quite a while, whore. On the off chance that I let you cum, what are you going to accomplish for me?"

Between pre-orgasmic stuns to her sensory system, Scarlett attempted to reply; however, battled to shape the words. Quietly, so just Leilani would hear her as she talked.

"Anything you need. I'll do anything you need."

"Would I be able to spank you?" Leilani inquired.

"Obviously."

"Obviously, what?"

"Obviously, Mistress."

"What about my pussy? Are you going to eat it each morning at the office after you finish with Mistress Natasha?"

"Indeed Mistress. Anything."

"What about your better half? Is it true that he wouldn't fret?"

"I don't know Mistress. I haven't let him know yet."

Scarlett was gasping in savage urge. Her legs were frail, and she was apprehensive that she was going to fall once more.

"Bella, did you bring my favorite item tonight?" Mistress Leilani inquired.

"You realize I always bring it for you, don't you?"

"Obviously. Be a dear and bring it for this flawless animal, will you?"

Bella left the room. Scarlett was imploring they were discussing some huge strap-on Leilani loved to employ against a defenseless slave. The rest of the ladies in the room appeared to appreciate this trade. Scarlett questioned it was the first one at Bella's sex party. Mistress Leilani stopped her panties and started to push them down. Even though Scarlett had not sprayed them, within was smooth patch of her juices and the substantial heaviness filled with her excitement. Leilani had them around her ankles and afterward off when Bella returned. Leilani spun Scarlett around to face her so she couldn't perceive what Bella was bringing into the room.

"Please your mistress now with your presentation and the remainder of the night can be quite simple and charming for you. Fuck this up and I'll whip your ass. OK?"

Scarlett nodded her approval. Leilani spun her back around, and she saw what Bella was holding. It was the biggest, thickest, and blackest dildo she had ever observed. It had a major suction cup at its base and a couple of huge balls hanging in front. The sides were ribbed, and the bulbous head was molded into an exact crown. On the side in white square printing were the words imprinted, 'Black Mambo' .Bella had Scarlett lick the suction cup. She, at that point, pummeled it down on the center of the coffee table. The sound was hard to portray. There was a sort of "thunk" as the air hurried out from under the cup. The dildo swayed to and fro entrancingly as the vigorous power dispersed.

Leilani instructed Scarlett to go down on "big black cock" like it's the last one on Earth. Scarlett stooped on the table. It was difficult to steady and position herself without the utilization of her arms. In any case, when she took the tip in her mouth, the silicone cock acted like the third leg of a tripod which made a difference. Scarlett was the ladies sitting behind her were getting an impressive perspective on her slobbering pussy as she put forth a valiant effort to suck off this beast of a cock. Scarlett experienced difficulty extending her mouth around the whole thing and could just take a couple of inches, her best-case scenario. She attempted and attempted to take more and hoped her valiant endeavors would be considered acceptable by Leilani. With a sharp smack on her ample butts, she revealed to her it was the ideal time for the following activity.

"I realize you need it. Screw yourself. Show every one of us what an eager cock hungry slut you are."

Scarlett didn't need to be asked twice. She would have liked to be known as a road-side pussy slut and compelled to eat Mistress Leilani's pussy right at that point, but she wasn't going to let an opportunity like this go amiss. She straightened back up to her knees and squirmed her way over to the dildo until her legs were straddling it. Scarlett checked out the room and every eye was hypnotically focused on her. Scarlett wiggled her rear end attempting to conquer the bulbous head with her pussy; however, it continued sneaking out.

"Excessively wet?" Bella ridiculed Scarlett.

"No, I can get this."

"Here let me help."

Bella gripped the base and steadied the silicone cock. Since it was pointing straight up, Scarlett experienced little difficulty taking the head and a couple of inches into her needful fuck hole. She had utilized some enormous dildos previously, yet in no way like this. She gradually brought down herself onto the bestial cock taking consideration to enable her pussy to extend around the intruder. The other ladies appeared to be in no hurry and enabled her to take as much time as necessary. Scarlett was clueless about the length of the cock when it started to penetrate her; however, she, at long last, decided it was enough. She couldn't take it anymore. All the more practically, she expected to get fucked and simply sitting on this dildo wasn't helping it.

Scarlett started to rhythmically slide up and down the monstrous phallus. Before long, she was lost in her own fantasy. The house could have been ablaze and she would not have known. Her animated psyche was devoured by just one idea. On the off chance that she was on the upstroke, the idea was tied in with getting her pussy filled once more. In transit down, her considerations were increasingly unpleasant about what that beast was doing to her drooling pussy and might she be able to ever screw a normal person again. She was certain that she was shouting and groaning in enraptured amusement, but her nerves were nearly closed down. Scarlett felt neither torment nor joy, just a serious sentiment of being owned and pride as she tamed the dildo that likely frightened everybody there. Her boobs were ricocheting fiercely out of the coat as she pounded herself up and down. Her hair was flying all over the place. She was certain that she was a magnificent hypnotic sight. And afterward, similar to a slug, it hit her. Without notice, she felt the inner walls of her pussy vibrating, the clit was trembling as it was set ablaze and she peaked tremendously. Firecrackers shot off in her mind. Scarlett was actually observing stars before her. She was certain about her boisterous screaming, but all she could intentionally recall later on, was bobbing off the table and crashing on the floor in writhing wreckage. Scarlett lay on the floor trembling as she was devoured by her powerful climax. Her whole world existed distinctly from the tips of her areolas to the base of her pussy. The world was a cheerful and safe spot. As she, at long last, started to quiet down, she heard applause appreciating her demonstration. Her eyes started to concentrate again and everybody in the room was standing and cheering up for her. Scarlett feebly grinned. She could hardly move.

Chapter 17

She was later informed that Bella had Clara licked the toy clean for her. Scarlett surmised this gathering liked to utilize that technique. She kept on lying on the floor recovering, while the ladies analyzed the toy and arranged to submit extra orders. A few ended up standing over Scarlett and giving her an unrestricted view up their skirts. Some didn't have underwear. She wished she could have sat up for a taste, but her body was still in no condition to move. At long last, Scarlett felt Leilani offering her hands and helping her to sit back up. She, at that point, helped her onto the sofa. Leilani tucked Scarlett's bosoms once again into the coat. Scarlett was certain she intended to tweak, pinch, and brush her areolas all the while.

"You were spectacular tonight, Scarlett. I have a present for you after we wrap up."

I sat on the couch viewing the last order getting composed. Clara had rejoined them in her normal public garments and took the sample cases and dresses out to the vehicle. No one had tried to bother Scarlett to redress as she sat in the coat, boots, and no underwear. Scarlett didn't generally mind. She was all set for home that way. At long last, when just Bella, Leilani, Clara and she were left, Leilani cut the leash to her neck and gave a pull.

"We will have a fabulous time at the workplace. I may even share you to Tom."

Scarlett just nodded and submissively pursued her to the basement entryway. Down they went over the thickly covered stairs into the "man cave." The cellar could have been a sports bar. There was what resembled an all around stocked bar with eight stools before it. Foosball, pool, and air hockey tables were positioned, and a dartboard hung on the wall. A poker table was positioned toward the side. What's more, a huge LED TV was placed on the wall. In case that Scarlett was Thomas, she would have never left. She couldn't comprehend what they were doing down here, at least not until Leilani led her through an entryway behind the bar. This room looked more like a genuine cave. Clearly, this was Leilani and Thomas' dungeon. It was dark. There were a couple of segments of reflective tape demonstrating a passageway in the negligible light from the other room. As Scarlett's eyes adjusted, it struck her. A large portion of what she could see was a reflection of Natasha's dungeon in the locker room at work. Mistress Leilani flipped a light switch and some dim lights in the roof woke up. In the center of the room was a pommel horse simply like Mistress Natasha had. Just rather than Scarlett being hung over it, Brooklynn was tied over its curved top.

It was then Scarlett understood what Thomas had been doing while they were hosting the toy get-together. Brooklynn must have showed up earlier than the rest of the party attendees, most likely riding home with Leilani from work. Possibly Thomas had been playing with her for the initial few hours of the toy party. However, he'd been away for at least ninety minutes, which implied Brooklynn had been in that position at least that long. She was wearing a hood with embedded earphones. Scarlett realized Brooklynn couldn't see the light, and she speculated she couldn't hear them either. Her non-verbal communication gave no sign she realized that they were there until Bella gave her a solid smack over her ample butts.

Brooklynn lifted her head in a vain endeavor to see who hit her. Scarlett looked as Leilani stopped the CD player appended to the earphones in her hood. She, at that point, unfastened it and pulled it off her slave. Brooklynn appeared to be alleviated and expressed gratitude toward her mistress. Leilani didn't utter a word. She pointed at Scarlett and twisted her finger. At the point when she moved toward her, she grasped her hand and pulled her before Brooklynn. Leilani nudged Scarlett's ass showing that she should draw nearer to her head and then gripped Brooklynn's hair and lifted her into position to lick Scarlett's pussy. Scarlett was all the while recovering from the fucking she inflicted on herself and her pussy truly wasn't fit to be utilized again unexpectedly early. It was sore and Brooklynn's tongue truly wasn't that satisfying as a result of it. Scarlett looked at Leilani with bitterness in her eyes.

"Mistress, I value the offer; however I'm simply not prepared for this at this moment."

"I comprehend. This was only a welcome to the club sort of blessing I needed to give you. Brooklynn would be glad to do this rather on Monday at the workplace, wouldn't you?"

"Indeed mistress."

"Then we have a deal. Monday after you finish with Mistress Natasha and me, Brooklynn will service you. Try not to wear underwear on Monday. All things considered, don't ever wear underwear to work from now on."

Scarlett was still in her post orgasmic bliss, so she just nodded. Bella accompanied her back upstairs to the room and assisted her out of the coat and afterward opened the boots. As she stood scouring her wrists and attempting to recover some circulation into them, Bella pushed her onto the bed and bounced over her. Scarlett was stunned and helpless as she pinned her assistant to the bed and started kissing her enthusiastically. She grabbed her wrists and held them tight against the bed over her arms. She, at that point, propelled herself up in a pushup position while holding Scarlett tight.

"I realized you had great potential from the day we first met. Starting now and into the foreseeable future, you are getting down to business shows for free simply like Clara does. You will be a provocative show model. We'll work out a timetable when you can help me, but tonight is the latest night you'll be getting a free pass. Think about that as a gift to you. Come over Wednesday night and I'll show you my private assortment of toys."

Bella viciously kissed Scarlett again and afterward moved off of her. Scarlett needed to rest as she watched Bella leave the entryway. She rested for a minute lying on the bed. Her hand floated down to her abused pussy. She was hesitant to stare at it. She realized it must be getting late, so she found her garments and got dressed. Bella was mysteriously absent and so was Clara. Scarlett heard the sound of a paddle impacting flesh originating from the basement. She plunked down in the lounge room to wait until Leilani was done with Brooklynn and immediately nodded off. She woke as Brooklynn was shaking her. Leilani appeared to be astounded that Scarlett was still there.

"Bella got pissed about something and left before I could get dressed," Scarlett said.

"Try not to stress. Brooklynn will drive you home."

"Thank you, Mistress Leilani."

"No worries. We pay special attention to one another."

"Mistress, would I be able to make an inquiry?"

"Obviously."

"Dominatrix Natasha said there are four mistresses in your exclusive club. I've met three. Who is the fourth?"

"The truth will surface, eventually. The reality of the situation will become obvious. I'm certain she will uncover herself when all is good and well. Trust me, I needed to take you in the workplace all week, yet I was eagerly waiting to make tonight's gathering awe-inspiring. It's something very similar with her. I'm certain she needs you at this moment, yet you'll need to wait somewhat more."

"Be that as it may, in what way will I know her? That is to say, I realize she has a tattoo. I saw that in the video. But neither you, nor Bella nor Natasha had one like it. So, how will I find her?"

"Trust me. At the point when all is good and right you'll discover her. She'll identify herself when she's prepared. Truth be told, you definitely know her. Presently, run along home to hubby. I'm certain he's pondering where you are."

Brooklynn hustled Scarlett out of the house before she could pose additional inquiries. She hushed up in transit home and would not respond to any inquiries concerning the sex gathering. They spoke a little about the secret dominatrix, yet nothing that would enable Scarlett to derive the name of the fourth mistress. Brooklynn confessed that she knew some of the different slaves. That truly disappointed Scarlett since she wouldn't recognize them either.

"All in great time. All in great time," was all Brooklynn would state. Scarlett needed to pause and discover when they were ready to be uncovered.

Scarlett spent the remainder of the weekend in reflection as yet wondering about and speculating who was the number four mistress in the group. Brooklynn had revealed to her that she knew some of the slaves. The only individual she could concoct was Helena, her neighbor. Scarlett knew Bella, hosted and facilitated the first toy gathering that she had visited and loaned her the little vibrator which initiated her transformation into submission. That made her a possible candidate. Her body type didn't exactly coordinate with the back view video Scarlett had in mind considering dominatrix number four. Still, she needed to make sense of an approach to be sure. Other than Helena, she clueless who else could be included. Brooklynn had utilized the plural adaptation of slave which implied Scarlett knew multiple people of the group already. Regardless of whether Helena was included, Scarlett was still missing at least several pieces to the riddle.

Monday morning unfolded with Scarlett no closer to settling the conundrum. As had become her daily schedule, she was in Mistress Natasha's office at 7:30 AM sharp. She was on her knees and servicing her pussy. Theresa showed up somewhat sooner than expected and ended up standing in the workplace watching Scarlett tributing to her manager's pussy. After Scarlett completed, she gave Theresa a sweet kiss so she could relish her manager's juice for the rest of the morning and afterward she headed upstairs. It was 7:55 AM when Scarlett entered her supervisor, Leilani's, office. She was sitting tight for her, as was Brooklynn.

This also would turn into a daily practice. Obviously, Leilani had a schedule. Scarlett was to service her at the beginning of the day at 8:00 am. Unlike Natasha, Leilani delighted in her tongue, yet in addition preferred her to finger-fuck her. That first morning, as Leilani had guaranteed, Brooklynn was told to lie on the floor and devour Scarlett while she bowed before Leilani and orally tribute her. It felt so great to encounter similar vibes that she was providing for her dominatrix. When Leilani could detect that Scarlett was drawing nearer to her peak, she helped her to remember the standard that Mistresses orgasm first and that it would be wise to hold back. This was a gigantic battle because Brooklynn was a gifted oral slave and appeared to be resolved to make Scarlett defy a rule on the very first day.

Scarlett was headed to interruption by Brooklynn's capable tongue and fingers. Clearly, she had substantially more experience than she had on the best way to satisfy a lady. Aptitudes that Scarlett realized she would need to learn were in exhibition and as she drove her consistently nearer to a tremendous discharge, her very own administrations to Mistress Leilani started to falter. Scarlett continued hearing Mistress Leilani state, "Don't you dare cum first." However, in the long run she quit licking her mistress and simply buried her head between her legs and hung on with a death grip. "Was their arrangement to make me defy a guideline so they could punish me? Likely. Had Brooklynn previously serviced Leilani so she wouldn't be as prone to orgasming before me? Possibly." Questions started to bombard her distressed mind. Be that as it may, as Scarlett held her Mistress' legs for balance, her climax tore through her. Scarlett realized she was in a difficult situation.

After she exploded, Leilani dismissed Brooklynn and Natasha to their cubicle. They didn't discuss anything as they plunked down; both their faces were iced with flavorsome female juice. Their two other cubicle colleagues, Molly and Cathy, didn't appear to take note. Around 10:00 am as they were getting ready to take their quick morning break, Molly stood up and strolled into Leilani's office. Scarlett had never seen in some way or another that either Molly or Cathy constantly missed morning espresso. Brooklynn and Scarlett were always there; however, one of the two young ladies was continually absent. Today, Scarlett took her espresso back to her work area lastly saw Molly leaving Leilani's office. She had generally remained in the lunchroom previously, but today, she kept watch on her manager's entryway. She saw Molly with the obvious sheen all over leave the workplace and heading toward the washroom. Clearly, she had completed what Scarlett had begun. At noon, Brooklynn tapped Scarlett on the shoulder and said, "Have fun with Natasha," as she strolled by her and into Leilani's office.

Scarlett hustled ground floor and was glad to see Theresa had not left for lunch. She realized she had violated a significant guideline and was hoping an excited performance to please Mistress Natasha. Possibly it might invalidate her offense. She spent the lunch break satisfying her mistress and at her request, Theresa. As the clock approached one, Natasha pulled a vibrator out of her work desk cabinet and gave it to Scarlett. She requested her to "give them a decent show" and revealed to her that she had only five minutes to make herself cum. "Hell, it didn't take almost that long," Scarlett wondered. She continued humming her clit and fucking herself as she rocked during her second climax of the work day. Scarlett was attempting to get herself her third climax of the day before her allotted five minutes was up. She nearly made it as well; however, just before she could cum, Natasha commanded her to stop. She, at that point, had her clean the vibrator with her tongue. Obviously, Natasha didn't generally need to instruct Scarlett regarding that. Scarlett had learned that rule long time ago in the past.

At 3:00 pm, she watched Cathy disappear into their manager's office. She presently understood the pattern. She had morning pussy pleasuring obligations and Brooklynn had lunch. Molly and Cathy clearly switched off on the morning and evening breaks. Again, Scarlett remained at her work area through this break. Like Molly, Cathy also left the workplace with a covering of Leilani's love on her mouth and headed toward the restroom. Brooklynn and Molly passed Cathy in the foyer as she exited. As they were reentering their cubicle, Brooklynn gave Scarlett's bosom a press and grinned at her. Molly did likewise. Things were unquestionably going to be all the more fascinating around the workplace.

At 4:45 PM, Scarlett's telephone rang. It was an instant message from Mistress Natasha ordering her to be in her dungeon down the stairs at five. Scarlett went into Leilani's office and showed it to her. She asked Scarlett to feel free to leave since Scarlett would be paying the tax in the security office before she would get the way in to the locker room. With a spring in her step, she set out toward the cargo lift. Trisha was on the duty starting her swing shift in the video observation room. Having seen Scarlett on the cargo lift camera, she realized the slave girl was coming and was prepared for her. Her jeans were at that point off and she was shivering with excitement when she showed up. Scarlett thought about whether Natasha had given her further advanced admonition since she was already wet and it didn't take long for the slave girl to get her off. Scarlett didn't generally think about the reasons. She was predominantly only happy to be done as Trisha gave the passage to the door. The whole exchange took under five minutes and not a single word was verbally expressed.

Scarlett hustled down the dark corridor to the locker room. As she had seen previously, she snared the bungee string around the entryway so it would remain open. As she pivoted to enter into the locker room, Scarlett was enticed to glance in the men's locker room. "Was there anything extraordinary in there? Did the male officials bring their slaves and conquests down here as well?" Scarlett thought inwardly as she shook her head to clear the distractive considerations and strolled into the locker room. It was still a couple of minutes before five, so she checked out the dungeon room and attempted to figure which apparatuses of torment she would be subjected to. She additionally gave careful consideration of which ones she needed to have utilized on her. Mistress Natasha had not landed by 5:00 pm on her watch. Scarlett chose to undress to speed things along. She flawlessly wrapped and folded her garments and inclined over the pommel horse so her rear end would be in exhibition when her Mistress would arrive into the room. At last, she heard strides on the tile floor of the washroom. There was obviously more than one pair of feet making the sounds. Indeed, it seemed like a party.

"Look what we have here," Scarlett heard Leilani shout from the entryway. "I see a decent ass prepared to be punished for defying rule number one."

Scarlett heard the gathered ladies snicker. She looked over her shoulder and saw Mistress Natasha, Mistress Leilani, Mistress Bella, Theresa, Brooklynn, Cathy, Molly, and Clara. Mistress Natasha was holding what resembled a sorority pledge paddle. Theresa had a little satchel. Scarlett assumed it was the ideal opportunity for her introduction. The group progressed toward her. Her level of passionate excitement was off the graph and she could feel the wetness streaming down her legs. Scarlett was home finally.

Scarlett looked out over her shoulder as the gathering progressed toward her. Mistress Natasha was the first to reach running her hand over her bare ass.

"It's smooth; however, not smooth enough," she reported.

Scarlett didn't have a clue what she implied, but Theresa gave her a satchel which everybody evidently anticipated. Leilani grasped her hand and guided Scarlett to a stool. She had her plunk down and spread her legs. Scarlett was eager to uncover herself before everybody and looked as Natasha pulled out scissors and a jar of shaving cream from the sack. Scarlett constantly kept herself slick and trim down there, yet she had never shaved everything off. Natasha likewise pulled out what resembled a little crack pot. Theresa connected it in.

Now, Scarlett was somewhat confounded. She had seen little heaters like that when she would get her legs waxed at the salon. On the off chance that she would get waxed, why would the mistresses and their slaves need the shaving cream? Scarlett didn't need to eagerly wait long to discover. Natasha gave her pubic hair a brisk trim to get it to the ideal waxing length. Scarlett had her legs waxed, yet never her pussy. It was somewhat more difficult than completing her legs because the skin wasn't as tight. Consequently, when Natasha started dragging the muslin strips adhered to the wax off, her skin pulled with it until at long last the hair tore out. Luckily Natasha had her strategy down. Immediately pulling a strip, she would rub the skin excitedly and powerfully which helped a great deal. She likewise utilized exceptionally short strips which limited how far Scarlett's skin would pull. At long last, Natasha applied a cooling gel when she completed with a zone. Scarlett significantly loved the gel.

Chapter 18

At the point when Natasha was done with her wax, she embedded two fingers into Scarlett's vagina. As her slave suspected, her fingers found no resistance and returned out shimmering to the cheers of the group. Her mistress could do pretty much anything to her now in their relationship and Scarlett would get wet from it. Having finished the waxing, Natasha had her slave turn over. She splashed the shaving cream all over her backside and scoured it to form thick foam. Someone had brought her a bowl of water and she started shaving her rear end. Scarlett never considered her rear end furry or rough previously. The razor floated over her soft flesh. She was certain it wasn't doing anything as she couldn't feel any hairs being trimmed. At the point when she was done, Natasha cleared off all remainders of shaving cream and the scoured baby oil all over her slave's uncovered ass. She, at that point, gave Scarlett a playful spank. The baby oil amplified the sound and again everyone cheered. What Scarlett didn't expect was the expanded agony. Mistress Natasha had given her slave a fun loving slap. It wasn't especially hard or horrible. She'd done that on multiple occasions to her and it in every case just felt better. As it was later clarified, the shaving of the butt with the razor evacuates the finely, thin hair there and the baby oil defuses the power of the spank over a bigger region. Whatever the explanation, the spanking was substantially more compelling.

Tragically not every person was as delicate as her mistress. Leilani and Bella turned her butts splendid cherry red before giving Scarlett over to their slaves. Scarlett needed to lie on every dominatrix's lap and get twenty-five spanks. All together for a slave to get a turn at her rear end, they additionally needed to consent to devour her pussy. Dominatrices didn't have this necessity as Scarlett could be commanded to service them whenever they pleased. Not the entirety of the slaves made the most of the chance, yet Clara and Theresa positively did. Clara particularly laid into Scarlett with her twenty-five vicious spanks. Scarlett was in tears when she wrapped up. Clara additionally didn't keep down when it came to licking her servile pussy. Theresa had been gentler at her rear and furthermore gentler at the pit of her womanhood. She appeared to be resolved to hear her fellow slave groan, yet not take her any further. Clara then again needed to hear Scarlett shout from stimulation at the two closures. She likewise appeared to be resolved to make her orgasm in front of everyone. Scarlett was glad to report that she prevailed in the two objectives.

After Scarlett exploded tremendously and no other slaves needed to spank me, Mistress Leilani declared it was the ideal opportunity for the "welcome to the club" spanking. She said everybody experienced this including any new dominatrices. Her rear end was already set ablaze and Scarlett didn't know whether she could deal with it; however, she bent back over the stool. Natasha took the first swing. As her mistress and support to the exclusive group, it was her entitlement to do as such. The paddle lit a fire through her ample butts into her pussy and up her spinal cord. It hurt more awful than anything she had ever felt in her life. Scarlett shouted like a banshee and drew back in torment. Luckily, she just took one swing. Her mistress, at that point, strolled before her and drew upward her skirt. Natasha wasn't wearing underwear, and she immediately situated herself before her slave's servile tongue. Scarlett heard the whoosh of the paddle from another person just before she felt the sting of its blistering hit. The power thumped her forward as her shout got muted by the delicate pink folds of her mistress's pussy. As Scarlett shook back, Natasha pushed ahead to brace her. A third swat pushed the slave again more profound against her mistress's succulent pussy. She was giving a valiant effort to orally please her mistress appropriately; however, the exceptional agony was making that troublesome. Three down and five to go unless Penelope or Trisha appeared.

The five slaves proceeded. Most paddled Scarlett as hard as their mistress had, albeit one was somewhat gentler. Scarlett couldn't realize what her identity was; however, she was appreciative for their restraint. After they all had their turn, she felt numerous hands starting to press and kneed her sole and blazing bottom. She screeched marginally when she felt two fingers attack her pussy and again when they pulled out, instead of reentering her pussy, they invaded her anal cavity. Her face was still squeezed into her Mistress Natasha's dazzling pussy and she kept giving her the best dedicated oral service to make her peak. Extra fingers presently invaded her pussy and both her openings were finger fucked until her dominatrix gave Scarlett her affection splash. As streams of ecstasy stained her face, Scarlett kept on devouring the flavorsome juice as much as she could. Natasha pulled away and Leilani, her manager, had her spot. At the point when Scarlett had her overwhelmingly satisfied, Bella showed up. At the same time, she was being fingered by the slaves who currently appeared to be resolved to making her cum. Scarlett was presently being slammed in the pussy and ass as another finger advanced over her clit. Bella was bumping her face and everything she could consider was "don't cum before she does."

It was getting harrowing as Scarlett crawled ever nearer to the edge; however, at long last, Bella grabbed her head and exploded in an orgasmic bliss. She accepted this as authorization for herself since there was no rule regarding one slave orgasming before another. Her pussy muscles contracted hard on the fingers invading her. Scarlett was certain whoever was fingering her anal cavity knew immediately. She curved upward away from Bella's pussy and gave a savage scream. Scarlett was currently a member of the exclusive club of slaves and mistresses. It had been a long voyage, an adventure she realized wasn't completed, but finally she had a place.

After her tremendous orgasmic peak ebbed, Scarlett was brought into the locker room to clean up. Her pussy appeared as if it belonged to some school girl. She resembled a young lady. Scarlett, at that point, turned her rear to the mirror and looked over her shoulder. Her rear end was cherry red adorned with blue stripes in between. It had unmistakably been abused.

"How am I going to disclose this to Jacques?" Scarlett said starting to cry.

She was encompassed by compassionate female embraces.

"I informed you not to stress concerning him," Natasha started. "The gathering deals with its own. Simply put on a long PJ top tonight. Jacques has been having an illicit relationship nearly as long as you. When you were picked as a potential member of the group, Jacques was lured. He's been sneaking around your back and having a great time."

"What are you discussing? Jacques's dedicated to me."

"No, he's not darling," supported Leilani. "See, clearly we're not intended to be monogamous. Your sexual coexistence was on the decay which provoked you to us in any case. We're generally married and our spouses. Most even participate... At the point when we let them. Jacques will be a similar way. Before long, he will find out about the presence of the club. As always, the situation with husbands and boyfriends, when they learn they will have the chance to fuck the greater part of these delightful ladies, they yield. Trust me. You'll be fine and your marriage will be fine. We recognize what we're doing."

Scarlett's brain was spinning like a cartwheel at the shocking revelation. She didn't trust them about Jacques, yet she likewise knew if she was going to proceed with the group inevitably, then he'd need to know and give his approval. Everything Scarlett could do was trust their instincts and measures to save her marriage. As she was dressing to return home, Bella pulled her aside.

"Scarlett, I need your assistance with something. I'm presently the only mistress with a single slave. I despise that. I need you to enlist another person for me."

"How am I expected to do that?"

"That is your concern. I'll give you an indication, be that as it may. Your neighbor Linda, that adorable youthful blonde that went to the first party that Helena hosted. I'd love to enslave her. She didn't purchase anything at the gathering and hasn't called me since; however I could detect she's ready for the taking. Your assignment is to figure out how we can enslave her and introduce her to the group."

Before Scarlett got an opportunity to react, she was gone and Leilani showed up.

"In case you experience any difficulty with Jacques, let me know. I'll loan you Brooklynn. To hear Thomas rave about her, you would think she developed sex or something. Arrange a threesome with her. That consistently works. He'll let you do anything you desire after that."

Scarlett's head was spinning. Natasha came over and gave her a major passionate embrace.

"We're all set now. Welcome to the club. Try not to stress over our fourth mistress. She and her slaves couldn't make it today; however, they will make their presence known soon. We will host a get-together with our husbands and boyfriends in about a month when everybody's time table can coordinate. I'm certain she'll need a little solo time with you before that, so anticipate that she would be getting in touch with you soon."

"Alright, mistress, I'll be waiting."

"Goodness, and remember to turn the key in to the locker room in. I think Penelope is back on service now. You realize what to do."

"Indeed mistress. It will be dealt with."

Scarlett was left alone in the locker room as every other person left. She wished another slave could deal with the room tax, yet she was the lowest ranking whore on the command hierarchy, so it came down to her. She bolted up and made the long stroll down the corridor. Turning to the corner into the security office, she was shocked to see Theresa on her knees with her face buried in between Penelope's thighs.

"She said this is your welcome gift," Penelope started. "Head on home and get a good night's rest. You'll be striving hard in the workplace starting now and into the foreseeable future."

Scarlett gave Theresa's butt a little tap and said much obliged. She heard a muted "the pleasure is all mine". But she didn't raise her head or stop her oral ministration of the powerful gatekeeper. Scarlett went to the service lift and took it up to the hall. Driving home, her contemplations were on two things. To start with, was Jacques truly taking part in extramarital relationships? Was it safe to say that he was such a primal sex-crazed creature, that his head could be turned that effectively by a lovely lady? It didn't take Scarlett long to address that question. Second, she thought of her blazing and aching butts. It was sore and simply sitting in the vehicle was agonizing. A long hot shower in Epsom salt was on the motivation for tonight as was sleeping on her stomach. With her luck, they were most likely lying about Jacques and he would need to do her doggie style tonight. Terrible, awful, corrupted considerations. "Everything will be OK. Everything will be OK." Scarlett tried to rationalize.

Scarlett showed up home and Jacques wasn't there. "Is it true that he is with his mistress? Is it correct to refer to that girl as a 'mistress' since she probably is a slave like me compelled to tempt him?" Scarlett thought and realized this was going to make her insane until it was settled.

Jacques came home soon thereafter. He appeared to be worn out and luckily didn't press his wife for sex. Scarlett was somewhat distraught because she figured that implied he was getting it elsewhere. She was additionally somewhat glad since he didn't find her swollen, bruised, and cherry-red butts. Early the following morning, Scarlett decided to go for a run. The air was cool, and the run was invigorating and helped her clear her considerations. As she was running up the sidewalk returning home, she saw Kathleen, her neighbor a couple of blocks up from them who was mowing her garden. She was wearing shorts and a shirt. She waved to Scarlett and she stopped to talk. She had not conversed with her since Helena's toy party. They didn't have any acquaintance with one another that well, even though they waved at whatever point they saw each other outside. Kathleen was perspiring more than Scarlett was and she saw her shirt sticking to the seductive outline of her voluptuous bosoms.

They discussed for a couple of moments about whether Scarlett loved the mowing and landscaping she had made and life stuff. Simply the typical girly talk and possibly a little neighborhood tattle, yet nothing excessively interesting. Simply the conventional low level chatter you make with somebody who you don't know that well. Scarlett revealed to her that she needed to return home, and she said she needed to return to the weeds. As she turned to go, Kathleen stooped down bending over to pull more weeds. The rear of her shirt rode up, and Scarlett saw the tattoo on the little of her back. It coordinated the one she had found in the video.

The picture of that tattoo had been scorched into her mind each time Scarlett viewed the video of her degradation. She had jerked off to that video a large number of times than she could recollect. She right away realized that the tattoo was a match. Kathleen must be the fourth mistress. Scarlett froze, gazing at her rear. Detecting her look, Kathleen turned her head and stared at her.

"Everything okay, Scarlett?"

Scarlett faltered out a yes. "I was simply considering something."

She made a hurried retreat back to the security of her home. Scarlett was shaking as she plunked down on the lounge chair. On the off chance that Kathleen was a mistress, then Helena could be her slave. It appeared well and good. She facilitated the party which started her adventure and transformations. In case Helena was a slave, then she most likely selected Scarlett just like Scarlett had been entrusted and tasked with enrolling Linda. Her head was spinning; her heart was pounding in her chest with all potential outcomes. In case Helena was Kathleen's slave, who else was likewise serving her? Bella had said she was the only mistress with one slave, so the fourth escort needed to have at least two slaves. Scarlett was getting a headache.

Scarlett chose to shower to flush away her running perspiration. She had an unquestionable inclination to finger myself as her mind replayed every one of the occasions of the past couple of months as she attempted to work through everything that had occurred. Kathleen must be the fourth mistress and she needed to realize Scarlett had seen her tattoo, both face to face and on the video. "For what reason didn't she disclose to me when she had the opportunity? Is it accurate to say that she was the one sleeping with Jacques?" Scarlett felt thirsty and a terrible heart-ache.

After her shower, she toweled off and got dressed. She strolled to the ground floor and saw Jacques holding an envelope.

"This came for you while you were in the shower. It's from Kathleen just a few blocks from here. She said she intended to offer it to you when she saw you today morning; however, overlooked it."

Scarlett took the envelope from him with a flimsy hand. Opening it up, she found a invitation to a "young ladies" night that very night at Kathleen's home. Scarlett comprehended what that implied and her pussy started to get wet. She told Jacques, and he said that was fine with him. His companion Robert had welcomed him over to watch the game and now he'd be free. Scarlett saw Jacques realizing that he was lying. He would have been with her. The way that she also would be with another person didn't make it any less excruciating.

Jacques left the house around seven. At 7:30 PM, Scarlett strolled down to Kathleen's mansion. She welcomed her at the entryway and led her in. Scarlett inquired as to whether her husband was home.

"Mike? No he's out this evening. It's simply us young ladies," Kathleen said.

Her answer made Scarlett anxious and animated simultaneously.

"Is any other person coming over?" Scarlett inquired if Helena would go along with them.

"Probably not. Just us. I needed to become more acquainted with you better."

The pieces were solving the riddle. Scarlett had no uncertainty that Kathleen would become more acquainted with her in the Biblical sense, in no time. She was attempting to make sense of exactly how to inquire if she was having any slaves and if she was a mistress when Kathleen gave her a basic command which removed all confusion.

"Strip."

Even though Scarlett expected to be stripped soon, the terseness of the command and speed at which it was conveyed after she strolled into the house amazed her. Even though Scarlett was astounded, she went along promptly which satisfied her.

"The other young ladies have been training you well. Generally another slave pushes back a bit. Good girl."

Scarlett grinned at her appreciation. She was by far the most physically forcing mistress in the group and Scarlett realized she would not like to jump on her awful side.

"Almost certainly you have invested some energy asking why I didn't make myself know to you sooner. That is impeccably justifiable. I guarantee you there are legitimate reasons, yet they shouldn't concern you. Tonight, I will demonstrate to you that we've managed Jacques."

Scarlett knew it. Jacques was taking part in extramarital relationships with Kathleen. She could see that. In spite of her muscle toned framework, Kathleen was still a wonderful lady. Scarlett could accept she could have allured him. Be that as it may, Jacques knew his wife was here this evening. Possibly he wouldn't be so idiotic as to appear except if he definitely thought about her secret life.

"Goodness, crap. Kathleen let him know, and that was the way by which she got her snares in him," Scarlett glared at her with perplexity.

"We'll discuss about him later. First, I need to put you through several obedience challenges and see what you've learned. I'm certain you progressed since I last fucked you."

Kathleen strolled over to an end table in the lounge and got a collar and leash. She commanded her slave to stoop down, and she clasped the collar around her neck. She instructed Scarlett to crawl behind her as she led her around the house. She gave her slave a voyage through their home even though Scarlett got a perspective of it. She was certain most people missed the details.

At the point when they got to the kitchen, there was a canine bowl filled with water. Scarlett wasn't astounded to hear her mistress guide her to take a sip. Kathleen was testing her level of submission and obedience and Scarlett was glad to show her. She, at that point, guided her outside into the back yard. Scarlett battled to pee on well-mowed grass. That was stretching thing excessively far in her animated psyche. Be that as it may, Kathleen was quiet and ordered Scarlett to pee on the grass. She hesitated and to which Kathleen replied that she could stand by throughout the night if need be. She reminded her slave the more she held up the more noteworthy the possibility that one of her neighbors would see her. Scarlett's heart was pounding in her chest. She froze in embarrassment, yet in the long run, loosened up enough to relieve herself.

"Excellent, doggie," Mistress Kathleen let Scarlett know.

Her applause satisfied the slave and she led her back toward the house halting just before the sliding backdoor passage.

"Sit. Stay," she commanded.

Scarlett stopped, hanging tight for her arrival as Kathleen strolled into the house. She returned possibly thirty seconds after the fact with two or three paper towels that she placed under her slave's pussy.

"Wipe yourself off with that."

Scarlett began to reach underneath her body to get the towel when Kathleen chastised her.

"Try not to utilize your hand. How could a decent doggie utilize her paw to wipe her pee?"

Scarlett was befuddled until she understood what her mistress was commanding her to do. She needed to set down flat on the cool hard concrete and attempted to bump the paper towel. Scarlett must have been a sight for Kathleen as she towered over her as she attempted to press her pussy into the paper. At the point when Scarlett had done all she figured she could do, Kathleen guided her to bring the paper inside and discard it. Scarlett got back on her knees and again began to go after the paper.

"What did I enlighten you concerning utilizing your paws?" Kathleen reproved.

Scarlett gazed toward her mistress uncertain of what she needed her to do.

"You do have a long way to go yet, Slave Scarlett. A decent doggie can't utilize her hands so she needs to utilize her mouth."

Scarlett surmised she ought to have been revolted, but in truth, she had been intensely turned on throughout the evening fully expecting being with Kathleen and her treatment of her was simply powering the fire in her spirit. Scarlett hurried in reverse, bowed down her head, and bit the edge of the paper towel with her teeth. It truly wasn't as terrible as she would envision. The edge of the towel was superbly perfect and there were just a couple of drops of pee in the inside. She could smell it, yet it unquestionably wasn't overwhelming. Kathleen guided her slave again into the house and over to the kitchen trash can where she had her dispose of the paper towel. Scarlett, at that point, pursued her mistress go into the family room. She positioned her slave parallel to the lounge chair. She, at that point, plunked down and her back turned into a footstool for her legs. Scarlett looked as Kathleen reached back to the table where the neckline had been and got a riding crop.

"My slaves are all around prepared. They are both pain sluts who can climax on order when I whip them."

Scarlett thought about whether this was the thing that Kathleen had as a top priority for her as the crop reached her rear end. It was anything, but a solid hit. It was really only an enticement and more delicate than the spanking and paddling. Scarlett had endured the inception. Still, she realized Kathleen could be a lot harsher in case she decided to be.

"Be that as it may, I am typically merciful with new slaves joined to different mistresses provided you do everything else decisively or questioning any commands. Do you get it?"

Kathleen snapped the crop somewhat harder over her rear.

"Indeed, Mistress Kathleen."

"Now, how about we become acquainted with you a bit," Kathleen started.

Scarlett was interrogated concerning all aspects of her life, her marriage, her adventure leading to the gathering, her associations with the party individuals, her turn-ons (many), her mood killers (few) and all things everywhere. Mistress Kathleen kept on warming her slave's butt cheeks and the backs of her thighs with the crop;

however, they were truly love taps not planned to exact a lot of agony and absolutely no harm.

Uncovering her most profound privileged insights, wants, and dreams to Kathleen had her pussy decidedly slobbering. Kathleen guaranteed Scarlett that the club took great consideration of its members and would put forth a valiant effort to ensure everything her slave could ever hope for worked out as expected. It appeared to be peculiar to Scarlett that the lady she was bowing submissively would be so worried for her prosperity; however, Kathleen sounded completely trustworthy and she trusted her.

Her arms and knees were getting exhausted, yet she dared not to stand. She figured it was at least 8:30 PM when Kathleen instructed her to service her mistress's pussy. Kathleen kept on utilizing Scarlett as a footstool steering her solid thighs around her head and her legs over her back. About 9:00 PM and two orgasms later, Scarlett heard Mistress Kathleen's telephone buzz as she got an instant message. She lifted her legs off her slave's back and strolled over to the kitchen to get her telephone. Scarlett stayed bowing before the couch since her mistress had not dismissed her yet. She strolled again into the lounge obviously reading her message.

"Your husband will be in position within a few minutes. We have to prepare."

Kathleen didn't try to indicate what "prepared" implied. She additionally didn't give Scarlett much time to consider it. Snatching the leash she drove her slave to the stairs where Scarlett crept behind her up to the second floor, down the passage and into her "dungeon." Scarlett had expected to be directed to the primary bedroom, yet clearly they utilized an extra room only for "visitors." Kathleen had Scarlett stand up and unclipped the leash.

"On the off chance that you have to go to the washroom, right now is an ideal opportunity," Kathleen said pointing back to the lobby. She was occupied with accomplishing something with a PC. Checking out the room, Scarlett witnessed an armoire, no dresser, a king-sized bed with a sleigh headboard and footboard with iron bars for vertical support, a few huge mirrors and a 60-inch LED TV mounted on the wall. There were likewise two enormous dog beds on the floor at the foot of the bed. Scarlett thought about whether that was the place her slaves slept.

Scarlett chose a quick trip to the washroom was a decent decision since it was offered. She didn't generally need to pee again, yet she needed to pause for a minute for herself. She sprinkled some cold water all over and gazed at herself in the restroom mirror. Every passing day was bringing her more profound and more profound into her trap of submission. "Where was everything going to end? Would it be a good idea for me to confide in the gathering about Jacques or was everything going to come smashing down when he shows up?" Scarlett surmised she was going to discover soon.

CPSIA information can be obtained
at www.ICGtesting.com
Printed in the USA
BVHW060853130121
597716BV00009B/397